A F
Wilderness

Book One of
'The Kingdom of Durundal'
series

S.E. Turner

Acknowledgements:

Daisy Jane Turner: illustrator, for the magnificent book covers.

Jeremy Boughtwood for formatting and publishing, without whom the book would still be in its manuscript form.

My friends and family for their enthusiasm and encouragement.

My three daughters who continue to inspire me.

Dedicated to those who are fighting their own battles.

ajeya carried her name with pride; she had been riding for most of the day and was taking the most direct route towards Castle Dru in Durundal. A blinding pool of crimson sunk low on the horizon and she found herself flanked by tall soldier pines and dwarf rogue bushes tinged pink from the setting sun.

Keeping her horse on a tight rein she moved carefully until the dense tangle of woodland opened up into a small clearing. From here, the eaves of the forest gave way and a cool green sheltered valley stretched out before her. The woods fell silent as she stared out over the wide open plain towards the great dark mass beyond.

The entire settlement was divided into three areas and set into a high hilltop plateau; while the walls that encircled it went further than the eye could see and set with a range of strategically placed lookout posts. The whole complex was a massive defence core that soared out of the ground like a giant's hand with its turrets and towers reaching high into the sky, and the arches of its windows and doors were born from its very roots.

She spurred her horse on, thundering across the plains, raising a cloud of dust on the dry summer land, gathering greater speed until the castle gates brought her to a halt. On this glorious evening the details were easy to make out as every one of the magnificent windows glowed with light, and torches were set at regular intervals along the roofline.

'Who goes there?' the sentry guard boomed as Ajeya pulled up her mount.

The platoon on the highest levels raised their bows, and with a well trained eye aimed their arrows in her direction.

A jewelled cap with small flaps hid most of her face; while a short tunic sat snug over brown britches and long riding boots were pulled high over her knees.

She was settling the white mare who shifted restlessly after a long exhausting ride.

'Make yourself known stranger. Who seeks entry into the kings' presence?'

'I am the Empress Ajeya, heir to the Empire of Ataxata; daughter of the Empress Eujena and I seek an audience with their majesties, King Lyall of Durundal and Namir, King of the Clans.'

She could see the guards vying each other, but she was expecting this reception; with an arsenal of atrocities going back several decades, gaining trust in the Kingdom of Durundal was never going to be easy.

The huge gates were slowly dragged open and two of the kings' guards stood ready to escort her.

'Alight your steed and surrender your sword!'

She dismounted as instructed but had no weapon to yield. The head ostler collected the reins that were left trailing on the ground and she was taken into the courtyard where a towering fountain with a massive girth took precedence.

Carved into the impressive inferno was a trio of figures made of hammered bronze: a wolf, a leopard and a hare, looking up to the skies and dancing in the water that rained down on them. She viewed it in awe and had to walk sideways to keep the guards in sight and take in the spectacle at the same time. They looked back at her with stern faces and quickened their gait, so she caught up and fell in line, though couldn't resist a nonchalant peek back at the masterpiece.

She was led through a maze of tiled courtyards with bustling markets, a school of learning, a place of worship, outbuildings and lean-tos, store rooms and ale houses; and beyond that, in a more scattered and varied formation in the lower town, she could see the dwellings where people lived. It was truly extraordinary and unlike any other place she had ever seen.

She followed them to a flight of steps, where, at the top, a pair of huge double doors stood open.

'This is the Whispering Hall, and where you will be greeted by King Lyall of Durundal and Namir, King of the Clans,' announced the guard firmly, viewing her with ever increasing caution.

Inside the yawning archway of the doors, she paused for a moment to let her eyes grow accustomed to the dim light and then she was able to stride forward with purpose again. As she entered, the solid oak floor seemed to stretch away forever into the shadows and at the far end of the hall she could make out the raised dais where two thrones of rich mahogany were placed.

Transformed from the same deep brown wood, the arms and legs had been sculpted to represent those of a leopard and a wolf, while the face of each animal adorned the back panel. Above, hung the battle standard of the clan; a mountain lion ready to pounce, with lips drawn back in a vicious snarl, exposing wicked incisors and its claws outstretched to attack.

And as the eyes of a generation of family portraits looked out of their frames and watched her every move, she waited patiently for her hosts, surrounded by rich tapestries and intricate carvings with a single red chair facing the regal thrones.

The young men entered and took their places on the royal dais. She noticed immediately that their stature was tall and muscular, with strong defined faces framed with locks of dark brown hair. Their smouldering good looks matched the gallant description she had been given by those who had ridden alongside them; for their reputation preceded them, and the air of nobility hung like a shroud over them; and yet, even though she knew so much of their history and had a couple of years advantage in age, she couldn't help but feel the tension in their presence.

She bowed low when Lyall acknowledged her and it was only when Namir nodded his head that the sentries retreated and took their positions outside the doors. 'Good evening,' said Lyall when the guards were out of earshot. 'We have been told who you are but not what you wish to discuss.'

'My lords, it is true, my name is Empress Ajeya, Governor of the Empire of Ataxata, and I come here to pledge allegiance to your standard and sign a treaty that seals us as allies. I am aware of the atrocities at the hands of the enemy and I seek to build trust between our two kingdoms and live alongside each other in peace.'

'Your brother said much the same thing some eight months ago, and I do not wish to have my life, or that of my family put in danger again.' Namir's reply was sharp.

Ajeya looked at him. 'I know of your turmoil and distrust. I know what you have been through; my people have suffered as well. But the days of bitterness between the Houses is firmly in the past and now we must look to the future. My lords, you have my word that I will work with you both to install peace amongst the lands, and in my position as Empress, my word is my oath.'

Lyall was still unsure. 'That is most gracious of you,' he said. 'But with respect, as we know so little of your past, you must share your background with us before any form of treaty can be considered.'

Ajeya was deep in reverie as a past life flashed before her. She was twenty two years old now and had only recently discovered that she was the heir to the throne and all the subject kingdoms of the Ataxatan Empire. Before this revelation, a harsh life had groomed her and those who knew her would say she was as strong as a man, braver than most, and clever in strategy. She was a quick learner being both attentive and intuitive and had all of her mother's strength, courage and perseverance. Few compared to her mother, who had been banished with her child by the Emperor when Ajeya was only two years old. And those who remembered the proud Empress Eujena of the Ataxatan Empire said that Ajeya was her double in every way.

'To disclose my background, I have to go back to the beginning of my life, and once you have heard my story you will see that my intentions are entirely honourable.'

The two young men viewed her warily amid the bellowing chimes of caution.

'I am sure you are a person of rectitude; you speak from your heart and I can see the integrity in your eyes,' said Namir with nobility. 'Nevertheless, appearances can be deceptive and words can have hidden agendas, so I hope you understand our concern and appreciate why we have to take every precaution; be it a man, woman or a child who seeks a treaty with us.'

'Of course I understand,' she answered sincerely.

'Please Empress, remove your helmet so that we can see your face,' instructed Lyall.

She sat on the chair provided and took off the heavily embroidered cloche. Long blonde hair tumbled from beneath it and fell easily over slender shoulders; she shook it into place and looked up at them. But as she brushed her hair behind her ears, an otherwise beautiful face was cruelly disfigured on one side and the two men felt instant shame. The right side of her face was stunningly beautiful, with high cheekbones and a graceful jaw on a long neck. Long dark eyelashes rimmed exquisite blue eyes that twinkled under the arch of a light brown eyebrow and golden strands of hair framed her face perfectly. But the left side of her face was quite different, it was as though the muscles there weren't working properly. Though the eye was a stunning azure blue it drooped slightly around the rim and the muscles over the cheekbone were less taut. This affected the curve of her top lip; until she smiled that was, and then her whole face lifted in a radiant warmth. But her eyes smiled all the time, they twinkled and shone out brightly and anyone could see in her eyes that she was honourable, content and happy.

Aside from the disfigurement she was a magnificent woman, standing tall and inherently strong. To adapt to the life she had led, her body had given her a frame of outstanding muscular definition. Her hands were worn and rough indicating she had become accustomed to lifting, carrying, chopping wood and tanning hides; while a life of living with a deformity had demanded another type of strength; the strength to survive.

When she felt that the men had seen enough, she flicked the hair from behind her ears to hide the disfigurement again. 'I was born like this,' she said in response to their shocked faces.

'Forgive me. I have been insensitive and harsh,' said Namir with a pained expression.

'There is nothing to forgive. I am used to it now, it is a part of me. Most see past the imperfection after a while.' Her eyes smiled when she thought of the man who loved her. 'But my father never could and he banished me from court when he couldn't stand the sight of me anymore.'

'That actually doesn't surprise me,' said Lyall with an air of disdain.

'I was two years old. My father said that I was not his, that I was a devil born from the devil's seed. He said that no decent man would ever want me and that he couldn't have a mutant living alongside him in the palace.'

The two men shook their heads with contempt.

'He told my mother to let me die when I was born. Of course she couldn't do that, she nurtured me and loved me more than any mother could. She tried to encourage my father to love me; I was a delightful child by all accounts; but the more he saw me the more he despised me. It didn't matter how much I laughed and played and wanted to hug him, all he saw was a deformed monster. So after two years he sent both of us away.'

'Where have you been all this time? How have you fared on your own?' asked Namir, totally appalled by what he had just heard.

'Where I have been and how I have fared is all part of my story,' she said stoically. 'Sometimes it's sad, occasionally it's heartwarming, but it's always full of strength; and without doubt, this disfigurement has defined me not only as a woman but has made me the person I am today.'

Lyall looked in awe at the figure before him and already the disfigurement had melted away. 'In your own time then Empress.'

Ajeya relaxed back in the chair, caressed the amber pendant around her neck and began to tell her tale.

2

Their new world was a grey unknown tangle, smelling of pine and moss and cold. A young woman and a small child were on their own, picking their way through the scatter of loose stones and scraggly trees. The child was about two years old and clung on to her mother's hand tightly. The mother was crying, the child didn't know why. Two days before they were enjoying the riches and elegance of a palace life, now they were outcasts and had nowhere to go.

'My lord, please, think about what you are saying.'

'I know exactly what I am saying and I have been lenient with you for long enough. I cannot bear to look at that monstrosity any longer; I swear it gets more hideous by the day and it makes me feel sick to the core. I asked you to leave it to die two years ago and you wouldn't, so now I want you and that 'thing' to go.'

'Gnaeus, you can see she is your daughter, she is fair like you; she has your colour eyes. I implore you to look at your child and accept her for who she is.'

'If you are saying that thing looks like me and is born from my seed then I shall have your head taken off this instance for treachery. That thing is not my daughter. That thing is the work of the devil and if you want to keep it, then you both have to go.'

'My lord you are so wrong,' she started to weep. 'Why do you say such things?'

He had his back to her now.

'What about Cornelius? He is only five years old, he will suffer without me.'

'Phharr,' the Emperor retorted loudly. 'A mother who sleeps with the devil will not be missed I can assure you. Cornelius will be better off without you and that wretched ogre that pertains to be his sibling. Now go as far away from here as possible before I change my mind and chain both of you together to rot in the dungeons.'

Eujena winced at his despicable words but appealed for a safe place for herself and her daughter. 'Is there an out-house we can live, or a safe dwelling outside of the city where you won't have to see us?'

'What?' his face turned crimson with rage as he faced her. 'Not only do you sleep with the devil and pretend that 'thing' is mine over the past two years, you now have the audacity to ask me to find accommodation for you both.'

'But my lord, where else can I go? The palace is my home and all I know, where can I go with a small child?'

'Well you should have thought about that before you slept with the devil and gave birth to that mutant.'

She grabbed on to him. 'Please Gnaeus I am

begging you.'

'Unhand me woman before I set the hounds on you.'

'Gnaeus, I implore you, I am your wife.'

'You are nothing to me, you are a devil who breeds devils. You have no place in this palace. You and that 'thing' of yours discredit me and my dynasty. No man will ever want to father a child with that monster and I will not support you or 'it' any longer. Now go to the hills where you belong, live in the caves with other monsters and find the savages that share your poison. I want you gone.' His look was enough to turn the warmest heart to stone and she was dismissed with the wave of a hand.

She turned to her children's maid. 'Where do I go Ariane, please help me?'

'Empress Eujena, I am so sorry that I cannot help you when you have been so kind to me,' Ariane dropped her face despondently. 'All I can advise is that you go to the clans, there are many of them north of here. You cannot stay anywhere near here, the Emperor will find you and imprison you both; and anyone who shelters you will be at risk. You must go and find them, they are the only ones who can give you sanctuary.'

'Will they accept my child?'

Ariane nodded. 'Of course they will accept her.' But her face concealed her uncertainty, because a child with a deformity was a different matter. The clans had strong beliefs about devils and disfigured children being possessed by them. And as the mother of a deformed child, Eujena would be viewed just as badly; as together they could bring double the harm and bad luck to the colony. Ariane sighed heavily as Eujena posed another problem and she felt wretched in her inability to offer a more favourable solution.

'But it's still only March and the weather is not yet warm.'

'Keep to the west ma'am, follow the streams and creeks that lead to the sea, and then go north, the weather will be gentler there. The setting sun will be your guide and the moon your friend. Food will be plentiful and soon you will find refuge in a clan.'

That night Eujena woke up screaming. She bolted upright; stark terror was sent charging through her veins, pounding in her temples and racing against her heart - she stared ahead at the imaginary shapes in front of her. A sharp crack made her jump and the following flash of light lit up her surroundings. She heard a tree split seconds after and felt the shudder as it fell to the ground. She pulled up her knees and sat there, hugging them close to her chest, warm tears running down her face. Darkness filled the void for several minutes where she was left alone with her thumping breast and nauseous sense of unease. Another bright shaft followed by a loud roar momentarily lit up the pitch of night, giving her one last glimpse of her life before she was banished forever. She pulled the sheets over her and buried her tear stained face beneath it. The thunder began to roll away and rumbled over the hills as dawn brought a misty morning and an overwhelming grief.

She hadn't left when the Emperor had demanded, she couldn't leave her son and was too scared to venture out on her own. Now she had no choice; the Emperor had sent armed guards to escort her off the premises.

Ariane had smuggled a few provisions to the desperate young woman before the guards had got to her. Some fresh meat, bread, apples and a sharpened dagger secured in a sheath.

'You will be needing these dear lady; may the gods look out for you and may the guides protect you both.'

'Thank you Ariane, thank you. I will never forget your kindness.'

'And I will never forget yours Empress; have faith and the gods will protect you.'

Eujena kissed the maid on both cheeks and as the approaching guards marched their way down the corridor, Ariane rushed off before she could be punished for fraternising with the enemy. Eujena was on her own now, she had to find the clans, there was no one else. She could never go back. She would never see her son again.

Birds filled the early morning with a chorus of twittering, chirping and loud raucous calls; a world of green still wet from the storm glittered in the morning sun. A hazy mist rose up from the plains and the air felt fresh and clean. A far cry from the stagnant air in the city she decided fairly early on. It was early spring and the young woman travelled west with her daughter, crossing many walkways until she reached a large flat plain, then she veered north. She found herself travelling most of the day with the child holding her hand or she bundled her up into a sling and carried on her back. She had to count her blessings she thought, she was still alive, her daughter was still alive, they hadn't faced the hungry hounds or been imprisoned in the dungeons.

They didn't really need much food to begin with as the protein from the meat kept them full and she found it fun searching for ripe berries with her daughter, turning it into a game and seeing who could collect the most fruit - she always let Ajeya win to keep her spirits up and to stop her getting bored. Eujena realised that she could turn up roots and dig out bulbs as well which satisfied a growing appetite, and alongside the leaves, berries and flowers, they seldom went hungry.

But the furore of instant freedom and gratification soon disappeared and those first few weeks that started as a game became extremely hard going and challenging. Ajeya cried constantly and Eujena had to carry her most of the time. The ground was hard packed and matted with old growth; so her blistered feet, not used to walking on such rough terrain began to bleed. And finally, the rations that Ariane gave her ran out. Scavenging for roots and berries, leaves and shoots, quelled a ravenous appetite, but she knew it wouldn't sustain them for the long trek that lay ahead.

After a few days she felt a change in the weather, the wind picked up pace and she saw the sky turn black with storm clouds. The rumble of thunder wasn't too far away and she had to run into the thick of a forest for protection. The rain began to fall softly at first, almost kissing her face with warm gentle drops, but as she hurried her steps into the safety of the glen, the heavens opened and she fell under a natural canopy where she sat it out and waited for the bombardment of the storm to pass. A sharp crack made her jump and the following flash of light lit up her claustrophobic surroundings. She heard a tree split and felt the shudder as it fell to the ground. She pulled her child close and sat there hugging her tightly while warm tears and cold rain ran down her face in droves.

Within a matter of hours her safe refuge had turned into a morass of devastation where upturned trees had been ripped from the ground and waterlogged trunks and broken branches littered her path. It now looked completely different and as she tried to find her way out again, she found herself trudging amongst a cobweb of trees, where every sodden branch, leaf and sapling slapped her in the face or caught her by the sleeve and tried to hold her back. An arduous task proved even more difficult as she tried desperately to fight her way through the enormous dense forest; for now it was a vast maze of muddy narrow tracks and passageways hindered by corridors of wet bracken, limp foliage and stinging brambles.

She looked to the sky and saw the birds of prey circling beyond the horizon. The deluge had forced the small animals from their burrows and now was the perfect time to hunt. 'Perhaps if I follow them, they will lead me out of here, for they must be hunting in the open plains.' She lifted her weary child on to her back and made another concerted effort.

Pushing through the matted undergrowth with Ajeya hanging on for dear life, was difficult enough, but tackling the sodden path with the added weight of a child slowed her down considerably; but undeterred, she continued to brush away the thicket with slow consecutive steps. Every now and then a small creature skittered away as her feet disturbed them. It always spooked her and made her jump. A wood pigeon or grouse was panicked into flight and that made her scream out loud. She tried to control her emotions for the sake of her child and she hoped she had nodded off on her back. The glade was now becoming all too familiar at every turn; trees, boulders, bushes, they all bore the same resemblance and she started to panic. Was she going round in circles she thought, did she trust her own instincts?

Ajeya buried her head into her mother's hair and instantly felt safe. She didn't once doubt her decisions or her navigational skills and she never flinched or felt unsettled. She knew her mother was strong and intelligent, stoic and resourceful and would never let harm come her way; and there she curled, quietly and resolutely, until finally the trees and vegetation began to thin out and the welcome sight of the wide plains opened up before them.

Though Eujena soon grew tired of her nebulous world; tired of travelling, tired of the monotony of the plains, tired of the unrelenting weather and the sores on her feet. Living on shoots and berries began to have a disastrous effect and Eujena found herself sleeping for long periods at different times of the day. She slept very badly and found herself waking at all hours, and when she did get a deep sleep, she was troubled by bad dreams and always awoke feeling abominable and listless.

'I should have let Gnaeus kill me back there,' she thought to herself often. 'Even a slow agonising death would have been preferable to this.'

They had been walking for many weeks now, sometimes it was a fairly quick pace with Ajeya on her back, but that proved to be exhausting. Then she developed painful sores on her shoulders as well; so mostly they just shuffled along at a very slow pace and didn't cover any distance at all. She began to wonder if her destiny was to roam these uninhabited lands forever, never finding her salvation or a safe place to stay. Either that, or until the day that death came knocking on her door. Totally disorientated and having lost her bearings, her fruitless search for the colonies cast a constant shadow of fear and worry on the young woman, and without any proper food in the form of protein, she was bordering on the early stages of malnutrition. She was tired and hungry, her lips were chapped, her eyes were sore and her throat was always dry and parched. As she dropped her child to the floor she closed her gritty eyes and quickly succumbed to the effects of exhaustion.

She dreamed of a better place where estuaries were flanked by paths and fields, grottos and glades, and the radiant gleam of the rising sun breached the horizon illuminating the plains with an intense golden glow. She saw wooded flanks of foothills and far reaching steppes under the glare of the sun, and a narrow canyon following a path of boulders with jagged rock faces edged with bearded moss and swaying trees. She saw the sun winking on the surface of a waterfall, its incredible power sent it gushing down into the river and that made her smile. Here, the green of the land was splashed with a rainbow of colours topped by the hazy hue of the skies. Birds drifted across the horizon where they darted in and out of the cascading rapids with the artistry of an acrobat and then swooped down to the river to gorge. Long limbed storks and oversized ravens tinged with green and purple scratched around the estuary looking for food. She saw one of them coming towards her, it was large and intimidating but she wasn't afraid; she held out a hand and beckoned it closer. It jumped, cocked its head and blinked. It looked around and jumped a bit closer. The raven flapped its wings and squawked.

'Come here,' she said in her dream. 'I won't hurt you.'

The bird took another step, and another, until it was right next to her. 'Here, I have some berries.' And she felt its beak on her hand, softly at first, but then she felt a stab of pain, then another and the bird was getting more agitated and impatient for food. She felt it tearing her fingers and instantly woke up to the large carrion bird digging into her flesh and as she struck out, the raven swooped over to take Ajeya who was standing at the edge of a precipice. Without hesitation Eujena sprang out of her subdued state and threw herself onto her daughter and screamed at the scavenger. Her heart was thumping and her dry throat suddenly got even drier. The scream had taken every last ounce of energy. She didn't let her go until she was sure it was safe, only then did she slowly sit up and trembling fearfully, held her child close.

She stroked her daughter's hair and brushed her face. 'I'm so sorry my darling,' she whispered tearfully. 'I have been so tired and clumsy recently, I haven't thought any of this out properly have I?' She hugged her child and closed her eyes and wished for a better life for them both. Ajeya hugged her back and as she looked over her daughter's shoulders, she saw it. She had to shield her eyes from the glare of the sun; but down below, a ravine was dancing in the shallows.

With jewels of sunlight skipping on its surface and tendrils of rich greenery dripping all around, it opened up a whole new kingdom. There was a river of sparkling water flanked on both sides by trees and bushes; and a gorge of rocky cliffs opened out into a sheltered valley full of growth. It was her dream, it was the same vision. She could now see clearly, this was her path; because this river and surrounding area would offer food and the gorge would offer shelter.

'Ariane told me to follow the rivers,' she said to Ajeya. 'She told me it would keep us alive.' Eujena got to her feet and taking her daughter's hand, led her down the path to the pulsating rapids where they could see that the river was full of fresh clean water and surrounded by a land that was burgeoning with life.

3

Their camp was a shallow stone bowl cut deep into the hilltop overlooking the river where they huddled close together and watched the birds of prey feast on a gourmet of nature's offerings. As the sprouting herbs and grasses tempted burrowing voles, shrews, mice, rabbits and snakes from their nests, so the great buzzards, kites and eagles began to gorge; and if they could feast on small animals, then surely she could as well.

She would make a trap to catch them and build a fire to cook them and get more sustenance that way. By watching the area carefully she could see the path that the animals took. She made a snare by using the stringy fibres from the milkweed plant; tied it to a small sapling and left a noose with some bait inside. She soon discovered that by catching her own game the food was plentiful, and finding wood for the fire was painless. Though getting the fire started was close to impossible and many times she felt like giving up and wept into the sunset.

Then she remembered her young son Cornelius telling her about a lesson where he had been taught how to build a fire using a fire drill and a hearth: as the stick spins an ember is formed, dried moss is added to create fuel and fire is the result.

But it was not that easy; her hands were raw by spinning the fire drill between her palms and it kept slipping on the wooden platform. It wasn't long before they began to bleed and she had to stop with the pain.

She ripped a section of her long dress to bandage them and looking at the little girl who relied so much on her for survival, she kept going beyond the discomfort. Eujena soon got into the rhythm of the movement, ignoring the sweat that formed on her brow and ran down into her eyes; her hands were needed to keep the momentum going, even a second delay could mean failure.

With the continual movement, the hole deepened and sawdust from the soft wood accumulated. She smelled the woodsmoke and saw the notch blacken and then she saw a wisp of smoke. That vision fuelled her, even though her palms were still bleeding and her arms ached all over, she could not give up now. With more glows and more smoke she held her head parallel to the hearth and began to blow on it; she watched it grow brighter with each breath and die down as she inhaled. She added tiny bits of shaved curls and continued to blow. Then a spark grew from out of the hearth which turned into a small flame. She blew harder, fed it more fuel and when it had taken hold, she added a few splints of kindling wood, adding larger pieces of driftwood when it had established itself.

And as she watched her man-made giant rise

into the air, it ignited a dormant emotion in her, a surge like nothing she had ever known before. She had accomplished something that had seemed unfeasible, almost unfathomable, practically impossible; but she had done it, on her own with sheer determination; and the satisfaction spilled out in a loud cry of sheer elation.

At that moment, in a lonely valley in the middle of nowhere, somewhere between the north and south territories, a young woman stood with her child by her side and she knew she could survive; she had ridden the storm, she had provided food and warmth. She knew that she was powerful, she knew she had the strength.

She stood up and danced, she took Ajeya by the hands and skipped round the flames, shouting, singing, praising the gods, thanking the spirits. The fire roared, the flames soared; yellow, orange, blue, magnificent, powerful, strong like her. She raised her arms to the skies to give thanks. Ajeya span around in circles. They were both drunk on happiness, they had both found their strength. And that night they feasted on succulent rabbit, seared to perfection and slept soundly with a belly full of food.

They didn't stay long in one place, they kept moving, and by keeping close to the streams, they always had clean water to drink, fresh meat to eat; and the plants and roots gave them a rich and varied diet. Eujena had now learned to take a variety of fish out of the rivers with wide mesh baskets made of cattail leaves and alder branches and cords made from stringy bark. She could gut them easily with the dagger that she had been given, and by doing this on frequent occasions, the fish provided them with a rich source of nutrition.

Survival, she surmised, was not so much about equipment, it was more about foresight and knowledge and making as much use of nature's harvest as possible.

She hadn't fully realised how constrained her life had been until she had tasted freedom; how dull and constricted it had become, answerable to only men without any voice of her own. Relying on servants for her every whim, learning about her children's progress from a tutor or a maid, and her hardest decision was what she should wear that day. And yes, this journey had been like climbing a perilous mountain at times, with the wind and the rain beating down against her, exposing her to all types of disturbing sounds and hidden dangers; but through it all, she embraced this new life.

She liked the challenge of making her own decisions, selecting her own food and choosing her own path; following the rivers and keeping the sun and moon as a guide. It was as if she had found the real person inside her soul, a person who could adapt and provide, who could face her fears and overcome danger. She seemed to quickly forget the life she had been born into, and soon, nothing from that life, apart from her child, was important to her.

The tiny girl was her only form of companionship, and although they only communicated in simple terms; it was wonderful to share the days experiences, to marvel at a discovery, to applaud an accomplishment, and for her child; with the hungry appetite and the fervent look in her eyes, she had to remain positive. She had to say that it wasn't much further, that they would find a clan soon to keep them safe, to give them shelter before the weather changed. She had to survive for the sake of her daughter.

Eujena had given the maid's bindle to Ajeya to store an abundance of ripe vegetation while she tore up more of her dress to make a small carrier for herself and had loaded it with her fire making materials and flexible baskets. The little girl looked around her with curiosity while they travelled, watching everything her mother did and she was particularly interested whenever they stopped to gather food. Eujena often gave her a bite of a fresh bud or a tender young shoot which ignited taste buds that had previously been lying dormant, and by doing that, even at this young age, Ajeya was building up a memory bank of plants. She quickly learned to notice the different identifying characteristics and began to smell and touch each leaf and every petal before making a decision whether to pick it or not.

As they ventured further north, the heavy brown barks of oak, beech, walnut and maple were intermixed with a delicate floral blossom, giving an early promise of a good summer with an abundance of fruit and other ripe delicacies. The terrain had been changing gradually as they travelled north and Eujena was recording each detail of the landscape that they passed through, especially the vegetation; and now she was entering territory where each shape of leaf, most height of stalks and every size of berry was an unfamiliar sight.

After finishing the climb of rolling hills interspersed with broad flat steppes, they stopped for the evening by a brook where Eujena made her characteristic snare and put some dark red berries in the middle to tempt a small rodent. She had made camp behind some rocks in a crude lean-to, snuggled up with her shawl over them both and watched for an animal to take the offering. They watched and waited as the stillness of the night fell around them; black leafed trees waved and fluttered in the twilight breeze, silhouetted against a darkening sky. Everything was stolid now and so very quiet; even the smell of night was different. She didn't want to light a fire just yet incase it deterred the curiosity of their meal; but even without the fire, not one animal was interested in the trap. Some animals ventured close, but whether it was the smell or a sixth sense, not one of them took the bait. Giving in to tiredness and going without food, mother and infant awoke to the pangs of hunger and a dry parched mouth.

But for Eujena, the shock of something in the distance melted those feelings to the pit of her stomach; for she saw in the middle of her snare, a dead animal. The snare had failed, but something hadn't, and the mammal had succumbed to the effects of another type of death where the noose had not killed it. Eujena told

Ajeya to stay where she was while she inspected the corpse.

She took a small bite of the berry, but the taste was rancid and instantly made her feel nauseous, she spat out the contents immediately, her mouth began to tingle and her tongue began to burn, she ran to the brook to swill out her mouth with fresh water, coughing and retching for what seemed an eternity. Ajeya ran over, clearly distraught at watching her mother suffer and wrapped small arms around her.

'I'm ok, really I am,' said Eujena. 'Don't worry, mother just has to be more careful in future.' She brushed the hair from her child's face and saw nothing but beauty.

'You see this berry?'

Ajeya nodded her head and was deadly serious.

'It's poisonous, it's what killed the rabbit, we must not eat it, even if it looks ripe and nourishing, these berries are not meant for us.'

She showed her the fruit, glistening and succulent in the morning sun; it looked so appetising and full of flavour.

'Can we eat the rabbit?' Ajeya asked, clearly hungry.

'No, we can't my love, the fruit is bad and will be inside the rabbit; we can't eat it little one. I will find us a better one to eat tonight.'

From that day on she had to perform a thorough test on any unfamiliar vegetation. If the taste made her tongue sting then she spat it out immediately. If it was palatable then she took a small bite and waited to see if there were any delayed symptoms by the next day. It was only after these thorough tests that she was able to identify what was safe for their consumption and what wasn't.

But it wasn't just poisonous plants Eujena had to watch out for.

On a bright sunlit day, when it was warm and tranquil with the beginning of summer, the trees were in full bloom and lazy flies tormented a week old carcass. A fresh breeze carried a pungent aroma and the moving sun sent shadows chasing the foliage across the slopes and steppes of a flourishing land.

They were walking through dense undergrowth; Ajeya was secured tightly onto Eujena's back with a sling; she was asleep while her mother foraged and selected the ripest berries putting them into her bag. She used her dagger to hack away the bracken and vegetation obscuring her path and hadn't realised how far she had gone, and it was there that she heard an unusual sound. Her ears tuned in to a disturbing grunting and snorting which seemed to be coming towards her. She stopped moving and hardly dared to breathe. She felt the child on her back, she would be safe there she decided. Eujena had to stay put, she couldn't turn and run because then her child would get the full force should the creature decide to attack. She had no choice but to wait it out as rigid as she could until the animal passed.

The sounds of snapping branches and moving bushes got closer; the muffled snorts of something feasting was perilously near, she had her dagger ready and crouched low. The waiting was intolerable and she tried to calm her pulsating heart and rapid breathing. The beaded sweat of fear ran down her face and despite the urge to wipe it away, she stood perfectly still.

But Ajeya moved behind her and suddenly, without warning, the animal burst through the thick growth, its large powerful body supported by short stocky legs, wickedly sharp lower canines protruded like tusks along both sides of its snout, small deep set eyes on a massive head were wild and it was storming towards her with the full wrath of a tempestuous tornado. As it got closer, the smell was nauseating, as the bristling hairs over a grey humped back covered cracked skin with ground in mud and faeces.

The wild pig glared at her. She threw a rock to deter it, closely followed by another one, but that only angered it further and the beast came roaring and scrambling. With just inches to spare Eujena thrust the dagger up into the creature's gullet, but it didn't stop the stab of a sharp implement in her thigh. With a splintering force, the pointed end of a huge tusk rammed into her. Blood quickly swamped round the incision. Her leg buckled beneath her and she groaned with the pain. With the tusk still in the top of her leg, she retracted the dagger and struck again. This time the boar gurgled its last breath and slumped to the floor. She pulled her leg free from the tusk and gritted her teeth to stop herself from screaming out loud and frightening her small child.

Her blood gushed out in spurts, which, running down to the ground, mixed an unsavoury palette with the red aqueous liquid pouring from the dead boar. Breathing heavily and trying to remain upright she ripped more material from her dress and applied a tight tourniquet round the penetrating wound. Ajeya was still sleeping. Shaking and gradually losing consciousness, Eujena found her way out of the undergrowth and back out into the open. Her head was swimming now and her leg throbbing, she staggered a few more steps, tried to catch her breath and then collapsed to the ground.

4

'What is it father?' asked the young boy.

'I don't know son, wait here while I take a look.'

The father pulled his horse and cart to a stop, just a few feet short of where Eujena and her child were laying. The horse snorted and swivelled his ears back and forth, he could smell blood and became unsettled; the young lad sat rigid in the front seat. The father jumped down and made his way over to the mound of clothes. He held his spear ready and advanced with caution. All his senses were alert. He listened for the sounds of breathing or any other disturbance of a predator hiding, he smelled the air for any distinctive odours and allowed his intuition to guide him as he carefully approached the obstruction.

Suddenly there was movement and the young child wriggled free from its swaddling. The young father stopped in his tracks, unsure of whether to proceed; he didn't want to alarm the infant. He held back while the girl's eyes adjusted to the light and her surroundings. He crouched low and looked around, he was still on the lookout for any unwanted carnivores. The girl nudged her mother; there was no movement. She walked around the body and hugged her.

The father looked back at his son; he was all right so the father edged closer, shielding his eyes from the bright sunlight and taking tentative steps. He heard a groan; it must be the child's mother he surmised. The child was getting distressed now and started to cry. Instinctively he waved aside his caution and moved more urgently to offer comfort and support and to ascertain the situation. But the first thing he saw was the mother's leg and that her life was pumping out through a deep intrusive gash. A makeshift tourniquet was soaked in blood and not doing much to protect the huge incision. He swatted away the nuisance flies that were eager to feast on the exposed flesh and untied the sodden bandage. He examined the wound, it was definitely the tusk of a wild boar that had inflicted this injury and judging by the amount of blood, he knew that an artery had been pierced. He spun round to see if the hunter was near. There was no sign. He immediately applied pressure to her groin with one hand then managed to take the shirt from his back and kneeling on one end, ripped a sleeve off with the other. He then looked around for a smooth stone for pressure and when it was wiped clean and put in place, he wrapped the whole leg in the temporary bandage. The force of his actions immediately stemmed the flow. He then looked at Ajeya, who by now, was covered in tear stained blood. He recoiled at her disfigured face. His hands flew up to his mouth as he stifled his shock.

'You poor lamb,' he cried out. 'The beast got you as well, how on earth have you survived?' He reached

33

out for her to offer compassion. The child held up her arms in response. 'Come with me; my people will take care of you both. Now I will put you next to my son Keao and then I will carry your mother to the wagon. Do not fear little one. You are safe with us. We will take care of you.' He lifted the small child up onto the front seat of the wagon where the twelve year old boy looked in horror at her disfigured side. 'It's all right son, there is nothing to be frightened of, it's just a small girl with a dreadful injury to her face.'

'But she must be in terrible agony and yet she does not scream or cry.' Keao looked on in disbelief.

'She is in shock, that's what shock does to you; it renders you speechless and stops the pain,' his father assured him.

The boy continued to stare at the child with his eyes set wide.

'Hold her hand son, then she will know that she is safe. I will get the mother.'

'What are we going to do with them?' asked the boy taking the little girl's hand.

'We are going to take care of them like any good clan member would.' He went back to where Eujena lay. 'It's all right, I am going to lift you now, so don't be afraid, I am not going to hurt you.'

As he put his arms under her fragile frame her eyelids fluttered and she moaned with the pain. 'My child, where is my child?'

'She is all right, she is sitting with my son, he is a good boy and is taking care of her.'

She felt herself being lifted by the strong powerful arms and put her own around his neck and instantly felt safe. 'Thank you for saving us,' she whispered, grateful for his intervention.

'You look like you've been out here for a long time,' he said with a gentle voice. 'Maybe you have lost your way.'

She tried to answer. But didn't have the strength.

'Don't speak now,' he said kindly. 'We can talk later back at the camp.'

'Camp, which camp do you speak of?' she whispered with an air of caution.

'The home of the Giant's Claw,' he replied proudly. 'We are clan people.'

He carried her to the back of the wagon and laid her down carefully. There were a number of blankets and animal pelts which he arranged to keep her warm. And then, for the first time in months, cocooned in the warmth of the furs and knowing that they were safe, she fell into a tranquil state of calm. The feeling warmed her bones from the tip of her toes to centre of her heart. She had found the clans at last.

The two children had turned around to watch him make her comfortable, though Keao found himself staring at the young girl's face again.

'Stop staring at her Keao,' the father said curtly. 'You will scare her. When she is all cleaned up and her wounds have healed you will see that she is as pretty as her mother.'

Eujena smiled at the remark, but almost immediately her body shivered under the layers.

5

As the rickety trap trundled along the barren path, Ajeya kept looking at her injured mother in the back. The young boy continued to hold the child's hand for comfort but couldn't steer his eyes away from her unsightly face.

'It's very bad manners to stare,' said the father, shifting his gaze from between the horse's ears to his son's glare. 'You will make her feel awkward and she's only little.'

'I can't help it though,' replied the boy still staring. 'How will she ever get better?'

'Of course she will get better, just like her mother will get better. The very clever medicine woman will see to it.' The father smiled and snapped the reins over the horse's rump.

Although being jostled for most of the journey, Eujena felt incredibly safe in the back and opened her eyes sufficiently to take in her new surroundings. She could see open meadows of grazing livestock and numerous fields yielding produce and despite her dreadful injuries, she was was able to focus on what was around her as this strange new kingdom got bigger and closer.

The bustle of village life got noisier and she strained to pick out a range of different sounds. The smell of cooking reached out to her first and she felt a wave of nausea rise in the back of her throat; food was the last thing on her mind. The wagon took her past clusters of homes where a hive of anxious faces popped out of doorways. Groups of working peasants looked up from their chores for the first time. Concerned murmurs from adults weaved amongst the anxious sounds from children, all shocked and aghast at the sight of the badly injured child.

They came to a halt outside the largest hut in the village and the father jumped down quickly. 'Wait here Keao, I must go and see the medicine woman first.'

The boy grunted an answer but continued to stare at Ajeya while she sat perfectly still and unfazed by the whole situation.

The Shaman's room was of a considerable size with rows upon rows of shelves, cupboards and tables, all crammed to the brim with stopped vials and glass bottles containing various coloured liquids. There were countless jars of dried herbs, stacked boxes of pressed flowers, an assortment of bowls containing every type of leaf, as well as piles of stripped bark and rolls of parchment everywhere. She had a herb or a powder or a liquid for everything, and that's why she was known as Ukaleq the healer; the great Shaman and alchemist.

An array of animal hide cushions served as lounging seats whilst layers of animal pelts and woven blankets befitted the sleeping arrangements. A cauldron and a kettle sat continually on the hearth and an old woman sat humming by the fire. The air was scented. It took a moment for him to place the sweet smell; a special essence used for the sick. He breathed in the incense and placed it as a waft from the yarrow flower. The healer opened her eyes calmly when he entered the room and her gaze fell upon his naked chest.

'Hagen, what a sight for sore eyes you are,' she smiled at him affectionately. 'So what brings you here today?'

A dipped smile camouflaged his flushed face until his predicament took precedence. 'It is a woman, she is not from our clan, but I found her on the plains. She has been terribly injured by a boar and her child is hurt also. But what concerns me most is that whilst the child's facial injuries are severe, I think she is in a deep shock as she displays no pain or distress.'

The medicine woman looked into his penetrating steel blue eyes for a moment; then, breathing in deeply, she placed her hands together as if to pray. She chanted a few times to summon the healing spirits and then opened her arms wide to welcome them. She closed her eyes and let out a sigh. 'The spirits have spoken and they will allow me to treat these women. Bring them to me and I will do what I can.'

The child was brought in first and laid down on a bed of animal furs.

'You will be safe here,' said Hagen. 'Ukaleq will take care of you now.' He smiled at her kindly and brushed the hair from her face. He shook his head in dismay at her injuries and looked despairingly at Ukaleq. The woman nodded and set to work while Hagen went to get Eujena.

Gently, but with experienced thoroughness, the healer washed Ajeya's face with an absorbent piece of rabbit skin dipped in the simmering liquid from the cauldron in which an iris root had boiled; then she scooped out the root pulp and put it directly on the child's face and covered the unguent with the same piece of rabbit skin. All the time she was humming and chanting and wafting the essence of mugwort over the child to induce sedation. A soft downy robe was draped over her body and a vial of soothing liquid from the yarrow flower was given to her orally. Ajeya didn't even notice her mother being brought into the room because she had given way to the aromatic smells and chanting and had succumbed to a peaceful sleep. Hagen put Eujena down on the prepared palette and whispered that all was well, that her child was being treated by the great Shaman and she should not be concerned. The healer then came over to Eujena and Hagen left the room.

As Eujena came to her senses slowly, a hazy light obscured the grey blur of sleep and she opened one eye believing that she was still in the wagon. But the sounds weren't familiar, neither were the surroundings. She didn't know where she was, but she felt safe and at ease now. She tried to pull herself up; though every fibre in her body felt heavy as she moved and became aware that she was laying on a pile of animal skins. She fell back instantly onto a soft plump pillow and breathed in the drops of ayahuasca bark which had saturated her head rest.

Ukaleq first of all cut away her long outer garments and carefully removed the tourniquet that Hagen had applied, she could see that the wound was seeping now and not pumping which was a good sign; Hagen had certainly saved this woman's life. She applied pressure to the leg while she washed the wound with an infusion of bugloss and the same astringent from the simmering cauldron. She cleaned it thoroughly, flushing the debris out and wiping away the congealed blood so that she could get a better look at the injury. Under the deep laceration she could see an artery had been cut, so she quickly went over to her stores of medicines and poured the ground up leaves of Lady's mantle to stop the bleeding. When she was satisfied with the result she took a needle made of splintered bone and a strand of wet sinew from a pot of moist snapdragon weed and began to sew the gash together. Eujena moved and twitched several times, but the bruised nerve endings and applied ayahuasca meant that she didn't feel any pain. Ukaleq managed to put eight knots along the wound and covered it all with a poultice from the mashed iris root. Covering her over with a thin blanket, she then went to get a vial of pure comfrey oil which dripped into the side of her mouth. Only then did the healer sit back on her heels and rocked as she chanted a healing melody. And while the nutrients and life giving properties were being administered into her body, Ukaleq noticed a smile creasing in the corners of the young woman's mouth, a dewy glaze fell over her face and a colour so subtle returned to her cheeks; and she knew instantly that this fragile woman had fallen under his spell and that she was dreaming of the beautiful Hagen.

But more than that, she knew that the child had not been cut, she had not been hurt, that there were no injuries to speak of; only a congenital malformation of the muscle and skin, and she really didn't know how the rest of the clan would respond to the intrusion of a deformed child.

6

As she watched her two new patients sleep, her mind was taken back to a time twelve years ago, a particular day when she had watched the spring rains wash away the last of the snow and the first crocus heads could be seen poking through the ground. The apple blossom had turned a subtle shade of pink and the first blooms had hinted at a blistering summer. For Hagen and his wife, this was to be a joyful day as they were about to welcome their first child into the world. She remembered how Hagen had come sprinting over to her hut in ecstatic excitement and began stumbling over incomprehensible words.

'It's Raine - she has started. It's coming. Please - it's her first.'

'Has she broken her waters?'

Her question was greeted with a furrowed brow and a quizzical look.

Ukaleq shot him a thin smile. 'I will come over. You go back to Raine and I will gather some of my medicines.

'Thank you.' He turned to go, but stopped at the entrance. 'You won't be long will you?'

'Hagen, these things can take hours, not

minutes. Now you just go and sit with her and make sure that she is comfortable.'

Hagen's face looked confused at the request and Ukaleq threw him an affectionate glance.

The Shaman had been concerned at Raine's pregnancy from the start. Spotting had been relentless but the sickness was the worst she had ever seen. She had given her regular doses of chamomile and meadowsweet throughout, both of which would usually cure a nauseous stomach; also the leaves from the mint bush and ginger root were made into a comforting tea, but that couldn't be kept down either. Ukaleq was expecting Raine to lose the baby at any time with the continued sickness, indeed she didn't know how it could grow to a full sized baby without any food at all. But grow it did, and whilst the foetus took every ounce of nutrition from its mother, Raine clung on to full term and was now ready to deliver. Ukaleq had collected baskets of raspberry leaf and willow bark to help with the contractions whilst a healthy supply of thyme was gathered to help her recovery and she would make a concoction to fight off any infection with the afterbirth.

She remembered that the contractions at the beginning were easy and Raine was managing comfortably with them. Hagen was sitting by her side continually offering support while the Shaman chanted and wafted aromatic essences round the room. All through the morning those women who had safely born a child, came into Raine's hut; it was considered a good omen if such women cast their auras over the new mother to be. Some stopped for a few moments while others sat with her for longer, offering their own tales and their own advice.

By late afternoon the contractions were getting stronger. As the pain mounted, the new mother took a deep breath and bore down with an effort that made her veins stand out and the beads of sweat collected in rivets in the wells of her collar bones. Her head swam with the exertion and she collapsed in a heap back on to the bed. Ukaleq gave her more doses of raspberry leaf tea and as the evening dragged into the next day, Hagen was becoming increasingly worried.

'There is something wrong, I know it,' he whispered to the Shaman with the guise of a vexed man.

'I can't lie to you, I am concerned,' said an anxious Ukaleq.

'Maybe you should go outside now Hagen. I will have to try something else to reposition the baby.'

'Are you sure about this?'

His question was not pleasantly received. 'I am the medicine woman, I know what I am doing Hagen.'

Raine lay in the bed, drenched with sweat, clutching the sheets on which she lay with white knuckles showing. She tried to stifle the screams as Ukaleq tried to reposition the baby by rotating her stomach, but in an already weakened state she didn't have the strength and her wails split the air.

'Your pelvis is too narrow,' said Ukaleq. 'And

the baby is oblique, I will have to try to move the child internally.'

Raine was given yarrow root to help with the pain and as the days and nights blurred together in a haze of suffering, even the Shaman was expecting the worst. With a huge loss of blood and in an already weakened state, the young Raine didn't have any more strength.

'She's too weak,' said one mother.

'She can't push,' said another.

'The baby will die,' came a third.

The Shaman now had but one chance to get the baby out, and without another minute to spare, she reached inside the mother and pulled at the baby, feet first.

For Raine, it felt as if all her insides were rupturing at once. That her body was being turned inside out. She felt a huge weight bearing down on her and thought that her very soul was being ripped out from deep within. Soon though, the worst was over, and a healthy baby boy with a shock of black hair, screaming and hollering with indignation, was lifted into the air and given to his mother for suckling. Then, when the baby had fed and the mother slid back down on the sheets for a much needed rest, the remaining mothers cleaned her up while Hagen cradled his new son.

'I shall call him Keao because he is the light of my day, and to my dear wife Raine, I salute you.'

But she was already fast asleep. Hagen placed

Keao in a cradle softened with a mattress of goose feathers and swaddled in layers of rabbit furs. The contented boy slept peacefully after taking the thick creamy liquid from his mother's breast and taking his wife in his arms, Hagen kept a vigil over his new born son.

That night a squall blew in; lightning crashed down from the sky and a searing white bolt split a hundred year old oak in a heartbeat. This storm had a fury like no other and as its thunder roared, it shook the very foundations of the earth to the core. A gap in their doorway turned the night to day and as Hagen hammered down the flaps, another streak of lightning shivered through the black dome of the sky and thunder cracked across the plains. His child slept soundly throughout, but his wife broke out in a fever and the bedding was as saturated as the ground outside. She tossed and turned in a delirious state and screamed out louder than the thunder when a gush of thick red blood soaked the sheets. He tried to settle her. He got strips of cloth and tried to wipe the constant sweats from her face but she pushed him away. He tried to give her warm water but she threw it across the room. He brought the baby to her thinking he would calm her down, but she gripped on to the bed with her white knuckles showing and the veins stood out on her neck. He had to put Keao back in the crib.

'I have to get help,' his voice was anxious. He tried to stifle the panic. 'I don't know what to do Raine, tell me what to do!'

She grabbed hold of him and held him for a moment; her eyes burrowing into his with the pain. She managed to mouth the words 'I love you' and then sank back on the bed and arched her back in agony.

The man was torn, he had to go and get the Shaman, but he didn't want to leave his wife. The storm was as its very worst now, but he ran faster than the howling gale to the Shaman's hut.

'You must come quickly Ukaleq, there is something wrong, seriously wrong, please come quickly!'

The medicine woman threw on her cape, snatched up a few herbs and rushed as fast as she could to the sick woman. But by the time they got there it was too late. The claws of Death had claimed his wife. A grey lifeless corpse was all that remained. The thunder rolled away taking the storm with it and Hagen chased it to the hills.

Hours later, the rain stopped and the thunder was rumbling softly in the distance. She found Hagen alone; sobbing, curled up in a ball and soaked to the skin. He had left his wife; she had died alone, and he would have to live with that for the rest of his days.

That was twelve years ago, and as Ukaleq looked over to the sleeping Eujena, she knew that Hagen had at last eased a heavy heart. He had managed to save the life of this young woman when neither of them could save his wife.

The next day, Hagen came in to see the progress of the two injured females. 'How are they today Ukaleq?'

'They are both fine,' she answered with great knowledge.' And they will both live, you will be pleased to hear.'

'Even the mother, she will live?'

'Even the mother Hagen.'

He span round on his heels a full circle and put his hands to his head. 'Thank you,' he cried out loud. 'Thank you so much.'

But the Shaman was humble. 'You saved her life Hagen, I just finished up, it's you she has to thank.'

'It's been a long time coming Ukaleq, but I feel at ease now. I have saved a woman's life when I was unable to save my dearest Raine,' he wiped away a tear.

'The spirits make life hard at times,' she said resolutely. 'Everything is sent to test our resolve.'

'I know, we all have to face our demons,' his tone was sombre.

'But we do have one small problem,' she posed the dilemma.

'Oh?'

'The child.'

'But you said they would both live.'

'And they both will live.'

'So what is the problem?'

'The child is not hurt, she did not receive an injury, she is not cut. Her face is a congenital deformity. She was born like it Hagen. It cannot be fixed.' The

Shaman's voice withered to a stony silence.

The colour drained from Hagen's face. 'But the clan won't let her live with a deformity.'

'I know - and that is our problem,' she sighed heavily.

Hagen looked everywhere for answers, he looked at the mother, and then pitifully at the slumbering infant. His eyes filled with tears. 'Ukaleq, I can't let another woman die, even if she is just a child. What are we going to do?'

7

Hagen came back the next day and the next and as the days rolled into weeks, the child grew stronger, though her mother took a little while longer. Ukaleq had decided to keep the child in the hut with her until Hagen had spoken to the mother and explained the situation. But by now the clan leader was aware and asking questions about the strangers.

'Ukaleq, I know you are the Shaman, and you are the wisest woman in the settlement, but as leader of this clan, I need to be aware of whom it is that we are harbouring.'

'I know Thorne, and you will be allowed in soon, but the child is not fully recovered and the mother still sleeps. It would be unwise to have too many different people coming and going.'

The leader rubbed his unruly grey beard between old gnarled fingers and narrowed his thin crinkly eyes. He took a long deep sniff of air. 'A few more days, then I will have to see them.'

'Of course.' Ukaleq bowed low and scurried back to her position by the girl and applied a fresh dressing of pulp and astringent to the disfigurement and called upon the spirits to help this child before the leader cast his disparaging eyes and sealed her fate forever.

'I thought you said she couldn't be fixed,' said Hagen entering the hut when he saw the leader had gone.

'She can't Hagen, but I am trying to make it look less obvious and asking for the spirits to help her.'

He looked over to the mother and heard her moan. Ukaleq handed him a mug of willow bark tea and gestured to him to give it to Eujena while she attended to the little girl.

'It's good to see you awake,' he said, and waited for her to acknowledge him.

Eujena propped herself on to one elbow and winced as she tried to move her leg. He immediately jumped to her aid and helping her up, propped up the pillows behind her to make her as comfortable as he could.

She smiled at his thoughtfulness. 'Thank you,' she said weakly.

'You are very welcome - so how are you feeling?' he handed her the tea.

As her leg throbbed, she recalled the force of the boar with a shudder and felt the sharp tusk penetrating her thigh. She remembered finding her way out of the gorse and then her mind went blank. She sipped on the soothing liquid and spoke as she recalled. 'I was attacked by a boar, I tried to fix the injury.'

'Yes, I found you, do you remember?'

She thought long and hard, but she couldn't

remember much. 'I remember being lifted,' she said.

He smiled. 'Yes, I lifted you into the back of my wagon.'

'I don't remember that but I do remember all the different smells as we came into the camp.'

He smiled at that. 'Yes, there is always food on the go here.'

Her nose began to twitch and she felt the pit of her stomach growl as the familiar odours of cooking stirred the pangs of hunger and she followed the trail to a cauldron of meaty broth simmering over the fire.

'Would you like something to eat?' He noticed the hungry look in her eye.

'I would, very much, thank you,' she looked around the hut anxiously. 'But where is my daughter?'

'She is over here with me,' she heard Ukaleq say, and noticed the old woman feeding her the very same broth.

'Is she all right? I mean, is she hurt?'

'Your daughter is fine, she is not hurt. I have cleaned her and she has rested,' Ukaleq's tone was reassuring to Eujena. 'Would you like to go and see your mother now?'

The child nodded and Ukaleq took her over to her mother's side.

'You see, your child is recovered.'

Eujena arranged a wisp of hair over the disfigured side of her face as if to hide it for the first time. The action didn't go unnoticed by Hagen and Ukaleq who looked uncomfortably at each other.

'This is Ukaleq,' said Hagen bringing over the broth. 'She is our medicine woman and has made you both well again.

The Shaman shook her head. 'I finished up, it was Hagen who saved your life. He saved both of you.'

'Thank you so much, I am indebted to you, we are both indebted to you aren't we my beautiful girl?' Eujena kissed her daughter's face and pressed the disfigured side to her breast.

'So who are you and where have you come from?' said Hagen at last.

'Well, my name is Eujena, and this is my very precious daughter Ajeya, who is nearly three now.'

'And how come you were all alone out in the wilderness?'

Eujena hadn't really thought her story through. She pondered for a while and bit her lip, she searched for the best answer that she could find. But there was none. She really just wanted to forget everything about her previous life and never speak of it again. A short trill laugh came from the back of her throat. She shook her head a couple of times and pinched her temples with her thumb and fore finger.

'You know what? I really can't remember. The fall must have caused amnesia. I am sorry, but I can't tell you any more.'

8

Whilst her mother was chatting with Hagen and Ukaleq, Ajeya managed to slip out unnoticed to prop herself up against a large rock and watch the activities of the people around her. The food and fresh dressing had revived her, so feeling safe and secure she stayed close to the hut, but it was far enough to attract attention. She was particularly interested in the cooking arrangements and spent the time watching the women set it up. In a large pit that had been dug out by a working fireplace, hot coals were placed on top of recently used ashes that lined the bottom. A layer of powdered, dried aurochs dung was poured on the coals, and on top of that was placed a large welded rack born from the furnace of the blacksmith. With a continued and sustained temperature of heat, whole carcasses were lain across the struts which would render a more succulent meat and make easier skinning and tanning of the hide. She had watched her own mother struggle with their cooking and she would try and remember this much more resourceful method.

Though while she was engrossed, a gentle breeze brushed the carefully placed curl from the side of her face and her disfigurement was cruelly exposed.

The passing clan members and working women glanced in her direction and muttering under their breath, kept a safe distance from the devil's child. She wasn't aware of the hostilities and certainly didn't understand the fierce glares. Nevertheless, not wanting to go too far from her mother, she stayed close by the hut and picked flowers to give as gifts to her saviours.

It wasn't too long before word got around and an elderly man appeared, and with tentative steps, he approached her. He smiled kindly so as not to cause alarm. She had never seen seen such a wrinkled skin in all her life, nor someone who was so bent over and walked so slowly. The unruly beard made her giggle and the crumpled crinkly eyes looked like those of a bird to her.

For him, in all his years, he had never seen a face so horribly disfigured and he found himself staring at the puckered skin, the drooping eye and the misshapen mouth. He found himself keeping his distance and not wanting to be too close incase he caught something from her.

But then she looked at him with her deep whirlpool eyes and smiled; and impetuously and with the uninhibited reactions of a child, she ran up to him and reached out to touch his face. Without thinking he bent down to her and gave permission. As she compared their faces with her small hand, touching his ancient wrinkled folds and then her own deformed side, she decided that they weren't very different at all.

Thorne was taken aback as she tenderly stroked

his weathered skin, for none of the children had ever reached out to him like that before. But she was not repulsed by him or scared of him, she didn't recoil in horror at the touch of his imperfect face. And that's when he found his compassion and looked at her beautiful innocence and found himself smiling.

'Would you mind if I sat down with you for a while?' he asked softly.

Ajeya took his hand and led him to her favoured spot where he sat on the boulder and she played at his feet.

'Do you know who I am?' he asked.

She looked at his face and shook her head.

'My name is Thorne, and I am the leader of this clan.'

She handed him a flower.

'Thank you,' he said and smelled the beautiful fragrance. 'No one has given me a flower before.'

She smiled.

'What is your name child?'

'Ajeya,' she said, and carried on with her interesting game on the ground.

'And your mother, what is her name?'

'Eujena.'

'What beautiful names,' he pondered for a while.

Then she stood up and reached out to him, he picked her up and sat her on his knee. She then put her arms around his neck and pulled his head down to rest her disfigured cheek against his own. His beard tickled her and she brushed it out of the way and snuggled in to the embrace of his ancient arms. He noticed her warm breath on his skin and felt her beating heart against his worn out bones. He found himself rocking the child and humming to her in a natural and comforting way. And then a tear ran down his face as he knew what he had to do next would be one of the hardest things in his life.

His emotions were stifled when the three adults came tearing out of the hut looking for her. Eujena didn't even notice the pain in her leg or her racing heart. She had just been told of the severity of having a disfigured child in a clan and what the implications entailed. With total shock and a deep sense of failure, she faced the leader with her daughter still sitting on his knee.

'Good afternoon,' he said. 'And you must be Eujena.'

She nodded meekly and an even quieter voice managed to say, 'yes.'

'I have been chatting with Ajeya here.' He brushed her deformed cheek and Eujena trembled.

The child kissed his loose jowls in response.

'I will need to speak with Ukaleq and Hagen now Eujena, I hope you understand.'

She nodded her head while stopping the nausea at the back of her throat.

He lifted Ajeya and put her back on the ground. 'You go inside with your mother now my dear child, and I will see you again in a few days.'

She reached up to kiss him again and gave him another flower.

'Thank you,' he said. 'Run along now and look after your mother.'

9

Thorne was fearful of the spirits, perhaps more than any one else in the clan. He had been brought up with stories about angry spirits all his life. Young men always had a tale to tell about visions they had witnessed or folklore they had heard and shared them on gloomy nights when the devils lurked and the undead resurfaced. These stories were always gruesome, carefully adapted myths and legends to strike fear into every living soul. Some were about angry demons who could turn spears around in mid air, driving the pointed wedge into the living flesh of men and causing death instantly. Others were about gods who inflicted dreadful illnesses with no end of suffering, and unexplained aches and rashes and the worst type of skin lacerations. There were tales about people, who's heads exploded with unbearable pain, and eyes and ears that would weep rivers of blood. This incredulous world of demons, ghouls and the undead, was all caused by defying the spirits.

He remembered the time when an older mother had given birth to a deformed boy. How the newborn had yelled and screamed when he was born after a long and difficult delivery.

The child was a much wanted baby, the woman had already lost many before they came to full term. With a series of miscarriages over the years and premature infants that didn't survive, hopes were fading as her biological clock was ticking. And so when she gave birth to a full term baby, albeit deformed, there was no way she was going to give this one up. The baby suckled at once, rooting for the breast and taking the life giving nectar.

'You can't feed him,' said the medicine woman, horrified by her actions. 'He has to go to the weeping caves. You cannot keep him. Don't make him strong when he will die anyway.'

'But he's my baby, he is not weak. The other ones I lost were weak and not strong enough to suckle,' she smiled at her miracle. 'Look at him Ukaleq, see how strong he is, see what a fighter he is. I can't let him die.' The mother continued to feed him.

'You know the rules Peira, you know it will anger the spirits. This will anger Thorne and the clan will be afraid.'

The new mother pulled her child away from the breast and watched as he screwed up his face and roared like an angry stag. 'I never thought I would have this baby Ukaleq. I thought there was something wrong with me, that I would never have what other woman have, a healthy baby to love and to cherish. This is my last chance, you know that, I am too old now. I cannot give him up.'

Ukaleq knew how much Peira wanted this baby,

her heart ached thinking how she had suffered with so many previous losses. The pain of giving this baby up would probably kill her anyway because she was right; she was too old now. She wouldn't have another chance. But Ukaleq also knew the customs of the clan.

'He is not healthy Peira,' she heard herself say, surprised at the sudden rush of tears that blurred her vision. 'He is deformed. Look at his twisted legs. He is not a proper human.' She sniffed her tears and blotted her eyes and then the truth was plain to see; that this child was an inhuman deviant, probably part demon; certainly not of this world, and who's very presence would cause masses of untold suffering to human life with an unsurmountable loss of livestock if he continued to live in the clan.

All the mother saw was a beautiful creation, who's legs would right themselves as he grew. All he needed was his mother's love and proper care with food and warmth and a roof over his head. 'I will take care of him,' pledged the mother sincerely. 'He will not cause misery to the clan. I promise you.'

The baby was still searching for the milk and nuzzling into her for warmth and protection. A huge wave of maternal instinct took over and the mother cradled him in her loving arms and looked at him adoringly. 'I can't do it, I have to feed him,' and she put him back on the breast.

The woman was still weak herself from giving birth and losing a lot of blood. She really needed to lay down and rest, but fearing her child would be taken away from her and left to die on a stone cold slab without her, she made herself stay awake and held him close. She wrapped him in a soft rabbit fur and then covered him in another blanket. 'I am not going to let you go anywhere my darling, I will take of you. You will be safe with me.' She clung onto him tightly when the medicine woman said she was going to get Thorne.

'I have to get him Peira, he has to see this child.'

'Tell him he has a son called Dainn,' said Peira, her voice struggling with emotion. 'Tell him he has a beautiful strong boy with the heart of a stag and the will of a god and you can tell Thorne that he will have to kill me first to take my baby.'

Ukaleq shook her head in despair and with a deep sigh of regret, disappeared out of the tent.

As soon as the medicine woman had left, Peira had already formed a plan what to take with her. 'I'll take my blanket roll to sleep on and a few rabbit skins for Dainn. I can carry a couple of extra blankets too. I am weak, but I have a strong son, he will give me the strength to survive.'

It was drizzling when Peira left the hut. It hurt to walk even a few steps, everything on her body ached. No one noticed the woman walking like a old hag with a newborn baby concealed beneath her cloak; and going the back way, she was almost invisible. She stooped heavily and took small steps. She wanted to stop, but the warmth and beating heart of her precious cargo kept her going. She didn't give in to the nausea or the dizziness that threatened to expose her in her tracks.

She felt her own warm blood running down the inside of her legs and her stomach cramped each time she lost more, but it didn't stop her. She pushed herself until she was ready to collapse and then she pushed herself further. Even when Dainn cried she didn't stop for him, instead she forced herself to get as far away from the clan as possible.

When Thorne came back with Ukaleq and entered the tent, his wife and son were no where to be seen. They had gone. He searched everywhere for her.

'She can't be far,' he kept saying. 'She is weak and losing blood.'

He searched for days, and the days rolled into months. He cried and screamed out loud in his search for her. He couldn't sleep at night and couldn't eat when he was awake. He aged considerably within a matter of weeks. Groups of men were dispatched at all hours of the day and then again at nightfall, searching far and wide, camping overnight in caves and looking for clues.

But no one could find the woman with a newborn baby; it was as though she had vanished into thin air. The clan fell into mourning, praying to the spirits and chanting choruses for her safe return. But it was futile because the harsh reality was that the wolves or some other carnivore had got both of them; and that was her punishment for not giving her deformed baby to the weeping caves.

10

A chilly east wind was blowing that day, hinting of the icier blasts and treacherous weather to come, but the sky was clear and the morning sun was bright in contrast to the sombre mood in the camp.

Ukaleq and Hagen hadn't said very much for a few days now, no one had said very much at all. No one knew what to say. It was only Ajeya who hadn't changed and continued to pick flowers and play games with the petals.

On that dreadful day, the Shaman approached Eujena with an expression of sadness and discontent. 'Our leader has made a decision,' she said in a low tight voice. 'You are both to come with me.'

Ajeya could feel her mother shaking and her hand gripped her own so hard that it hurt and the child knew instantly that it was more than the wind that was making her mother shiver so much.

The leader was standing at the mouth the standing stones where his face matched the weathered granite and his eyes were as grey and opaque as the menhirs themselves. He moved slowly to the altar, his head hung low with the weight of the overwhelming burden that he had to deliver. He trod the path that still bore the traces of those who had walked that way before; but had any of them sentenced a child like he was about to he wondered. Was this the epitome of his leadership, to pass judgement on a child born from a woman, but according to his clan, was not of this world and therefore should not be allowed to live.

The rest of the clan followed silently and awkwardly with not one of them raising their eye line above the ground; not one of them wanted the finger pointed at them and so they filed in dumbly and uniformly and positioned themselves in a circle ready to witness the fate of this poor infant.

'Eujena,' said Ukaleq quietly. 'It is time.'

Eujena looked at the Shaman, her eyes were dull and uncomprehending. She didn't want to cry, she wanted to remain proud and show all of them that her daughter was not deformed through weakness; rather, that she had the strength far greater than any of them and whatever sentence was passed that day, her legacy would live on, where theirs would quickly fade.

Her heart was strong but her legs were weak and they buckled under the pressure. Hagen put a protective arm around the terrified woman and led her into the middle of the stone circles. Her saviour's arm jolted her back to awareness and awakened an undefinable fear as she was led in to face the leader. She could see the stern hard look in his eyes had been replaced by true compassion and a deep sorrow, and she knew then what he had to say.

'Eujena,' he said aloud, and continued with a low

tone that was more befitting of this terrible occasion.

'You were brought into our clan by a great man that we all deeply respect, a man who has suffered a great loss himself and has had to acknowledge that the spirits made that decision and took his wife from him. Then you were attended to by our great Shaman, Ukaleq, who, with guided hands and a deep ancestral knowledge, got you back on your feet so you would walk with fellow women again. The spirits looked down on you favourably that day and decided that you should live.' He looked up to give thanks to the spirits, and then lowered his eye line with hers again. 'But we are an ancient civilisation, with strong beliefs and deep rooted traditions. These customs have been passed down for generations and every clan member knows the traditions surrounding birth and death. If a child is brought into this world of a different body to our own, then we do not accept it. To us, that child is not ready for our world, and the spirits tell us to leave it to die in the weeping caves and it will be returned when the body is whole again, in another time, in another life.'

Eyes instantly fell on the small deformed girl who clung on tightly to her mother, totally unaware of the severity of the situation.

'And our traditions make no allowances, you must understand that Eujena. Many children of parents who stand around you right now, who were born with defects and imperfections have been surrendered to the weeping caves, so that they might come back stronger and without imperfection when they are ready.'

67

The sound of whimpering and sniffing back tears reverberated round the stones. Eujena's tears fell silently down her face.

'I have no choice Eujena, the spirits have spoken.'

Eujena felt the blood drain from her face and a knot tie in the pit of her stomach. She fell to her knees and dropped her head into her hands. No, it cannot be, she wanted to scream. I have kept my daughter safe and she has lived when any other child would have died. Who are you to decide my baby's fate? The words stuck tight in a dry mouth and not one decibel escaped from her lips.

Ukaleq began to wail a high pitched octave. The mourning began to start. But the sound was cut off as the leader held up his hand.

'I am not finished.'

With the echoes of the Shaman's wails still reverberating round the cold stark granite menhirs and the mourners looking to the skies for answers; a hushed curiosity was launched around the assembly.

'Ajeya is not clan,' he began. 'She was not born from a clan woman, she does not have a clan father. Clan totems do not run through her veins, so they will not be vilified.'

Eujena's heart began to race and she looked up at Hagen.

'Ajeya shall live,' hailed the leader. 'But she can't live amongst us for fear of reprisal from our totems and the spirits of dead children who have gone before her. You both will have to leave before the sun sets on this day. But you will be dispatched with prayers for your safety in this hostile kingdom.'

The leader looked at Ajeya and smiled. She smiled back at him, and she saw him open his hands, and in his hands were the flowers that she had given him only a few days before.

At that moment Eujena went through a range of emotions; relief because her child was to live, but despair because a second man had decided to outcast them both from the community because of a disfigurement. The assembly were making their way out of the stone circle, Thorne had his back to the clan now, holding his arms high as if to propitiate the spirits.

She stood up slowly and hooked Ajeya closer to her body, and waiting for him to finish, she spoke out with passion. 'Thorne, please, may I be granted one last request?'

The assembly stood still, any murmurs ceased immediately; the leader turned round. Hagen appealed to her, Ukaleq tried to silence her, the congregation looked on in utter bewilderment; no one had ever dared to answer back when a judgement had been passed.

The leader looked severe and his eyes hardened. 'This is most unusual,' his voice was gravelled.

'Please,' she appealed to him.

Thorne looked at Ukaleq, who couldn't face him. Hagen had his eyes closed and was biting his bottom lip anxiously. The only one who looked at him was Ajeya and she beamed up at him.

He nodded his head once to allow Eujena safe passage to speak.

'Thank you for your leniency and fairness in allowing Ajeya to live,' she began nervously. 'I am indebted to you my lord. But please, I beg you, cast us out when the bad weather has past. My child is still young and I fear we would not survive in such brutality. If the weather doesn't get us, then the starving beasts would. Please my lord, we will go at the first thaw - I give you my word - I will not ask anything else from you.' She appealed to his compassion, for she knew it existed. She knew he saw something in her daughter where few others had even tried.

Thorne looked at the two fragile flowers in his hands, withered and limp outside their natural surroundings; where, without protection, they would be dead in a few days. He remembered his own wife and child and his eyes filled with tears. He looked at the two vulnerable women and his heart melted, for without their basic needs, they too would succumb to the elements. His eyes softened and the weathered years of age took on a different guise. The assembly waited with bated breath, for most of them thought they would be put to death on the spot.

'Ajeya, come here.' He held out his hands to the youngster.

Trusting this man with her child, Eujena released her to him. Gasps abounded and hands flew up to shocked mouths. The little girl ran over and as he bent down to her level she wrapped her arms round his neck.

'Would you like to stay until the bad weather has passed?'

She nodded her head.

'And if I let you stay, can we sit on that boulder and talk from time to time.'

She nodded her head again.

He looked at her disfigured face and he touched it gently. Now he knew that this beautiful child with the smile of an angel had been sent by the spirits to him; she was a symbol of life and beauty; not of death and misery. No more would the weeping caves take disfigured babies to die in there alone; naked on cruel slabs of rock, waiting for the death to take them in the dark, numbed with cold and hunger, crying for their mothers and terrified. Ajeya had shown him that this ancient practice was wrong and the spirits had frowned on it. But she was a tool of the spirits, and he knew that he could not keep her. She was not his to keep. He was only borrowing her. He would have to let her go to other clans and do the spirits work, but he had to keep her safe. The old man pushed himself up and looking at the concerned expressions concertinaed around the camp, heralded his decision.

'The spirits have guided these two women into our care. The spirits have already decided that these two women should live. They have let Ajeya survive where many others like her have died. If we let them go into the wilderness to face the freeze alone, we will be contravening those wishes and we will anger the spirits. Therefore, I agree, you can remain until the thaw.'

71

Hagen let out a long sigh of relief and Ukaleq bowed low to the great Thorne and ushered her charges in to the safety of her hut.

11

It was only one week since the leader had cast his decision and the full brutality of the unforgiving northern hemisphere was under way as the biting east wind was preparing its gusts of icy blasts. By day the sky was a shimmering blue gauze that sprawled out over the horizon and by night the sky was full of grey swollen clouds and a polished drizzle scattered over the surface of the ground making most areas impassable and dangerous. Life stood still in these torturous winter months; everything had to conserve its energy until the thaw.

It had been a long summer and the harvests were bountiful, the spirits had been generous that year and there was enough laid by to see the clan through the harshest of winters. The tribe were ready for the chill by stocking up with their regular supply of meat, fish, eggs, berries, nuts and vegetables. The orchard trees had been stripped of their fruit, ready to be made into wines. Fish and meat had been dried and salted and wrapped in layers of animal hide.

The smaller mammals where brought in from the pastures and put in the barns. Some families kept a few in their huts for added warmth even using their droppings as a heat catalyst on the open fires. The mighty aurochs with their thick hide and woolly coats were undaunted by the biting winds and gathered in groups when the temperature plummeted where their breath loomed in clouds; hovering, momentarily suspended in the freezing air. The mountain range of the Giant's Claw was arched in a series of majestic peaks and it sparkled like a gigantic luminous amethyst when the sun was at its highest and hollowed into a huge white orb when the moon was at its fullest.

The first snow had sifted in silently during the night. Pristine whiteness softened the contours of the familiar landscape creating a magical dreamland of fantastic shapes and mythical plants. Bushes appeared to grow tall hats of soft snow overnight while the grand old conifers were draped in exquisite glistening soft plump robes. Clouds of smoke hung in plumes above the thatched roofs and frigid icicles clung like jewelled pendants from every eave and crevasse. For those who ventured out in their huge oversized coats of animal pelts, crunching the snow with well padded feet; the biting air fought hard to chaff their skin and ice cold flakes found uncovered patches and froze instantly where ever they landed.

The second snowfall had no magic at all for the clan, and the temperature dropped sharply. This was going to be a harsh winter and as the cold took a grip, the squalls grew, and with the squalls and the freeze came the blizzards.

This blizzard lasted for many days and

imprisoned most of the clan in their huts unleashing several feet of snow. For those who had to go out and rescue stranded animals, the deep snow drifts left them exhausted, and many of them took hours to return home as the driving sheets caused temporary loss of bearings. By the fifth day the blizzard was howling with an unrelenting full force and a number of hardy animals had already perished. Many trees and bushes would never recover and the lakes, rivers and streams would surely flood.

'Thank the gods you found the strength to ask to stay,' said Ukaleq for the hundredth time. 'You would have surely perished by now. Without food, shelter and warmth you would have frozen to death, or become entombed in a snow drift or even been taken by wolves.'

'I know Ukaleq, that's why I had to appeal to Thorne, I knew that we would never have survived a winter here in the north.'

'Where do you get your strength from dear lady. What are you guided by?'

Eujena looked over to her daughter who was sitting by the fire mending baskets. 'She guides me Ukaleq - and everything else that I need in life.'

There was a long pause while the two women digested her words and looked at the young girl with a deep affection.

'Do you remember anything about your roots? We know you are not clan by the clothes you wore, so do you remember anything at all now. What about the winters, what were they like?'

For the first time in days Eujena shivered. 'I really can't remember anything, but I don't recall being imprisoned in mountains of snow for days on end.' She drew a thin smile.

'Yes, our winters can be particularly cruel, though this has to be one of the worst, and I have seen some harsh ones.' She handed Eujena a mug of meaty broth. 'Here take this, you need to keep your strength up.'

They both looked over to Ajeya who was still mending baskets with dexterity and precision.

'She learns quickly doesn't she?' noted the Shaman.

'She certainly does, and she is both perceptive and strong.' Eujena sipped on the broth. 'But she needs to be doesn't she?'

After seven days the storm had finally blown itself out, and when the wind finally stopped blowing, the last of the snow sifted down. A scraping could be heard outside their hut and Hagen appeared at the door like some hideous monster draped in a heavy winter coat with an oversized hat covering his head and a scarf that was stuck to his face. He had a wooden shovel in his hand and had cleared a path for the women.

'It's good to see you Hagen,' said Ukaleq with a jubilant smile. 'Is everyone from the camp safe?'

'Yes, the tribe is safe, though we have lost a few animals sadly. Some to the weather and many to the wolves.'

'That's too bad,' said Ukaleq shaking her head.

Eujena swallowed hard as that could so easily have been her.

Keao followed his father in. 'Would Ajeya like to play in the snow?' he asked Eujena. 'I have brought a warm coat for her.'

Ajeya stood up excitedly, she hadn't been out for several days and really needed to run about.

'Of course,' said Eujena. 'Thank you Keao, it will do her good to get some fresh air.'

Eujena wrapped up her daughter and putting on a few more layers herself, watched from the entrance as she took her first few tentative steps on the glistening spread of snow. She observed Ajeya looking at her own footprints that left an indentation in the freshly fallen blanket and laughed out loud at her first attempt to build a snowman and chuckled as she ran about with Keao, throwing mis-fired snowballs at him and trying to dodge his perfectly aimed ones. She had never seen her child laugh so much and roll around so happily. Keao was so very good with her, even her own brother hadn't played with her like this.

Though perhaps it had been forbidden.

She wondered what Cornelius was doing now, how was he faring without her, was he all right on his own? She shivered again and pulling her shawl around her, shook those thoughts away. There was nothing she could do about it and it did her no good to reminisce.

At that moment she felt a glow transcend

around her as Hagen approached, and holding a mug of broth, stood beside her to watch the two children play.

'It's good to see them getting on so well.' He sipped from the mug that was piping hot and spouting small wisps of condensation into the chilled morning air.

Eujena looked up to him and smiled. 'It really is Hagen, it warms my heart to watch them.'

The sight of them playing and the sound of laughter had the two adults spellbound for a long time, but Hagen had something to say and his mind kept playing it over and over until at last he could hold it in no more. 'You know, I have been thinking...' he breathed out heavily and waited for the right moment again. 'I have had a long time to think during this bad weather.' A thin smile crept across his chiselled face.

Eujena looked at him, wondering what he was going to say.

'I'm thinking of coming with you when you have to go,' he blurted out in a single breath.

Eujena was stopped in her tracks momentarily, slightly unsure of what she had heard. 'Leaving here with me?' her tone was one of shock and surprise.

'Yes, leaving here with you,' his smile was broad.

'But Hagen please, these are your people, this is your life. Your son has his friends here. Please consider what you are saying.'

'Eujena, I have done nothing else since Thorne passed his judgement. I have been to talk to him about

78

it and he agrees that I should go with you, to take care of you and Ajeya and make sure that no harm comes to either of you.'

'Hagen...'

But he stopped her. 'Eujena, Thorne has spoken, he believes that you and Ajeya have a higher purpose to play here, that you are both instrumental in bringing about change and that we can leave nothing to chance. We cannot leave you to wander the wilderness again, exposed to dangers and battling the elements. No, we cannot allow it. I was the one who found you and saved your life, and it is my destiny to continue to protect you.' He thought long and hard while Eujena took it all in. 'But it in all honesty I want to take care of you, not just because of what Thorne says, or what the spirits expect of me - I want to.' He emphasised those last three words and sighed as he recalled a past life. 'I have been on my own for twelve long years Eujena. My son and I, we look after each other, just like you and Ajeya. But both of us are continually reminded of a dreadful past - probably a bit like you - where we have lost a part of us and we are trying to find our way again.'

She put a hand on his arm.

'People have supported us and been good to us, especially Ukaleq and Thorne, but I can't sit back and watch you venture out into the wilderness on your own and risk your life out there again.' He looked to the mountain still weighted down with snow and eased his own heavy heart. 'The spirits have brought you to me Eujena, just like the spirits brought Ajeya to Thorne;

and is my destiny to protect you.'

She was moved and tried hard to stifle her emotion. No one had wanted to take care of her for such a long time and she feared for the safety of her child more than she did for herself. 'I don't know what to say Hagen,' she began. 'I cannot express how I feel, this is most gracious of you, giving up your home for us and I cannot find the words to thank you enough.'

'Do not thank me dear lady, it is I who has to thank you for giving me my life back.' He took her hand and kissed it, and as a spark of something ignited in both of them, a freezing cold orb suddenly exploded on his face and the sound of laughter trailed away as they watched Keao and Ajeya running off into the distance.

12

The winter finally released its frozen grip and the last icy breaths that covered the land were exhaled. Fresh ripe buds on the trees heralded spring and the pulse of the earth quickened as life started to pump through the soil once again. New shoots and a variety of colours patch-worked the contours of barren grey moors. The sun made a welcome appearance and beat off the blistering attack of winter. Rivers thawed and ran freely. Shivering transparent icicles slowly dripped away.

Evergreens pumped up their sagging branches, shaking off their top hats of moulded snow. Mythical plants robbed of their identity were exposed once again and bushes that had been concealed for months reappeared. The animals were back in the meadows now and a spring cleaning ritual began in the huts.

Many hands helped with burning the stagnant stale straw, the old embers and the animal hairs. The chimney was brushed. The floor was scrubbed. The eating area was cleaned. All the animal hides used for keeping out the driving rain and bitter cold were hung out and beaten rigorously to get rid of the accumulating mould and the stench of confined herbivores. Doors were left open to welcome in the new season and the fresh air burst in. But a change in the weather meant it was time for the group to leave.

'I said I would ask no more of Thorne, so I have to keep to my word,' said Eujena packing away her few belongings.

'I know Eujena, you can't ask any more of him; but you being here has made such a difference.' Ukaleq was pouring various potions into vials and sorting out roots and herbs into baskets that would come in handy over the next few days.

'Really! How so?' Eujena stopped for a moment.

Ukaleq looked up. 'Because the ancient laws on leaving disfigured children in the weeping caves to die will be phased out immediately.'

Eujena smiled at the revelation. 'That is wonderful news Ukaleq and I am so very pleased. And I will pray for all those children and their mothers who have had to endure such unnecessary suffering.'

Ukaleq sighed with a thin smile and carried on with her sorting.

'You see how strong Ajeya is,' continued Eujena. 'Yes, she may have a weakness on one side of her face, but she has the strength of a gale to bring about change.'

Ukaleq's smile grew with admiration and came over to give Eujena the tonics and medicines. 'Thorne believes that it is Ajeya's destiny to make a difference to the way people view life, so he will want you to keep on your path to seek out other clans and civilisations.'

The herbs were accepted with appreciation as Eujena continued. 'Yes, I believe that too, Ajeya has a purpose to play here, she is more than a precious daughter that I have been blessed with; she is a gift from the spirits.'

Ukaleq was searching through her cupboards now and rooting through drawers. 'That she is to be sure, and now you have Hagen to look after you both.' She stopped to face Eujena. 'And I know you are resourceful and strong in your own right and you are a wonderful mother that Ajeya is blessed to have; but even you need looking after occasionally Eujena.' She carried on searching for something. 'Mother nature is a force to be reckoned with and out there on your own is not easy.'

The Shaman's words were honourable and well meant. At last she found the jar of comfrey oil that she was looking for. 'My favourite herb; it has so many properties you know.'

Eujena took her friends hands and kissed them. 'I will never forget you Ukaleq, you have saved me.'

'I have enjoyed every minute of it, and it is my honour to have had two great women in my care.'

The two older women embraced as Hagen came in through the flap in the doorway. Eujena smiled at him and gave once last hug to her friend and went over to Ajeya to let Hagen say his own goodbyes.

He took Ukaleq by the hand. 'Dear lady, there are so many words I could say right now but only one will cover it all, and that's thank-you,' he sighed with appreciation. 'Thank-you for everything; your kindness, your compassion, your guidance, your friendship.'

He wiped away a tear, and the great Shaman hugged him.

'Who is going to be my sight for sore eyes now eh?' She tried to make light of the situation but sniffing back a runny nose made it impossible. 'Just you take care of these two women my dear friend, and the spirits will take care of everything else.' She hugged him again.

'You know I will,' he assured her.

Eujena carried out her small bindle and Hagen lifted Ajeya up into his arms. Keao was already on the front seat of the wagon where Coal, the black gelding, was fidgeting noisily with the snaffle between his teeth.

'You help your father now won't you?' shouted out Ukaleq to where he sat.

'I will, I promise,' he beamed back at her.

Thorne had already heard the roll of the wagon disturbing the well trodden path and could be seen making his way towards them. Ajeya saw him and struggled to get down; Hagen released his hold gently and she ran up to meet him. Though unsteady and shaky, the great man was still able to bend down to her level and pick her up. She felt his cheek, just like the first time she had met him and placed a kiss on his old wrinkled skin. Then she threw her arms around him and squeezed his neck. Everyone was out now and smiling at the spectacle.

Thorne was aware of the tear running down his

face. 'You know, I night not have been blessed with any children of my own, but to have spent these last few months with you is all that I needed to give me hope for the future.'

Ajeya didn't fully understand the sentiments, but she was aware of the kindness in his voice.

Eujena heard him though and moved forward. 'Thank you so much Thorne, for everything.'

The wrinkles in his face moved to either side as he smiled and took her hand to plant a kiss. 'Hagen finding you was a blessing for us all, and this little lady here will remain in my heart forever.' He took out a pendant from his pocket and put it round Ajeya's neck. 'A small gift to remind you of me.' His voice was breaking now.

Ukaleq recognised it straight away and smiled thoughtfully.

Thorne nodded his head at the memory. 'I was seeking refuge in a cave after a day's hunting. I was a young man then with strong arms and an even stronger heart. Not bad looking either by all accounts,' he smiled at the thought of his former self. 'I had caught a few rabbits and a couple of quails, but the winds were howling and a storm was brewing, so I knew I had to find shelter quickly. It was very dark in there, I couldn't see very much at all, so I made a fire to give me light and keep me warm. I also needed to eat, so I prepared one of the rabbits. As the fire took hold, I noticed something gleaming amongst the rocks. So I went over and picked it up. And do you know what it was?' He looked at Ajeya who shook her head. 'It was a deep golden stone. I had never seen anything like it before, it was beautiful.

Brushing it off, I looked at it closer. And encapsulated within the smooth transparent stone, was a complete winged insect. I couldn't believe it, how could it be? How could a living creature, however small, become part of a stone? It had one part of a wing missing, even though the other wings were delicate and shimmering and the bluest of blue that you have ever seen with intricate patterns like spidery veins; it wasn't entirely perfect.

I thought it was a sign from the spirits, that perhaps it wasn't perfect enough and had died in the weeping cave. That the spirits had entombed it to show me that the ancient belief of surrendering malformed babies to die in there was a true and just cause. I took the stone home and made it into an amulet and have worn it ever since.' He touched the smooth orange exterior.

'But you know what? I was wrong. And I have only just discovered the true meaning within the last few months. That the insect was perfect, it was beautiful, and the stone was a sign to show me that everyone is perfect in their own way. That perfection is what you perceive it to be; and you, Ajeya, have shown that to me. So I have to pass this amulet on to you, because you are the rightful owner.'

He handed the child over to her mother and kissed her forehead. 'And your mother will tell you the story of how you came by this amber necklace, and that the great Thorne gave it to you, because you taught him a valuable lesson.'

Eujena put a hand on his withered arm and dropped her gaze in a humble appreciation. There were no words left to say now. The camp was stifled into a soul searching silence.

Hagen shook the great man's hand and looked into the eyes full of experience and wisdom. 'Thank you Thorne, you are the greatest man I know and have been like a father to me.'

Thorne took both of Hagen's hands in his own and tipped his head in acknowledgement. The tightness in his throat had rendered him speechless.

'Look after Ukaleq for me,' said Hagan. 'She needs you more than ever now.'

Thorne nodded with reverence.

Then he helped his charges onto the front seat of the wagon and shook the reins over the back of his horse. And as they trundled out of the camp forever, Ajeya looked back at the great man waving back at her until she could see him no more.

13

As they continued north, the land gave way to flat open plains crossed by rivers and streams of runoff from the great Giant's Claw mountain range. They kept to the valleys for shelter from the elements and were able to hunt for food within the massive reserve of wildlife.

The river was a blue green ribbon shining in the morning sun. Reeds grew thick in the shallows along the banks and Ajeya squealed when she saw a water vole skimming across the surface spreading ripples as it went. The mountains opened up upon a vista of green fields, and stretching out before them were the great grasslands with their bountiful source of life; displaying yet another face of the renewing cycle as the party travelled. Young flowers began to unravel in their camouflaged cocoons while others were already in full bloom, and the waves of softly billowing grasses turned the meadows into a beating heart once more.

Mother nature was at last peeling back her worn outer dermis and revealing the vibrant new life beneath. Trumpets of the earth heralded her return and the long fingers of the sun's rays fanned across the fields to open up an artist's palette of rich hues, blushed tones and a blaze of colour. The sweet breath of a westerly wind flew in from the wings of the sun and the pulse of the earth returned to camp. Birds, bees, butterflies and dragonflies were increasing in numbers along the flight path of the biggest star, while trees released their buds and fruits. This was the beginning of spring and with it came renewed energy and an abundance of life.

As they crossed a fjord, Hagen noticed the thunderous swell of grey clouds jostling for position and within seconds the calm of the weather was turning into a storm. The force of the wind intensified as Eujena and Hagen surged forward, and though it was just past dusk, the light of the moon was dimmed by moving clouds of dry loose sand billowing up from the dry ground. Soon they could hardly see their way through the windblown dust while flashes of lightning cracked around them and thunder growled and rumbled over the hills.

In a blaze of light, Coal reared up in terror as a bolt flashed the white of his eyes. Hagen had to get down from the seat and lead the terrified animal by foot. 'We have to find shelter,' he called back to Eujena. 'We will stop at the next crofters lodge.'

Holding the snaffle and shielding his eyes, he battled hard against the gale force wind and a driving dust storm that blackened the sky and came perilously close to not finding anywhere at all.

But these pastures were full of scattered crofters huts that offered protection for stranded shepherds and it wasn't long before Hagen spotted a refuge. The children were ushered inside quickly where they found last season's straw on the ground and a couple of rush mats as bedding. A table was in the corner with an old wooden bench underneath and very little else.

Hagen unharnessed his horse and brought him inside with them, the precaution was to stop him bolting in terror with the lightning and jeopardising their only means of transport. A grey gloom instantly filled their haven and made the room appear darker than it actually was. Eujena stood by a window and looked out into the night and the rain.

Somewhere above them a lightning bolt crackled across the sky, brightening the room for a couple of seconds. When a clap of thunder followed some six seconds later, Coal startled and whinnied. The lightning flashed again and the thunder rumbled after ten seconds, Coal reared but was held back with a secure rope. He tried to bolt but couldn't get away. He pawed the ground with his hoof and nearly sat back a couple of times as his hind legs buckled with fear. Hagen went to the colt to calm him as another streak of lightning raced across the sky and the thunder shook the rain from the storm clouds.

'It's all right boy, settle down,' he stroked Coal's soft velvet muzzle and breathed gently into his nostrils.

As another splinter of lightning raged across the sky and lit up the surface of a lake, Coal remained still and composed, he didn't buckle or rear. This time he was hardly aware of the thunder as it responded to the storm's veil of light. Hagen continued to stroke the colt and spoke reassuringly until he heard the thunder rolling away in the background.

'You must have a magic touch,' said Eujena noticing the instant calmness of the young horse.

'Animals need to be reassured and shown there is nothing to fear. It's all in their mind you know. These magnificent beasts, so strong and powerful, can be the most timid creatures sometimes.' He stroked Coal's ears and patted his long smooth neck.

'You are still very good.' Eujena smiled and thought about her own fears of the dark and how she had to overcome them for the sake of her child.

'The storm will have long gone by the morning and we can be on our way again. Come, make yourselves comfortable and we will be on our way at first light.'

He brought in a few provisions and a flagon of water that would see them through the evening; a more substantial meal would be sought on the morrow. The family sat round the table and feasted quietly on chunks of bread and strips of mutton as the distant lightning continued to light up their sparse surroundings. The storm was moving away now and when Hagen untied him, Coal settled down on the floor. Eventually the storm passed by uninterrupted and the rumbles were soon several miles away. Coal was sleeping peacefully and the warmth from his body kept the chill at bay while the family positioned their mats and bedding around him for their first night together.

In the morning Hagen was up early to prepare a light breakfast of field mushrooms and quails eggs. Coal was led out of the dwelling where he found a nice barren area and blew the dirt with his nose, then, when he was sure it was free from debris, he dropped to his knees and onto his hide where he rolled from side to side with his legs in the air and stretching his neck joyfully. Then he stood back up, shook the dust from his shiny black coat and cantered off to drink from the cool of the river.

Hagen watched dutifully as Eujena followed him to the river's edge to bathe. 'Don't go far,' he shouted out, stirring the pan of food over a low fire.

'I won't, I will just sit at the edge to freshen up,' she called back.

The sun danced on the ripples and it looked like all the stars from the night before had fallen from the sky and had landed in that very river. It sparkled and glistened with a thousand jewels while the current teased it and caressed it and guided it gently along its path.

Hagen watched from his vantage point and smiled with a growing affection. He saw her dip her feet tentatively in the shallows. He could tell that the water was freezing cold when she recoiled quickly with the shock, but slowly and carefully she eased them in until they were completely submerged. The warm sun beamed down on her skin and it felt good to peel back the weathered signs of winter. She closed her eyes and looked up to the orb, feeling the rays warming her face and neck. Breathing in deeply she embraced the spring air, it made her feel alive, her skin tingled and she felt refreshed. She swirled the water around her legs with the tips of her fingers and wriggled her toes in the folds of silt. Her hands scooped up a palm of water and she splashed it over her face. Tiny fish swam up to her and she giggled like a child, they nibbled her toes and the feeling was actually quite therapeutic she thought. She watched as Coal moved away from the water, he shook his head and found a mound of succulent grass to munch on. His tail swished from side to side as he moved forward with each carefully placed step to another healthy patch to feed on.

Suddenly she was jolted back to reality by a piercing cry. 'Someone, come quickly,' she heard the panic in his voice. 'She's choking!'

Eujena hurled herself out of the water and ran like the wind to her child just as she was losing consciousness. 'What happened?'

'She was eating an apple and a piece got stuck,' came Keao's frantic reply.

The remains of the offending culprit was discarded on the floor, though the chunk draining her life still remained lodged in her windpipe. Eujena reacted calmly and quickly and holding her daughter firmly she struck her back with a force hard enough to dislodge the obstruction but not to hurt her or damage her small back. Nothing happened. She did it for a second time, then a third. Still nothing happened. Precious life saving minutes were ticking away now.

She picked the girl up, sat down and put her across her lap, then reached into her mouth with a finger to see if she could find the blockage. She couldn't feel it. It had to be trapped quite a way down, so Eujena stood up, turned the girl round and held her around the middle with one arm so that her head and arms hung down and struck her sharply between the shoulder blades. Then, from behind, she put her arms around the limp child and pulled in with a jerk. Still it did no good, nothing moved, she was frantic now and desperately trying to keep her composure.

Hagen and Keao clung on to each other, biting down hard on their bottom lips and feeling useless because neither of them could help in this life and death situation. By now the little girl had stopped breathing, she was limp and lifeless and her eyes glazed over. Eujena hurriedly lay the child flat and tilted her chin up to open the airwaves, then, pinching her nose to stop the air getting in, she placed her mouth on top of hers to form a vacuum. Then she began to suck the obstruction out. The minutes were still racing by and Ajeya was now blue. She didn't have long left.

Eujena sucked hard until her lungs could hold no more, and as her suction created a force from above, the obstruction moved, and whether or not the previous attempts had dislodged the offending object, but this attempt worked and the offending piece of apple flew out into the back of Eujena's mouth. She spat it out immediately and continued to breathe life saving oxygen into her child's lungs; and as her chest began to rise and fall, the men could at last breathe again with her.

Eujena held her daughter tightly as she began to cry, and took in gasps of life giving oxygen to fill her lungs again. She wiped her face and hugged her tightly. 'You're all right now my love, you are safe, you are always safe with me.'

Ajeya's cry had reduced to sobs now, but Eujena cradled her until her breathing settled down again.

'Will she be all right?' asked the ashen faced boy.

'Yes she will be fine Keao, don't worry, she is just shocked that's all. Thank you for calling me straight away.'

'How did you know what to do?' asked Hagen.

'Just intuition Hagen, something inside me just instinctively knew.'

'And I'm supposed to be taking care of you both.' Hagen's voice was thin.

Eujena reached up to kiss his hand. 'You do a fine job Hagen, don't you ever think otherwise.'

The blockage had gone now and Hagen led his family back into their hut to eat. He poured Ajeya a soothing drink of nettle tea and sat back on the bench as she sipped on it.

'You gave us quite a shock back there,' he stumbled, clearly still visibly shaken.

'Sorry,' the little girl said. 'I was hungry.'

Eujena pulled her closer into her breast and held her head close. 'Come, Hagen has got the breakfast ready, let's eat together now, but I will be watching you very closely now little madam.'

And in the background, Coal was still munching his way along the field, his tail swishing in the breeze and his shiny black coat glistening in the sun.

When the wagon reached a large plain, they saw a variety of deer and aurochs near a river grazing in a meadow trimmed with various oaks, beech and pine, with succulent vegetation dotted around the perimeter. This land was rich with black soil, with wide slow moving rivers, and hundreds of small lakes that shone like mirrors in the sun. Wheat, corn and barely grew high in its fields and some distance further Hagen noticed a large pile of recently felled trees, a dense stand of them with baskets of kindling wood on the ground beneath. Here, the ground was littered with blown leaves and still damp from last night's rain. Coal seemed to like the soft feel of the saturated carpet and bounced his head up and down in appreciation.

'We must be near a clan,' Hagen hailed excitedly. 'Only a clan would live so close to large herbivores amongst woodland and water.'

Eujena was still looking in awe at the Giant's Claw, an impressive mountain that carried the torrents of a thousand waterfalls winding and gushing to the bottom some two miles below. She smiled at his revelation. Of course he knew best, he always did.

The travellers rolled across the plains towards the

camp, and from their elevated position they could see that the living accommodations were made from wooden slats that reached six foot high out of the ground, though Hagen said another two feet was underground for added support. They were solid and sturdy and held together with wattle and daub to fill the gaps. The leader's house was obvious, a big timber hut with a huge wooden roof with neatly stacked logs arranged outside with his own water pump and bowl which clarified his status. There were cook fires all around the settlement with something burning on all of them; whole hogs, racks of mutton and a huge wild boar crisping nicely. Eujena winced at the sight of the hideous beast.

People were going about their daily chores; men sharpening wooden spears, youths sparing with timber staffs, young boys were fletching arrows and women smoothing glistening blades. There were girls running errands, babies crying in their mother's arms and as their wagon rolled into the settlement, a gathering of sheep, goats and geese were sent spinning in all directions.

The door to the leader's hut opened and a young man with a strong jaw and searching eyes came out to address them. 'Good evening travellers, welcome to the Clan of the Mountain Lion, my name is Laith and I am the clan leader. How can I help you today?'

'Good evening to you too sir,' said Hagen most humbly. 'We are travellers seeking employment and wondered if you could spare some accommodation in return for work.'

'That I may,' said the leader still searching. 'Have you come far?'

'From the Clan of the Giant's Claw,' said Hagen with his strong voice.

'I know it very well,' responded the young man. 'And I trust that Thorne is in good health.'

'Yes all is well,' assured Hagen. 'And Thorne still has the heart of an aurochs.'

'Excellent news, that's what I like to hear, and any friend of the great Thorne is a friend of mine........ Did he send you to me?'

Hagen looked at Eujena then at the leader. 'Yes, he said that you would help us.'

'He was right,' smiled Laith.

'Thank you, we very much appreciate your kindness,' responded Hagen.

Laith smiled. 'So, are you going to introduce me to your family?'

'Where are my manners? Please excuse me. I am Hagen, this is Eujena and these are our children ,Keao and Ajeya.'

Laith studied them all with a kind face, until a woman came out of the entrance and took his attention. Her beauty mesmerised each one of them and her presence was as breathtaking as the morning dawn on a summer's day.

'Artemisia, we have guests,' hailed the leader.

'I can see we have new arrivals dearest - and I heard that Thorne sent you all.'

'Yes he did,' answered Hagen.

'Well, like Laith has already said, any friend of Thorne is a friend of ours and we extend the hand of friendship to welcome you into our clan. Please, all of you, join us for some refreshments.'

14

A heavy curtain of aurochs hide covered the opening, which was high enough for Hagen to walk through comfortably; the arched doorway led to a roomy area where a large fireplace sat in the centre with a massive cauldron of water over it. A range of chairs and tables were scattered around, while eating bowls sat stacked on shelves and other utensils dangled from hooks on the walls. It was warm inside the timber hut and the occupants didn't need to wear layers of heavy clothing. There was a hole in the top of the roof that let out the smoke and extending out from the walls, around the sides, were wide benches with thick furs piled on them. Underneath were the sleeping arrangements; all very plush and comfortably attired, which befitted the stature of the clan leader.

'Please, sit where ever you like, you are my honoured guests. Thorne knows I am establishing a new clan, and I expect that's why he sent you.'

Hagen smiled beneath a look of uncertainty. 'He didn't mention that this was a new clan.'

'Yes, we are a very new settlement and haven't been here long ourselves,' Laith said.

Artemisia was pouring some mugs of tea for the

new arrivals and handing them out generously. Eujena warmed to the woman who stood before her. Slightly built with a good bone structure, firm jaw, rounded chin, high cheekbones and deep set eyes framed with long dark lashes. Her glossy dark hair was piled high on her head and she wore a smile that would melt the heart of any man. Laith took the mug and his smiling eyes thanked her.

Ajeya was still wrapped around her mother and slept soundly against her breast. Keao sat between Eujena and Hagen, rigidly observing the fine youthful leader who looked a good ten years younger than his father.

'So where have you come from then Laith?' asked Hagen, fully aware that this man was his junior.

'I grew up in a place far different to this. We both did,' he looked at Artemisia fondly. 'But we shun the trappings of wealth and prefer to live off the land.' He took a slurp of tea.

Eujena took a gulp of breath. 'What sort of place?' she asked, realising that they were indeed more akin to each other than she had initially realised.

'I grew up in a castle dear lady, alongside my wife to be,' he looked at Artemisia. 'A huge grand fort, where the only decision I had to make was what I should wear that day.' His smile was thin as he reminisced. 'But I respond to the wild and surviving off the land, living with my own choices and making my own decisions.' He pondered for a moment as he recollected his calling. 'But I soon realised that starting a community on one's own poses its own risks and dangers, from all ends of the scale. So I invited a few people to join us and gradually we have built up a small settlement.'

The sense of familiarity continued for Eujena. 'Do you ever regret leaving the castle and all its luxury Artemisia?'

'Not at all,' she answered. 'Not once have I ever yearned to go back, I have never felt afraid and I have never felt alone. My life is here and it gives me everything that I need.'

Laith took her hand and continued. 'In the Clan of the Mountain Lion, we encourage our children to learn early on; so young girls will learn about plants and their life giving properties, while the boys will begin to hunt small animals and learn how to use a spear.'

'Can the girl's hunt and use spears?' she continued, looking at Laith.

'To be honest with you, most girls prefer to weave baskets and learn how to cook alongside their mothers; relying on passed down family recipes and making a home. But if a young girl wanted to hunt with the boys and learn how to use a spear, then I would have no problem with that.'

'How old is your little girl?' asked Artemisia feeling a stirring in her belly.

'She is three and a half now,' said Eujena proudly, noticing the swell in the woman's girth.

'She is so very beautiful.' Artemisia noticed.

'Yes she is, I am truly blessed.' Eujena pulled Ajeya closer into her embrace and kissed the top of her head.

'Our first child is due in another six full moons,' announced Laith noticing the subtle exchange.

'And we are to be married in the month of June, when the day is at its longest, for that is sure to be a lucky day for all of us,' continued Artemisia.

'So only another three full moons till your wedding day,' said Hagen observing the small time scale. 'There will be much work to do before then.'

'That there will dear friend, so you have arrived just in time.'

The two men laughed and clinked their mugs together.

'I thought we had new arrivals,' said a kindly voice coming in to the room.

'Zoraster, where have you been? We've been making acquaintances without you,' Laith teased his friend and stood up to greet him. 'This, good people, is my oldest friend and we go way back.' Laith put his arm around the young man. 'He is our physician, our teacher, our medicine man, our healer and what Zoraster doesn't know isn't worth knowing; so if you need the answer to anything, then this is your man.'

Hagen stood up to shake Zoraster's hand and introduced his family. 'I am Hagen, this is Eujena, this is Keao and this small sleeping child is Ajeya.'

'We welcome you,' said the healer. 'We always like to welcome new travellers and as this is a very special year for all of us, you are most welcome.'

'We have told them our news Zoraster,' said Laith. 'But do you think a little celebration is in order to welcome our new guests in true Clan of the Mountain style?'

'What an excellent idea, because there is always something worth celebrating in clan life,' he agreed.

'Come, you probably need to rest a while and freshen up,' offered Artemisia. 'Let us show you to your new accommodation. We have a lovely little hut just a short walk from us where your wagon can be kept under the lean-to and your horse can go in the adjoining field.'

'This is indeed very gracious of you all,' said Hagen appreciating the hospitality.

'Nonsense, like I said, Thorne sent you to help us in preparation for our busy year ahead; and if you treat others how you would wish to be treated, then kindness will be repaid two fold; that's what I have always found anyway.' Laith held the hide open for them.

Artemisia led them along a well trodden path to where a vacant hut stood. 'It might be a bit stagnant in here after the long winter, but a few baskets of pine cones will freshen it up nicely for you.'

'Thank you so much,' said Eujena under a wave of emotion. 'This is more than adequate for our needs and so very kind of you.'

A drape of thick leather hung over a long wooden pole and the entrance led in to a room very similar to the one they had just left. It was smaller of course and much more sparse with a hearth full of logs and straw on the floor, but with a little bit of thought it could easily be made into a beautiful home. Two palettes full of sheep wool were at one end of the hut and two feet above those were benches covered in furs and animal pelts. On the adjacent walls hung more animal skins and a small wooden table was near the door.

'I love it,' said Eujena. And with her hands on her hips started to mentally arrange their new home.

'We will leave you good people to settle in, and when you are ready, join us for some food, and maybe a little singing and dancing.' Laith hooked an arm around his wife to be and disappeared back to their own dwelling to prepare.

Hagen came in from settling Coal in the field, and with the help of Keao, brought in their belongings from the wagon. They both looked around with wide open eyes and were obviously both thinking the same thing about getting to work making a few more essential items; like a couple of substantial beds, a few more shelves and at least four comfortable chairs.

'This is grand isn't it Eujena?' Hagen said putting down the bags.

'It really is, we are so incredibly lucky.' Eujena's voice was bursting with pride.

Ajeya sat on the palette and asked for some food. Keao gave her a wedge of bread and a flagon of warm water; meagre as it was, that was all they had.

'I think a feast is planned for tonight, you will get a lot more food then,' he assured her.

And that night was indeed a feast with such food that they had never seen before; course after course, menu after menu. There were great haunches of aurochs roasted with carrots, joints of venison braised with leeks, grilled bacon and flat mushrooms, roasted mutton with mint, peppered boar with cranberries, stewed goose with barley. And for afters; baked apples in wine, wild pears in honey, cinnamon cakes, spiced wine, chilled ale, weak mead, iced lemon and honeyed beer.

The huge outdoor fireplace burned hotter and hotter as more ash and wood was added and formed a centrepiece as the clan began to move away from the tables full of food and into the centre to celebrate with song. A drum began to beat rhythmically and people began to tap on anything that was near; the ground, a mug, a knee; then the wind pipes came in; a haunting melody that was lifted by the breeze and transcended around the camp like a plume. Women began to hum a high octave while the men thrummed a deep guttural sound. A woman's voice began to sing out with passion and the beating got faster and faster. Then the same woman put an instrument to her mouth and began playing on a jaw harp. The most incredible haunting sounds seemed to connect all of nature and the surrounding cosmos in a staccato of octaves.

The harp trailed off as the drum took over and in

a burst of exuberance, Laith landed in the centre of the group with his feet thumping and his hands clapping; he pulled Artemisia into the centre and together they danced in perfect time with each other. She moved forwards and backwards with him, meeting together then out again, taking a turn round the edge of the circle, skipping and jumping, but laughing most of all. Round and round they went and then started the whole thing over again.

Laith lifted her into air amid a cacophony of shrill excitement and then put her down gently to make her exit. But then Zoraster entered and in an amazing display of high kicks and long leaps, began to weave his way round Laith. The crowd were shrieking with laughter as the two men linked arms and in a series of acrobatic moves and dare devil antics, entertained the throng with their much admired theatrical displays. There were shouts of joyous approval, feet stomping, hand clapping and those who still had a beer in their hand, slurred it all over the dance floor in unrivalled appreciation. Women began to join them, the children were dancing as well, and as the music changed tempo again, everyone by now was moving in time to the beat.

Keao was dancing around a tree with Ajeya; her shrieks and howls could be heard above the other children who had joined them. The light from the fire pits lit up their joyful faces and not one person even noticed the child's disfigured face. Eujena was laughing and singing with the rest, she was swaying in time to the infectious music and letting her body move as if no one else was watching. Only Hagen noticed the beautiful temptress with the engaging smile, swirling her hips and twirling her arms to the rhythmic chants. He sidled up behind her and put his arms around her waist and nuzzled his face into her hair. He began to match her body and sway in time to the music. She tingled within his warm embrace and held onto his strong arms tightly.

'It's intoxicating isn't it Eujena?' he whispered into her ear.

'This is truly wonderful Hagen, I have never been so happy.' She reached up to caress his face but then someone grabbed her loose arm and dragged her into the centre of the ring. Hagen still had his hand on her other arm, so he too was snatched in. The stranger who had interrupted their moment of passion immediately left the two of them in the middle and they had to suddenly improvise their own form of wild exotic dance to the sound of the beating drum and the loud intoxicated voices.

The north had turned pitch black now and the stars were hanging in a clear sky; and as the moon looked down on them with her own graceful smile, Eujena felt the tears of laughter running down her face and felt that she never wanted this night to end.

15

She picked up a few handfuls of pebbles from the edge of the stream and gave them to Keao. He had positioned a range of utensils on some tree stumps and took out his catapult to get some practise; a V shaped piece of wood, born from the branch of a maple tree, which he could bend and manipulate to hit what ever he chose, over any distance. The stones were placed in a leather pouch attached to either side of his apparatus; and with extraordinary accuracy he pulled back on the leather strap and hit each of the utensils in quick succession. The little girl jumped up and down excitedly and ran to put the targets back on their plinths. Again, in the speed of an arrow, the targets were toppled from their positions.

'Ajeya, let me try something else.'

She ran up to him eager to please.

'Let me hit something that sits on your head.'

He placed a small metal mug on the top of her crown and walked away. She stood perfectly still and didn't take her eyes off of him.

'Don't move, you must not even blink. You promise me.'

She didn't say a word. She trusted him, even at

that young age she knew he wouldn't hurt her and he knew that she understood. From several feet away he sized up the target, he steadied his left hand that held the shaft and pulled back on the sling with his right hand, he held it there, closed one eye, then, with the accuracy of a hawk that was diving at full force, the stone hit the centre of the mug and knocked it cleanly from her head.

'Again again!' she cried out excitedly.

'Ha ha,' he laughed out loud. 'Come on, it would be better if I teach you how to hit a target, not become one.'

Using a sophisticated form of stick he had engineered this basic device to suit his requirements and had constructed a potentially lethal weapon. He lined up the utensils once more and with unsurmountable amounts of patience and confidence, he began to teach the young girl his craft. Ajeya watched Keao intently and listened to everything he said. She was fascinated by his skill and even though she never hit a target, she knew that she was learning and that by experimenting and practising, with his help she would improve.

'Everything is an illusion. See the butterfly with its dappled wings? They have those to blend in with the different colours of flowers and leaves so they are not eaten; and this insect here, see how it changes colour to camouflage itself in the undergrowth. And look how those deer in the meadow flash the white of their tails to evoke a sense of size. Everything in nature is an illusion to outwit and outmanoeuvre. Remember that Ajeya.'

'Is it pretending?' she asked with a small wrinkled up nose.

'Yeah, it's kind of pretending,' he smiled at her analogy.

'I can pretend that I am beautiful then.'

He was sad that she even thought that. 'You don't have to pretend Ajeya, you are already beautiful.'

She looked happy with his response and he noticed the delight in her eyes.

'Son, what are you doing over there?' called out Hagen coming into the clearing.

'Just teaching Ajeya a few survival skills,' he winked cheekily at the little girl.

'I need you to help me now son,' coaxed Hagen. 'We have got a few bits of furniture to make, remember.'

'Yes, coming father.' He tucked his catapult into his belt and bent down to the small girl. 'You run off now my beautiful, we will do this another time. Your mother will have some work for you to do now.'

She ran back through the tall golden grass, bent with the weight of ripened seed heads, and a cool breeze chasing her heels. In her mind's eye she was carrying a catapult, and the wind brushed a strand of hair over the disfigured side of her face, but still she remained focused, nothing would impede her illusion. Then, searching for the balance point, and steadying her aim, she released the stone into the air and hit her target full on. She jumped about with joy and did it again and again. By the time she got to the hut she was slightly out of breath and fell into the room where she found her mother sweeping the floor.

'Ajeya darling, there you are, where have you been?'

'Practising with Keao.'

'Practising what?'

'With a catapult and I'm really good at it.'

Eujena laughed softly. 'I'm sure you are my love; but now it's time for boring stuff and I need some help getting this place in order.'

'Keao says I'm beautiful.'

Eujena stopped what she was doing. 'Well that's because you are.'

Ajeya found herself grinning again and took the broom from her mother to sweep the floor. All the while she thought about and memorised what Keao had told her.

'Look to the skies to see where the eagles are hunting, smell the change in the air and feel the pace in the breeze that brings the storm. Watch the habits of animals for they are more in tune with nature than any man, and observe the weather at all times, for the skies rules everything.'

He was teaching her how to feel the outside world through smell and touch. He was making her aware of the different sounds in the air. He was showing her how to look for different colours that would tell her what season it was. He was preparing her for the rest of her life.

After several hours of cleaning, sweeping, beating the animal hides and getting a fire going; a welcome visitor appeared. 'Am I interrupting anything?' said Artemisia peering round the doorway.

'No not at all Artemisia, we were just about to sit down and have a break, weren't we Ajeya?'

The little girl nodded and went to sit down on a bench.

'Would you like some dandelion tea, Artemisia? I also have some cinnamon cake that was left over from last night.'

'That would be lovely Eujena, thank you, but I just wanted to see how you are settling in and if you all enjoyed last night.'

Eujena busied herself preparing the tea and took three slices of cake from its muslin cloth. 'We had a wonderful time, I haven't laughed so much in all my life and I don't remember dancing so much either.'

Artemisia chuckled. 'My sides were aching watching Hagen dancing around like a man possessed.'

'I know, he was so funny,' agreed Eujena wearing a wide grin. 'It must have been the strong ale that disguised his inhibitions.'

'Yes, it always works,' smiled Artemisia. 'I swear they make it stronger every time.'

Eujena laughed. 'Please sit down.' And she guided her to a seat next to Ajeya and offered a mug of tea and a slice of cake.

'You've got a good man there Eujena.'

The young mother smiled.

'Are you from the same clan?' asked Artemisia, eager to know more about her new friends.

'Not exactly,' Eujena stammered. 'He saved me one day. I was out collecting berries for Ajeya and myself and I was attacked by a boar. It inflicted a terrible injury on my leg and I would surely have died if he had not passed by and seen me.'

Artemisia winced at the thought. 'So where had you come from?'

Eujena allowed the fragrance of the tea to swill round her mouth for a few moments and let herself enjoy the warmth of a velvet smooth taste before she could answer the question. 'I don't know Artemisia. I have suffered from amnesia ever since. But I was miles from anywhere so I must have escaped something.' She tried hard to camouflage the deception and felt dreadful having to lie to this special woman.

'Makes it even more remarkable that he was in the right place at the right time,' said Artemisia sincerely.

'I count my blessings every day that he saved me,' remarked Eujena with the sting of tears in her eyes.

Artemisia refrained from asking any more probing questions that obviously stirred painful memories. 'And did you have a nice time last night Ajeya?' she addressed the young girl.

She faced her and nodded, and for the first time

114

Artemisia noticed the disfigurement. She looked wide eyed at Eujena and nearly choked on her cake. 'I'm sorry, I must slow down when I eat.' She took a few sips of tea to regain her composure. 'I'm so glad you had a nice time Ajeya, I saw you dancing with Keao, and he looked like he was looking after you.'

'Everyone was nice to me,' said the little girl with the glimpse of innocence in her eyes.

'We try to be nice here at the Clan of the Mountain Lion. We want to build friendships with everyone from all walks of life and that's why we are so pleased that you chose us to come and stay with.' Artemisia's voice was kind and gentle.

'I like it here,' said Ajeya tucking into her cake.

Artemisia leaned over to hug the child and kissed her forehead. 'I quite like it here too.' She felt a flutter in her belly. 'I think my baby wants to say hello, I can feel her kicking. Would you like to feel her?'

She nodded eagerly and placed her small hand on the bump while Artemisia began to sing softly.

'The wild wind blows through valleys my love,
The wild wind blows through the trees,
The wild wind blows o'er the rivers my love,
But will n'er get close to thee.
The wild rain storms through the valleys my love,
The wild rain storms through the trees,
The wild rain storms o'er the rivers my love,
But none will get close to thee.'

She stroked Ajeya's hair when she had finished the lullaby. 'Did you feel her kicking?'

Ajeya's face lit up and her face was full of wonder. 'Yes I did.'

'You know what? I hope my little girl is as gorgeous as you, because you are as pretty as a meadow full of flowers.'

The girl beamed up at the beautiful lady.

Eujena felt the tears spill over. At last she felt safe; at last her daughter was accepted and she sat down to enjoy the afternoon with her new found friend.

16

The long awaited Spring Festival was a celebration of appreciation; it also welcomed new life with strong ties in the camp and promises of a good yield of crops for the coming seasons. With a joy and respect that could only come from those living on the edge of survival; this was the clan's most celebrated ritual.

After a long hard winter the thaw was a welcome sight and those that survived the brutal hostility of a northern hemisphere blast could only thank the spirits for their good fortune. To witness the vibrant green of the valley meant that life was pulsing through the land once again; and to celebrate the new life that they needed so much to survive, the beginning of spring had to be blessed with a festival.

Everyone took part in the preparation and groups of men, women and children had been out for days fishing, hunting, trapping and gathering buds, shoots, bulbs, roots, leaves and flowers of every description. Some plants were gathered for sustenance, others for flavour and many were used for teas and medicines. The rivers were plentiful at this time of year and the clans most staple diet was a rich variety of fish. Though for a feast such as this, wild boars were hunted, stags were killed and the newly laid eggs from every type of creature were collected.

But this time, there was to be another addition added to the usual proceedings.

All children of the clan had a totem as a guide, and as they were not clear about Ajeya's origins, Artemisia and Laith had decided that this auspicious occasion would befit such an honour; and it was after dinner one evening that they suggested this tribute.

'And that is why we offer this ceremony to protect our children, to give them a guide and extra powers, you do understand this custom don't you Eujena?'

'Of course I do Laith.'

'We all need protection, every one of us, but children are so very vulnerable. Sometimes only the spirits can help.' Artemisia's words sat deep.

'Does Keao have a totem?' Eujena asked Hagen with a searching look.

'Yes he does, just as Laith has said, all children of the clan do?'

'Well then, as Ajeya is a clan girl now, I think its only fitting that she has her own totem to protect her.'

'I think it's a very good idea Eujena. All children need protecting. It's a very harsh kingdom out there.'

She touched Hagen's hand, grateful for his advice and nodded her head in support of Laith and Artemisia. The three onlookers tipped their heads in agreement.

'If it helps at all, she was born under a blue

moon. I have always thought that was a sign of protection and strength.' Eujena looked at each of them in turn.

'Yes that is very special sign,' said Artemisia, her voice uplifted.

'Indeed it is,' declared Laith. 'And there is only one totem that can befit such an honour.'

Eujena raised her eyebrows in anticipation.

'Ajeya's totem is the Hare!'

'The Hare?' Eujena's voice went up an octave.

'Yes, it is a very important symbol especially during the Spring Equinox,' replied Laith almost aghast at her response.

'It is a figure of independence and infinite wisdom,' said Artemisia noticing the subtle exchange.

'With high expectations and heightened intuition,' said Laith.

'It's a fine totem to have,' heralded Hagen nodding his head in admiration.

'So when will she be given this symbol?' Eujena asked.

'Tomorrow of course, the Vernal Equinox, the first day of spring.'

The commanding words mingled with the wisps of smoke from the fire and the waves of shimmering heat were sent as spiralling plumes through the roof and out into the cool evening air. Streams of grey particles weaved around the outside trees to cast their own powerful shadows, and the last dim afterglow outlined a hare in the wilderness silhouetted in the hazy moonlight.

The same time the following evening saw the giant obelisk loom over them in a humble epitome of enormous power. And with the needle of the dome pressed high against the orb of a bright new moon, the tribe filtered in with heads bowed low and hands pressed together summoning the spirits to offer their guidance. There was not a sound, not even a quiver. A subtle gesture from Zoraster invited Eujena to move forward and stand with her child before the grand menhir.

In the silence, the sound of breathing grew loud, and the crackling of the fire intensified. Moving air was an invisible presence and a soft chanting honed in on the community. They didn't even notice when it began, how the humming monotone became a tool to beckon the spirits and then a rhythmic chant evoked a further sense of power and fortitude. The woman with the jaw harp began to unite all of nature with its surroundings and hailed in the spirits of all those lives who were part of a distant past. The whole group began to feel like one entity and their hearts began to beat in unison. They breathed as one and had the same thoughts flowing through their sub conscious. Soon the solitary standing menhir had control over every single person in front of it. The jaw harp faded and a drum beat softly and finally Zoraster held up his hands to welcome the spirits.

Laith waited patiently for the right moment to begin the ceremony. The bright full moon looked as if it would burst when the leader broke the tranquil silence and began the proceedings.

'Comrades; citizens; people of the mountain lion; we welcome a new child into our clan and she and her family are very much welcomed into our community.' A wave of bobbing heads acknowledged the new arrivals and Laith continued. 'We offer all of them our love, our protection and other offerings of wealth in front of the menhir.' He bowed to the grand stone and took in a deep breath as he addressed the clan again. 'But this is also our celebration of spring to call forward the spirits and pray for continued sustenance in a rich and varied land. This is a special time for all of us to renew our own vows with Ajeya as we remember that nature is connected at an unseen level. That animals, birds, plants and rocks all have lessons to teach us and messages to share. These messages are instrumental for us to survive; they have been passed down to us from the gods and our forefathers providing direction, protection and healing. Citizens hold your thoughts within this circle and pray for continued good fortune as we feast with the spirits tonight and give this daughter her guide.'

As Eujena led her child to Laith; he continued. 'Each child is given the spirit of a chosen animal by the leader of the clan; this will protect and guide the bearer in this life, the next life and throughout eternity. The spirit guide and totem for this child is the Hare as it exhibits great courage with swiftness and speed; it has total awareness of its surroundings. But above all else, it represents love and infinite wisdom. The Hare will serve its bearer well.'

The jaw harp started up with a low vibrating drone as the tribe held their own thoughts and then as the drums and reed instruments accompanied the melancholy sounds, the clan filtered outside of the menhirs to begin a night of celebration.

They filed out towards a spectacular spread of trestle tables where exposed plates of exquisitely presented food was waiting for them; wild boar and steamed fish, roasted venison with minted sauce, boiled eggs with pine nuts, potatoes glazed with honey, carrots dipped in ale. And for deserts was a range of sweet breads, cinnamon cakes, apple dumplings and dried figs.

Then the first few notes of the reed pipes began to shiver across the dance area. At the fourth quatrain, the couples joined together and slowly began to move. Hagen held Eujena's face in the palms of his hands and kissed her gently. As he did so, they kept their posture graceful and their stance defined. They moved with subtle gestures as they circled around each other; seductive, passionate, empowering. He took her hand and pulled her into him, she felt his strong arms around her as she fell back, confident that he would not let her fall, and felt his beating heart as she rose again and pressed her breast to his chest. She spread her arms wide and he lifted her high into the air, and as she dropped to the ground, feeling almost weightless, the drumbeat started. Without conscious thought they both slipped into the arise, parted, hands raised, meeting for the merest fingertip touch, parted again and then he lifted her high into the air before letting her slide down against his body till her feet touched the floor. They held the embrace until the music stopped and then wrapped their arms around each other as a final embrace.

The clan erupted with shouts and whistles of appreciation and the music and feasting started up once again.

17

The spring warmed and the days lengthened and the weeks that followed were a haze of preparations. Preparing for a wedding, preparing a comfortable range of furniture for their home and preparing a little girl how to defend herself.

Keao devoted his time to modifications to improve Ajeya's performance with the catapult; even making a smaller more adaptable version for her to use. He had assured her that even with a good working weapon, they would both need to practise for several hours a day. Though in the end, it was teaching her the way of the kingdom that filled most of their days.

'Why was I given the Hare as my totem?'

'Because it is a very special animal that is why.'

'But it's so little.' Her face was one of disappointment.

'You don't have to be big to be powerful.' His words were monumental.

'What is your totem?'

'I have an Owl.'

'That's much bigger than mine.'

He got down to her level and looked her in the

eye. 'Did you know that if you look into the sky when the moon is at its brightest, you can see the image of a hare in the moon. The hare is so much bigger than anything else and it looks down from its highest position and sees everything.'

She smiled at the enormity of her totem and stood up tall and proud. 'It sees everything?'

'Everything.' He nodded with a serious face.

'So what can the owl do?'

He sat back on his heels and breathed in deeply. 'The owl is the greatest predator of the forest. It has total awareness of its surroundings so it can hunt in the dark using sound alone to guide it to a kill. It will watch the movements of its prey for hours before choosing the right moment to strike. It has perfect patience and perception and its stillness makes it invisible.' He looked beyond the forest. 'Have you ever seen the bird behind the call?'

She shook her head.

'That's because it is special and can hide. But the hare can see it, the hare can see everything. It will be a very special guide for you because it will know where everything is, good and bad, and it will protect you.'

She thought long and hard, wrinkled up her nose and creased the fold where her eyebrows started. 'So with me watching everything and you as a great hunter, we can work together.'

He laughed affectionately at her proposition. 'Of course we can, let's give it a go now.'

She watched him climb a tree and he wedged

himself between a sturdy branch and the trunk. He looked down at her and put his finger to his lips. 'Be like an animal,' he had told her. 'They slow their heartbeats to a near standstill, so their body heat drops and their scent disappears. They become invisible.' So when she saw his signal, she knew instantly to be quiet and conceal herself. Insects buzzed around her and landed on her face and in her hair, birds flew so close that she could feel the whisper of their wings. Red ants crawled up her legs and bit her, but she didn't flinch. To them, she was a statue. A roe deer nibbled her way to where she crouched; invisible, silent, unmoving. Only the leaves on the trees stirred and the bows creaked; animals knew those sounds. These humans couldn't be detected.

Keao spotted a buck rabbit chomping contently on the remnants of a healthy dandelion. The buck sat upright on its hind legs and sniffed the air; his nose twitched trying to detect any threatening odours while his long ears shifted, locating any sounds that would give him the advantage to disappear into the safety of his burrow.

Thud! Thwack! One after the other, two rocks hit him full pelt in the temple and he fell instantly to the ground. He wouldn't have even felt it. Ajeya looked up at Keao, his catapult was still swinging from the exertion. The Owl and the Hare had hunted and a buck rabbit would make a fine stew tonight she thought.

Eujena had decided to start making clothes for each of

them. The primary reason was so they would look their finest for their host's big day, but the second reason was so they had more than one outfit to wear. Therefore, with the long light evenings, and with Ajeya and Keao out for most of the day, she had ample time to do it. Artemisia had given her a bundle of old clothes to adapt, and she found the whole process so interesting and the garments so intriguing that she was able to match the elaborate beading and fine quillwork onto all of their garments. So good was she with the splint of a bone as a needle and the tendril of the mugwort as a thread, she worked tirelessly and easily to provide a set of clothes for each of them. She even made bed spreads and curtains with the left over fabric. Artemisia made her promise that she would teach her skills after the wedding.

Hagen had chopped down trees and split them where they lay, then lathed them by hand, sawing and pummelling till well into the night. Hours of rubbing down to give a smooth finish and then carving out intricate patterns gave his work a personal feel. Two beds he made, complete with wooden slats and headboards, as well as four chairs with arm rests and two stools for milking the goat that they had been given. And as the weeks rolled into months; the shell of a building that they were provided with, soon became the epitome of a home, adorned perfectly to their tastes and somewhere that they could call their own for the very first time.

That evening, the sun was just going down when she arrived back from having supper with Laith and Artemisia. She knew that Ajeya and Keao were still out practising together, and that Hagen was chopping up logs for the hearth.

It had been a nice evening with Laith and Artemisia. A rich meaty stew had been served with lashings of dumplings and legions of carrots. The meal was delicious and washed down with copious amounts of last season's wine.

'So when are you two going to get married?' The alcohol had certainly distorted Laith's perception of etiquette.

'I'm not sure,' said Eujena slightly startled, remembering only too well that she was still a married woman.

'Laith really, it's not our business. I'm sorry Eujena, I think my husband to be has had rather too much to drink.' Artemisia rolled her eyes as she got up to collect the plates and put them in a large metal bowl outside the front porch. Then she returned to her husband's side.

Eujena smiled at the bond that these two people shared.

'But they make such a wonderful couple; like us.' He reached over to kiss her cheek. Artemisia reached for Laith's fingers and entwined them with her own.

'One day perhaps, when we are settled,' she said.

'But you are settled here, surely,' Laith remarked.

'We are getting there,' Eujena smiled.

'Have you seen what Hagen has done with their home?' said Artemisia. 'He is a wonderful carpenter and his workmanship is so skilled.'

'I have my dear, and he is undoubtedly very talented.'

'And the clothes that Eujena has made, the curtains and the spreads; their home is one of the finest.'

Laith smiled and raised his eyebrows as he agreed with her. 'I know, and have you seen how that young boy has taken Ajeya under his wing and teaching her the way of the forest? It truly is inspiring.'

'She loves it here,' said Eujena recognising her own good fortune. 'We all consider ourselves very lucky to be able to call this our home.'

Artemisia took her hand. 'This will always be your home, always,' she smiled tenderly. 'And Laith,' she continued, noticing his heavy eyes. 'This fine lady has promised to teach me how to make clothes after our wedding.'

'Do you think you will have time my love? You will have your hands full not long after.' He tilted his head in the direction of her growing bump.

'You will be wonderful parents, your child is very lucky.' Eujena's tone was melancholy, and she shivered at the memory of Ajeya's biological father remembering how he had never accepted their only daughter.

'I am a very lucky woman and I thank the gods every day for guiding me.' Artemisia kissed Laith's hand. He leaned over and nestled his head on her shoulder.

Eujena pondered on the good fortune of these two people, finding each other and falling in love; making a home together and now bringing a new child into the world. What blessings they had been given; nothing on this earth could part these two and she smiled on them with affection.

'We are all lucky,' he slurred, but was completely in control of his chosen words. 'Lucky to have such good friends and family.' He knocked back the last of his wine and struggled to keep his eyes open now.

Eujena stood up to go. 'I think it's time I went, so I can let you two get some much needed rest. When that little one comes, you won't be getting any sleep at all. Your whole life will change in an instant and...'

The sound of snoring cut short her words and the two women laughed.

'How can men do that?' chuckled Artemisia. 'Just fall asleep wherever they are?'

'I know, I can't do that. I need a nice warm bed with plenty of soft downy blankets.'

'Me too,' agreed Artemisia. 'I had better get this big lump to bed - or shall I just leave him there?'

Eujena wrapped a woollen shawl around her shoulders. 'I would leave him there, you don't want to do anything too strenuous now do you?'

'I heard that,' mumbled Laith.

'Eujena laughed. 'I will call by tomorrow to give you a hand with the dishes.'

The fire was out when she got home and the house was dark and gloomy. It seemed really empty without her family there. Even though the new furniture adorned the room and her curtains and bedding added vibrant colours and warmth, it still felt very cold and very empty. Outside it was eerily quiet punctuated by the occasional noise. Something rustled outside. Then came the screech of an owl. And finally, the scream of its victim. Silent wings carried the kill back to its lair.

She lit the fire, boiled some water and made a cup of dandelion tea. She sat down on the bed. It seemed a long time that she was alone in there. The warmth of the embers made her sleepy and the tea relaxed her. But falling asleep was full of disturbed dreams. She dreamed of Keao fighting for his life in a troubled land, she dreamed of Hagen driving Coal through the dark in an attempt to get away from something dreadful. In that dream she was left on her own again with Ajeya to battle through the wilderness. Bats and other mythical creatures swooped down on them and tried to peck at their eyes and claw at their skin. She woke in a sweat of fright. She got up and stirred the fire, then warmed her tea and sipped it. At last she heard laughter and familiar voices and a smile swept across her face as her family returned to their home safely.

That night as they lay sleeping, Hagen looked over to the slumbering woman, he breathed the smell of her and watched the rise and fall of her breasts. A wispy tendril of hair lay across her face and moved with each breath she took. He reached over and gently moved it aside. He covered her with the soft downy blankets to keep off the chill and then her breathing changed; it became slow and heavy. She rolled over onto her side and in her sleep she murmured: 'Strong and handsome, my beautiful Hagen. I wish that one day we too could get married.'

18

It was the day before the wedding and something about the way the trees creaked that evening sent a shiver down Eujena's spine. Even though it was the eve before the longest day, the air was heavy and full of uncertainty. The trees bowed and twisted as Hagen drove his family through the forest, so much so that they didn't even resemble trees any more; rather, they took on the form of hideous deformed monsters trying to hide away from the stretch of the sun. The huge oak towered over them with its bulbous arms weighted down with a harvest of leaves and its gnarled claws crawling out yonder in search of life giving sustenance. Coal nickered and became skittish, he too was spooked at the squawks and hoots that came from the overhead limbs clustered around them.

'We should be back soon,' assured Hagen.

'Yes, I still have a few alterations to do on Ajeya's dress and need to catch the light.'

'I will get you back in time and make sure all the errands are completed for the wedding.

'It will be a wonderful day Hagen, I really can't wait to see them married.'

'You have become very close to Artemisia

haven't you?'

She looked at him tenderly. 'I really have. I don't remember ever having such a close friend - well, apart from you of course.' Her hand found his and she knitted their fingers.

Hagen smiled at the touch. 'And look at those two in the back, see how close they have become.'

'I know,' Eujena's voice was tender. 'Ajeya loves Keao, and he is so good with her.'

'He's teaching her to used a bow and arrow now, they practise every single day.' Hagen's voice was full of pride.

'Yes, she is always practising with the one he made her, even when he is off doing something else, she will carry out his instructions and fill her days.' Eujena smiled at the thought. 'But it's good for a girl to know how to use a weapon, don't you think?'

'I totally agree,' Hagen nodded. 'It's a sign of the changing times we are in.'

Eujena gripped his hand tighter and smiled with ease; until a raven landed on a broken branch above and gave a harsh raucous rattle of distress. She looked up in alarm; the last time she saw a raven like this she was close to death. She noticed it had blood on its wings and it opened and closed its beak in fear of something. She shivered and leaned into Hagen. 'Can we go a bit faster my love, I feel I am getting a chill.'

'Of course we can; come on Coal, let's get home,' and he snapped the reins over the horse's rump. But the smile vanished from his face when a terrible scream split the air and he pulled the cart to a halt immediately.

'What is it?' cried out Eujena, looking around to whence the sound had come.

'I don't know I can't see,' Hagen's response was shocked and his heart quickly accelerated as he hunted for the source.

'Children get down! Keao, get that blanket and pull it over you!' The acuity in Eujena's voice was hushed.

Then they saw a great rush of men, women and children running in all directions followed by soldiers on horseback. With a thunder of galloping hooves, an army of devils descended on the vulnerable clan; with swords flashing and bayonets charging, they attacked anyone who got in their way. Those that fell or turned back were cut down by the long swords, and as the horsemen advanced, their horses rode over the bodies of the wounded and the dead. Terrified, the people of the clan had nowhere to go; and even the men armed with spears and arrows were brutally cut down before they could fire a shot.

Eujena recognised the colours of the army and the blood drained from her face. 'What do they want?' her voice was a faint whisper; Ajeya was camouflaged in the back; listening, watching, pretending.

'I've got to go and help them,' cried out Hagen jumping down from the wagon and reaching for his spear. 'Keao come with me, and bring that catapult with you.'

135

The boy did as he was told; throwing the covers off him, he jumped down and covered the little girl again.

Eujena clung on to his arm. 'You can't go in there Hagen, you can't!'

'I will not leave these people on their own Eujena, look at them, they are being slaughtered out there.'

Still she grabbed onto him. 'They are the Emperor's men Hagen, they are here to find me.' Her voice was frail and breathless.

'What do they want with you?' He was getting impatient as more of his kinsmen were getting mowed down.

'I can't tell you right now, but my life is in danger and I have to get out of here,' she spoke quickly sensing the danger she was in.

Hagen looked at her. 'Why do they want you though? What have you done?'

The four of them were frozen in suspension and time moved slowly as Hagen was torn between duty and honour. It was his duty to take care of Eujena and Ajeya, but it was his honour to look after the clan. The trees camouflaged them but didn't spare the stench of death and blood.

Cruel fires burned rapidly, devouring homes and precious possessions, corpses were cremated where they lay and columns of black smoke rose up to stain a deepening crimson sky. An old man writhed on the ground in agony, screaming at the grey belly of smoke above; his flesh was on fire and no one could help him. The flumes of burning wood filled their lungs and the constant wail of screaming reverberated around the camp. The reek of burning skin was worse.

They dared not move a muscle, even Coal didn't flinch. Eujena watched the leader of the invaders ride by on his horse, she saw him clearly in the light of the setting sun, those eyes were as cruel as a devil hunting its prey. That face terrified her. She thought her thumping heart would give them away it was beating that hard. She recognised him at once, even under all the armoury and the royal disguise, she would never forget that face. Why couldn't he just leave her alone? She had gone like he had demanded. She had found refuge in the clans like Ariane had said. Was he now punishing the clans and going to put her and Ajeya to death after all?

The Emperor of Ataxata looked straight through the blistering scene with his eyes fixed in her direction - her heart missed a beat - had he seen her?

'He will kill me if he finds me Hagen,' her voice matched the panic on her face. 'He will kill Ajeya, he will certainly kill you for harbouring me - I was married to that monster and he banished me for having a disfigured child. He said if I didn't leave then he would let me and Ajeya rot in the darkest dungeons. He made me go into the wilderness and left me to die out there, and I know that if he sees me now he will kill me.' Her eyes ran with tears as she begged and pleaded with the only man who could save her.

Hagen dropped his head to the floor and breathed heavily with the weight on his shoulders. Which one should he help?

The soldiers brought in the caged wagons, and as the remaining survivors were herded in a beleaguered line, the horse and cart that protected the woman he loved and the children he had sworn to take care of, slowly rolled down the hill quietly, steadily and out of sight.

'Right, now that you are paying attention, I need a little information.' The Emperor marched his horse along the long line of terrified villagers, trying to find the weakness in the clan. 'And you have seen what I am capable of.' Still he walked purposefully while the clan trembled fearfully. Then he stopped in the centre and faced them.

'I need to know the whereabouts of something.'

The clan looked at each other in total shock, what could they possibly have that he needed?

'And I will remind you that lying to me is punishable by death.'

The clan's eyes fell on the remaining soldiers kicking anything in their path and crashing through burnt out homes.

'I am looking for The Seal of Kings.'

Terrified expressions abounded, because they really didn't know what he was talking about.

'I have been told by a reliable source that the Seal of King's whereabouts is known by a clan member.

So I ask you again, who can help me with my enquiries?'

Still, there was nothing from the crowd except the guise of fear and trepidation.

'I will give you one last chance. Now, before I really lose my temper, where is The Seal?' His voice shook the ground so hard that even his grey mare paced about nervously.

'We don't know my lord,' came a pitiful voice. 'We are peasants and know nothing of such things.'

The Emperor rode menacingly close to the owner of the voice but kept his words slow and even. 'I don't believe you and I should take out your tongue right here you miserable wretch.' His eyes narrowed and a sinister smirk grew too easily. 'But I am a lenient man, and because you are the only one who spoke up to spare your clan, it is you who I shall take as a prisoner.' The sickening grin widened menacingly.

'No, please have mercy, we do not know what you speak of, please spare him,' cried out his wife.

The smile vanished and his lips were thin. 'Another woman asked me for mercy once, I didn't listen to her pleas either... Lock him in the wagon.'

The berating clan tried to stop the soldiers advancement but were cruelly beaten back with fists and clubs and anything else that would inflict a cavernous wound.

Suddenly the air cleared and a movement froze the proceedings. 'Leave him. Take me!' An exhausted but authoritative voice took precedence.

The Emperor tipped his head, and grinning, looked straight at the owner of the offer. A strong young man with the air of grandeur and leadership about him had spoken up. Gored with battle wounds and leaning on a blood stained sword, he had no fight left in him. He would be no trouble. But this would do nicely. This was their leader. So much better than a mere peasant.

'Laith, No!' A woman screamed.

Artemisia stood at the entrance of their hut, tears streaming down her face. 'Laith please don't go, it's our wedding tomorrow, our unborn child needs you, I need you, please don't leave me.'

Zoraster put an arm around her and tried to hold her back.

'I have to go Artemisia, I am the leader here, I cannot let another man take my place.'

Artemisia ran out and clung on to him. 'Please Laith, please.'

'I will return soon; I promise.' He held onto her tightly and kissed her face.

The Emperor looked at them and sneered with total disregard. 'In your wildest dreams,' he thought.

'Take him!' came the order. 'Lock him him in the wagon and we'll be on our way.'

19

The plump grey clouds seemed to follow their route, and the rain fell soft and steady, muffling the sound of Coal's steps and camouflaging the tears that fell in pools down Eujena's face. They rode in silence as if the woods were full of ears. The children slept peacefully in the back of the cart and following the road north they took a barren path that meandered through sparse woodland where the trees leaned drunkenly on each other and created a wall of black through which no stars could shine. Coal nickered nervously and Eujena glanced over her shoulder to make sure that no one was following. In the pits of darkness all she could see were monstrous shadows taunting her, so she pulled her shawl tighter and leaned into Hagen.

By nightfall, the clouds had emptied their heavy load and now only a fine drizzle fell around them as their journey led them to a vast open space. The stars could be seen shining brightly from here, straining to break through the cracked and pitted black barrier of the night sky. The moon was full and her light cast hideous shapes across a desolate landscape while the bark of a fox and the howl of a wolf made Coal skittish again.

Strange nocturnal sounds in the distance told them that an unseen world was close by and the screams of a victim were evidence that a hunting predator had taken its prey. The dark concealed many secrets, some were so grotesque that they would only play out silently in one's owns thoughts. Sometimes they became real and turned into folklore and fables to tell over a camp fire by men high on liquor. For if left alone, they would surely grow into something more terrifying. So when it got too much to bare and Hagen couldn't stop his exaggerated thoughts, he had to know the truth.

'Will you tell me what that was all about back there Eujena?' his voice was barely audible.

Eujena felt her heart beating faster and the nausea in her stomach rose to the back of her throat. She remained silent, unwilling to divulge her past.

'Eujena, please,' his voice was an octave louder.

She began to sob quietly. 'I'm so sorry Hagen, I truly am.'

'What are you sorry about?' his tone was puzzled.

'Everything, simply everything.' Her face was stained with a thousand tears and for the first time he was aware of the weight that she carried on her shoulders.

Hagen looked at her as the wagon rolled along on even ground and the darkness weighed down heavily on them. Neither of them felt scared anymore though, the night with all its secrets and concealed monsters were of little consequence now; for both of them knew that what she was about to say would consume them more. She looked back at the children to check that they were both settled and that they wouldn't hear what she was about to divulge. The deep sounds of sleep from both of them told her that they were immersed in pleasant dreams.

'I was married to that man back there,' she began, her voice was a little over a whisper. 'It seems like a lifetime ago and I have had to put it to the back of my mind. But the truth is, that monster is my husband and Ajeya's father.'

'But there were a lot of men Eujena, which one are you talking about?'

She looked at him bravely, she was trying so desperately hard to conceal her fear and the mere mention of his name made her want to vomit. 'The one on the grey mare, the one in the golden helmet and red cape. The one standing back and giving the orders.'

'The Emperor?' his voice was incredulous.

She nodded meekly.

Hagen looked at her unable to conceal his shock. 'The Emperor is your husband?'

'Estranged husband, but yes, he is.'

'So you are an Empress?' his tone was still one of bewilderment, but still he kept a tight rein and Coal plodded onwards.

'Not any more I am not, most certainly not any more, and Ajeya must never know about this. Her past is in the past. It is forgotten and of no importance to

143

anyone. I am only telling you because of our circumstances and what has just happened. But Ajeya is a clan girl now with the totem of a hare to protect her. She must never know Hagen, please give me your word.'

'I give you my word, she will never know of this from me,' Hagen's voice was low and sincere.

'Thank you,' the sound was breathless with emotion.

'But I need to know what happened to you. Why were you on your own with a young child when you had such privilege, wealth and safety in the city. You were an Empress Eujena. What happened?' He wasn't entirely sure that he needed to know, or indeed wanted to know, sometimes ignorance is the best policy. But he had opened this pot of worms and he couldn't stop it now.

Eujena found her strong voice and began to tell her story. 'That man cast me out. When you found me I had been wandering for months in the wilderness trying to survive, trying to keep my child safe. I don't even know how long for. I honestly can't recall very much. The days and nights all roll into one. All I know is how alone and vulnerable I felt and many times I wished that I was dead.'

His face saddened but still his inquisitive side searched for answers. 'But why did he cast you out?'

She sighed heavily. 'He said that Ajeya wasn't his, that she had been born from a devil's seed, that no offspring of his would take on a form so hideous. He told me that no decent man would ever want her because of her disfigurement and that she would discredit the dynasty. He accused me of sleeping with the devil and told me to take her and live in the caves or he would make us end our days in the dungeons,' her throat was tight and she struggled to speak; she needed a few moments to find her composure.

'But what made him wait until she was two years old? He must have loved her before then.'

Eujena threw him an unsavoury look and bit her bottom lip as she breathed deeply. 'He never loved her. He told me to let her die when she was born. After two years he said that he couldn't bear to look at her anymore, that she made him feel sick,' she dropped her gaze to the ground.

Hagen found a rage burning inside of him and needed time to control his fury.

'We had been travelling for months when you found me. You were my saviour then and still are. Hagen, please don't be angry with me and cast me aside now. I know I lied to you about my past, but I was scared. I thought you would abandon me and I couldn't bear the thought of being out there on my own again. Please forgive me, please I beg you.'

He stopped the cart. A strange silence descended. The predators were no longer hungry, their prey were no longer unsafe. The only sounds were those of the sleeping children still immersed in their own innocent dreams and a dragon moth fluttering by taking advantage of the cool night air.

A chaos of emotion surged through his body at once; love and sadness, fury and fear. He relived the moment that he found her bloodied body, barely alive but still hanging on to something so strong. He felt the joy when Thorne gave them his blessings and allowed them to part as the family he had always yearned for. He could still taste her kiss from the evening of the Spring Festival when Ajeya had been given her totem and the energy that he had felt when they had danced until dawn. He longed for the warmth of her body as they slept together and he knew that it was her skin that gave him comfort, not the bed or the covers that had been so lovingly made. He heard the screams of the clan he had just left behind; and he felt an anger so strong because the Emperor had tried to destroy the people he loved most in this kingdom. He wanted to cry out but nothing came out. His voice was dry but his tears flowed silently; because the strongest emotion of them all was the love he had for this woman.

He looked at her and managed to whisper. 'I love you Eujena and I love Ajeya as if she were my own. You make me laugh and you make me happy and I would do anything for you.' He kissed her hands. 'I am sad that you think I could be angry with you and cast you aside, like a monster with no feelings. We are on this journey together and we face everything together.' He took her face in the palm of his hands and kissed her passionately.

She held on to him and sobbed. 'I love you too Hagen. I always will.'

He held onto her tightly and let those words of love fill the air; then something entered his mind and he spoke out what he was thinking. 'Is there anything else you need to tell me?'

She thought for a while, and decided that she should have no secrets, that she had to tell this gentle man everything. 'I have a son called Cornelius. He is three years older than Ajeya and is not disfigured, in fact he is a very handsome boy, so the Emperor acknowledges him as his own. But I worry for him Hagen. He does not have a good father like you or any honourable father figure to look up to or aspire to. He is surrounded by hatred and greed and I fear for him.'

Hagen didn't say anything. There were no words to say. This poor woman had suffered so much. He pulled her close to him and held her there. He kissed the top of her head and made her feel protected. 'You are safe now, I will look after you. To everyone we meet from now on, we are husband and wife; Ajeya is our daughter and Keao is our son. Keao will be told in the morning. Ajeya is too young to remember much; but she will grow up believing that Keao is her brother. We are a family now looking for work.'

Her sigh was long as she nodded with relief.

'But in light of what you have just told me do you think we should change your name, just incase he comes looking for you again and asks if anyone knows Eujena?'

'You are right Hagen, I hadn't thought about that. He didn't find me back there so he might continue his search,' her voice became anxious. 'I shall change my name to Jena; perhaps we could tell Keao that I have decided it is a more appropriate clan name.'

'That's a good idea,' he smiled.

'What about Ajeya, should we change her name?'

Hagen took in a deep breath through his nose and let it out slowly through pursed lips as he thought about it. 'I'm hoping it won't be necessary, it is you whom he wants to silence. Ajeya is a child and is no threat.... she will have no memory of him. You on the other hand.......' He let Eujena work it out for herself.

'You are right, Ajeya shall continue to be called by her name, and from now on, I shall be known as Jena.'

He kissed her hand as if to seal the pact.

A stirring came from the back of the cart and Keao popped his head up. 'Is everything all right father?'

'Everything is fine Keao, I was just checking that we were on the right path and now I know we are.'

'All right, just shout if you need me,' and the boy snuggled down again and pulled the covers back over his head.

Hagen nodded his approval and snapped the reins over Coal's back.

It was almost dawn by the time they reached the next village. People were waking, shutters were opening, spilled voices still hushed from sleep. Further off came the creaking sound of the waterwheel and the droplets glistened under the rays of a rising sun. It was midsummers day and the woodsmoke hung lazily over squat flat roofs.

'We shall try this clan,' Hagen's voice was more optimistic now, and Eujena's remorseful eyes were brighter.

The village was surrounded by fields and a stream whispered beneath a wooden bridge. Beyond that were about a dozen houses around a common green and a beautiful oak tree stood proud, festooned with different coloured ribbons dangling like rainbows from the gnarled and twisted branches. A dog started barking at the sound of the wagon and a flock of geese started honking and hissing at the approaching horse. Hagen steered the party through the village, following the twisting lanes between the homes. People were emerging and setting about their work. One group of lads were armed with sickles and heading off for a day in the fields, another group were off to the barns to see to the horses. Women with baskets of grain were feeding a gaggle of geese followed by young girls throwing seeds to a brood of hens. Gates were being opened; doors unlocked, wagons and carts wheeled out ready to take their loads. A hive of activity spread out before them and the sun blazed down as though the colour stolen by the night was returned in an even brighter hue. Most people tipped their heads at the young family making their way through the peppered bridle ways. It was a peaceful spot, still and tranquil and lovely to behold.

Hagen jumped down from the cart. 'This is good land and good soil,' he said, picking up a handful of dirt and rubbing it between his fingers. 'Fertile and rich, this is an excellent settlement.'

'I'm glad you think so,' came a booming voice.

Hagen stood up and smacking his hands together, dusted himself down.

A tall man stood before them with long white hair that reached his shoulders, his eyes were kind and his mouth arched into a gentle smile. His breeches were worn and his white shirt crumpled but a strong hand was held out as a sign of friendship. 'My name is Colom and I am the leader of the Hill Fort Tribe.'

Hagen responded with a firm handshake. 'Good morning Colom, I am very pleased to make your acquaintance. My name is Hagen, this is my wife Jena, my son Keao, and my daughter Ajeya is still sleeping in the back I believe.'

As Colom walked over to greet Jena, they couldn't help but notice he had a slight limp, whether it was one leg slightly shorter than the other or a deformity they couldn't tell, but as it didn't really seem to bother him, they decided that it shouldn't bother them either.

'Have you come far?' asked Colom after shaking hands with Jena and Keao.

'About a days ride,' said Hagen sincerely. 'But I am looking for work and I would require

150

accommodation for all of us if you can spare it.'

Colom turned around and looked over the settlement; he rubbed his chin between his thumb and fingers and grunted to himself. Hagen looked back at Jena and shrugged his shoulders. Jena began to look uneasy.

'I'm a good worker,' he chipped in, hopeful that his aptitude would make a difference. 'My son Keao is fourteen years old and he can put his hand to anything; really, he is a good worker and very strong.' Fumbled words seemed to fall on deaf ears.

Jena looked to the ground despondently. But then her eyes lifted to see a woman walking towards them. She was wiping her hands on a white apron that fell over a long woollen dress.

'What's all this Colom?'

'It's a young family Peira, they are asking for work and lodgings.'

'Well we can accommodate them can't we? I mean we have a lot of work at this time of the year and we can always do with the help.'

'Of course we have work my love, I was just thinking which lodge we could put them in.'

'That one over there father, that one's empty.' A young boy appeared from behind his mother, both his legs were in wooden splints and held in place with a thick leather strap, they had been made by an expert craftsman and were designed to fit him perfectly. Apart from his legs he was a sturdy lad, and with a mop of golden curly hair he looked like a little god sent from above. Jena was taken aback by his beautiful face.

'You wouldn't think he was only six years old would you. He's got a good head on those shoulders, always telling us how things should be done,' his mother laughed and hugged the boy affectionately.

Colom took his hand. 'I believe you are right young Dainn. Come, let us show our guests to their accommodation.'

20

Colom whistled to a stable lad to take the horse and wagon. Hagen lifted the sleeping girl out of the back of the cart. Jena carried the blankets.

'Where are your belongings?' Peira asked in a perturbed tone, looking for their bags.

Jena looked to Hagen to answer.

'We had to leave in a hurry, some of the children were being unkind to Ajeya.'

Jena rolled her eyes at him. Hagen shrugged his shoulders in response.

The look didn't go unnoticed by Peira. 'Why were the children being unkind to her?'

Hagen showed Peira the child's face, she threw her hands to her mouth and gasped. 'The poor lamb! Children can be so cruel. My own boy has suffered taunting from an early age, what with his legs and walking, but I soon put a stop to it, with the help of his father of course. He cannot abide it either and suffered extreme mockery himself. But it must have been so hard for you.'

Jena bit her bottom lip and shook her head discreetly. But what was the alternative? Tell them the truth, that they fled the Clan of the Mountain Lion when it was being attacked by the Emperor and his army! No, Hagen had probably come up with the best and only explanation.

'Your boy walks well though,' noticed Jena.

'He does now,' replied Peira. 'But it wasn't always like that.' The mother looked at him lovingly, reminiscing and remembering a more difficult time. 'The splints will be coming off soon, he only has them on for a couple of hours a day now,' she revealed. 'He doesn't really need them, it's his father, he just wants to make sure.'

'Really, that is good news,' enthused Jena.

'And then he will be able to play with Ajeya.'

The two women smiled at each other and watched as Coal was led off to a stable and the wagon was stabilised under a lean-to.

'Your horse will be well looked after,' said Dainn. 'I go to the stables every day to help. Maybe Ajeya would like to come with me one day.'

'She would like that very much Dainn, thank you.'

They followed their hosts to a comfortable sized building that had a long veranda at the front and a wide porch leading into a spacious family room. The veranda had a seating area and a wood pit. Various kitchen utensils were stacked in a bowl on a small wooden table. Inside the family room there were curtains up and rugs on the floor and a huge wooden table ran along one side with two long benches underneath. Cupboards, drawers and shelves were scattered opposite. There were three doors leading off into the bedrooms. Each subsequent room had wooden beds strung with timber slats. Goose down mattresses lay on top of the slats and pillows full of eider feathers were at the head. A neat pile of blankets and finely woven sheets were stacked at the other end.

'This is perfect,' trilled Jena.

'We get our own rooms at last,' hailed Keao.

Hagen laughed and put an arm round the lad's shoulder.

'I am glad you like it,' Peira was pleased.

Jena quickly made up a bed and lay Ajeya down. Peira helped her cover the child with blankets and as she did so, the amber necklace was exposed and glinted in the sun.

Peira gasped in astonishment. 'Where did you get that?'

'She was given it Peira, it was a gift. It's beautiful isn't it.'

'It certainly is, but who gave it to you?'

'By a great man called Thorne, leader of the Giant's Claw.' Jena's voice was full of pride.

'But she is disfigured, why would Thorne do that?'

Suddenly Jena became concerned. This was more than admiration of a trinket. Peira knew something. She knew Thorne.

'I think it's time we went,' said Colom to Hagen and Keao peeping round the corner. 'I can show you where you will be working. And you young Dainn, you come along too.'

'Can't I stay here? Mother is upset.'

'No you can't stay, you come with us. I need you to help me. Mother is fine, she just needs to talk to Jena.'

'But...'

'No buts - come on.'

The men left. The women looked at each other.

'Come and sit down, you look shocked.' Jena led Peira to the long table and sat down next to her on the bench.

'I'm so sorry, I shouldn't have alarmed you,' croaked the older mother... 'But the necklace brought back memories.'

Jena was still in the dark about the meaning. 'Thorne gave it to Ajeya. It was a gift.'

Peira started to weep.

'What's the matter, please, I don't understand?'

Peira composed herself and lifted her head high. 'Thorne was my husband, I was married to him,' she sniffed back the tears. 'For years I tried to have a baby and each one I lost. It was either still born, or I lost it in a pool of blood. There were so many that I lost.' Her voice trailed off.

Jena put her hand on the woman's knee.

'When I gave birth to Dainn, he was born with twisted legs and I was told I would have to surrender him to the weeping caves,' she started to cry and then composed herself again. 'I'm sorry.'

'Please don't be,' said a compassionate Jena.

'I was a much older mother Jena, it would have been my last chance to have a baby. I know that. Everyone knew that. So before they could take my baby from me, I ran away.'

Jena held her hands up to her mouth. 'You poor woman.'

'I remember being weaker than I realised, and certainly older than I gave my self credit for; a much younger version of myself would have moved much faster and been far more nimble in any type of terrain; but creaking bones and stiff muscles added to the trauma of just giving birth and it made the journey nearly impossible. And the wet weather added to my burden further, creating mud pools where I trod and the winds tried hard to beat me back.'

Eujena listened sympathetically as the woman recounted her traumatic experience.

'You are not having my baby!' I yelled out to the elements, fearful that they were blasting me from above. 'Yes you are trying to send me back, I know you are, but you will not beat me. I am stronger than you give me credit for and I am not going to give him up to you, or to the clan, I am not going to give him up to anyone!' I remember opening my cloak to look down at him, I saw that he was sleeping peacefully and then covered him up again and braced the unforgiving wind and the unrelenting rain.'

But unbeknown to her, the wind and rain were aiding her escape, because as the wind howled past her, it whipped away all evidence. Her tracks, her smell, any fibres left on branches; it was all caught up with the gusts and dispersed of. And as the wind worked hard, the rain came in from behind and washed away anything that was left; so there were no signs of blood, or footprints to follow. After climbing for what seemed like an eternity she found a small hole carved out of the mountainside. The vegetation there was ripe and in vast quantities. She knew it would keep her sustained; but now, all she wanted to do was to sleep. She bundled her small baby inside the cocoon, lay down her sleeping mat and holding him close, slept for the first time in about twenty four hours. Dainn finally woke and started crying for food; she felt groggy but in her semi conscious state put him to her breast and closed her eyes as he suckled. She started to stroke his legs, very gently, so very carefully, and as she stroked them she gently manipulated the soft bones of his tibia. He didn't like it of course and squirmed; so she stopped, kissed his head and let him feed in peace. But it was something that she would continue to do on a daily basis, just for a few minutes, to try and straighten out his limbs. When he had fed, she wrapped him in the rabbit fur and lay him down to sleep while she went to forage for food.

The sun was up now, but she could see the rain clouds in the distance; she needed to stoke up before another deluge soaked her to the skin. New shoots and bulbs were big and juicy now, full of flavour and essential nutrients. Clovers, dandelions, wood sorrel, purslane and if she was really lucky she would find some mint and marigold to help wth her stomach cramps and stem the flow of blood. She had to get water too, but that was more difficult. Looking around, she saw many disc sized boulders, so she arranged them in wells and grooves so they would catch the rainwater. She also needed to clean herself and she could do that by ripping up one of the old blankets that she had brought along with her.

The next day Peira had tried to make a fire, there were still a few sticks of dry stalks left around from where she had foraged and thin strips of wood in the form of debris made a handy tool. She twirled a stick between her palms against another piece of wood, but she didn't have the endurance to maintain the effort required to make it smoulder, and it was fortunate for her that she couldn't. A few of the search party had found their way to the mountain meadow while she and her baby slept. If that fire had been started then the men would have smelled it and found her. As it was, they walked so close to the cave that if Dainn had whimpered in his sleep they would have heard him. But he was so well fed and kept so warm in his mother's arms, he never murmured, and the entrance to the small hole in the rock wall was so well hidden by the thick bushes, they didn't even notice it.

The leaking swollen sky had turned the bank of her shelter into a basin of mud and washed away all traces of her; so experienced hunters, used to following tracks and disturbance had nothing to go by, and where she had dug up roots and bulbs, the rains had laden the stalks down and flattened those too.

But she couldn't stay in the cave forever. She had heard the men talking outside, she was still too close to home and knew that she had to push on. She couldn't stay on her own either, she needed to find another clan who would accept her and her child. So she left her refuge when the rains had stopped and the ground was duly quenched with water and began hunting and foraging and learning to cover her tracks. She found herself in the forest and feasted on wolf spiders, fat and juicy with their eggs sac still attached, so hungry was she that she swallowed them whole. The towering trees were entwined with tendrils of ivy and creeping vine, and a delicacy of slow moving grubs and fast flying insects feasted on the leaves and then hid themselves away. But Peira searched them out as food, and with a keen eye and nimble fingers found their larvae to be a good source of protein as she continued to suckle her baby. Life was teeming in the forest and there was no shortage of food or water. She noticed a fallen oak, and in the warm glade a fawn could be seen hiding while the hind was feeding on flower heads.

'Another mother protecting her young,' she thought. And smiling at the newborn, she moved quickly on.

Then one day, in the distance, peeping through the windows of the forest, she saw the fort. She could almost touch it now. She heard the water wheel groaning and creaking, and the droplets of water that escaped from each rotation seemed to dance towards her like the fireflies in the forest that she had become accustomed to. She could smell the rich succulent aroma of fresh meat cooking on a spit. Her mouth began to salivate, her stomach growled in response. She looked down at her son, pulled the cloak around her and made her way to their new home.

'Colom found me, disorientated and confused. He took me in and has looked after me ever since.'

Silence filled the air as the two women shared the painful experience and discovered a bond.

'Oh Peira, what a sad story, but what a declaration of your love for Dainn. What a testament of your strength.'

Peira wiped her tears. 'So you see, the locket is a symbol of death to me, and that my son could have so easily been taken and left to die if I hadn't gathered my strength and run away with him.'

Jena composed herself and allowed time to pass before she told Peira the true meaning of the necklace. 'I am so sorry Peira that you had to go through that. But I truly believe that by meeting Ajeya and her beautiful spirit and contagious laugh, Thorne realised the error of the tradition. He gave her the locket as a symbol of life because he knew that nothing is truly without imperfection. Perfection is a state of mind of how we perceive things. The tradition and customs paved the way but they had been misinterpreted all the time. Dainn is an example of that. Ajeya is an example of that. Look how strong they are.' Jena sighed. 'He gave it to Ajeya for her to tell everyone that it was he who gave it to her and why. He has changed Peira, he really has. The weeping caves are a thing of the past now. No more will babies be left to die in there.'

Peira listened intently to what she had been told and digested the words carefully. 'I am glad. I really am. Too many babies have died. Such wasted lives.' She wiped away her tears.

Jena's feelings for Thorne were humbling. 'Why don't you take Dainn to see Thorne, to show him what a fine boy he is. That his son didn't die, that he is alive and well. Thorne is a good man.'

Peira looked horrified. 'No, I can't do that, never will I do that. He believes that Colom is his father and I won't do anything to change that. I would have to explain to him why I ran away and I can't do that to him.'

Jena dropped her head in shame for she knew the burden that Peira carried.

'You know what I mean don't you?' Peira's voice was all knowing.

Jena nodded her head.

'Is your story similar to mine dear lady?'

She nodded her head again.

'Tell your story to me Jena. I think we share a common ground. I believe we have been drawn together. The gods have paved our paths. We were meant to meet, don't you agree?'

21

'I can't believe you didn't recognise her Hagen, it was only six years ago that she went.'

'I really can't remember her; I didn't pay much attention to what was going on around me at the time - I was quite busy,' he finished his tea in three gulps.

'But she was Thorne's wife, you must have been aware of her going and all the agony that surrounded it. She just vanished and no one knew where.' Jena was wrapping a few chunks of bread in a muslin cloth and sealing a flagon of fresh water.

He pursed his lips together and shook his head. 'I think I remember something going on now you come to mention it. But Thorne kept it all hushed. I thought she had died.' He put the mid morning meal in his bag and slung it over his shoulder.

Jena knew she was on delicate ground now and decided to leave it. 'You get to work now,' she smiled. 'I will have some lunch ready for you at noon.'

His kissed her goodbye and went off to work to start his first day in the fields mending fences.

Keao sat on his stool in the byre, his hands drawing hot milk from the udder of the patient cow and watched the dawn creep up over the misty land. The milk hissed into the wooden pail in rhythmic spurts, the notes growing deeper as the pail filled. The cow tugged hay from the bulging net before her. A young girl sat next to him doing the very same thing to an equally patient Holstein.

Keao noticed how the sun rose over the rim of the furthest hills and the burning bright orb tinged the ground tangerine before his very eyes. He was sure he saw a barn owl in flight and when he saw it rise with a field mouse in its talons his heart raced for a minute and he felt its elation.

'It's a beautiful setting isn't it,' said the young milk maid coyly.

He was so focused on the owl that he didn't hear the young girl and continued to look at the spectacular scenery.

'I said it's a beautiful setting isn't it?' her voice became an octave higher.

He snapped out of his daydream and for the first time noticed a pale complexion peppered with pretty freckles; red hair was tied up in a scruffy bun and moist lips matched the same shade as her hair. Bright green eyes shone out at him and smiled before her lips curved.

'Yes it's beautiful, really beautiful,' he was mesmerised.

'My name is Red - because of my red hair - so what's your name?'

'I am Keao, my family has just moved in.'

'I thought I hadn't seen you before,' her eyes still smiled.

The cow swung her mournful head to gaze at him.

'See, even Buttercup is checking you out.'

He laughed softly. 'A cow checking me out eh, now that is funny.'

Buttercup swung back again to snatch another mouthful of hay.

'I guess she's not interested,' he laughed again.

'I like cows,' she said.

'Well that's just as well seeing as you work with them.'

'Do you like cows?'

'I do.'

'Why do you like them?'

'I like all animals. I find them calming and beautiful. I like the power they have to see anything and hear everything. They give so much and yet receive so little in return. I like the simplicity of the life they lead; the grass they eat, the smell they have. I like any herd animal because of the way they group together and can feel each other and are in tune with each other. I like the sounds they make. A cow lowing is music to my ears, their milk feeds my very soul.' He breathed in the rich smell of the milk and saw the froth of bubbles in the pail.

Red was enchanted. The cow turned around again and swished her tail, the end of which tickled his ears. Red laughed. 'She likes you.'

'I like her too,' and he carried on with his work.

When they had finished the mornings milking, Red took the pails into the buttery and Keao took the cows back to the field where he waited for her to bring fresh sandwiches and a flagon of fresh warm milk before they went to see the goats and do the same thing all over again.

He liked being with Red, she was the same age as him and he found her to be the most prettiest girl he had ever seen. And back at the lodge, a little girl practised alone with her catapult, and for the first time since she could remember, she didn't have anyone to practise her craft with.

After a couple of days, Dainn appeared. 'Do you want to come and see the horses with me? I can ride one on my own today because my splints are off.' He ran around the yard in front of her to show her that his legs were straight and muscular, and now he had the freedom to do all the things he wanted to do. Ajeya laughed and ran around with him. Round and round they went and she followed him to the stables. Jena saw them go and smiled to herself.

He tacked up his mount and led it out into the paddock where he trotted around and went over some jumps. He watched Ajeya following him with a keen eye and he offered her the chance to have a go. It was the first time she had ever been on a horse, so she was a little apprehensive. The sheer size of the animal was huge compared to her small stature.

At first she just sat there, passive, rigid, hardly daring to move. Then he began to walk her round a bit and she got used to the motion. She didn't know how to squeeze with her thighs or pull on the rein, she wasn't really strong enough; but she was most content to just sit up tall, swaying from side to side as the horse trundled along.

It was a mutual training period, each learning from the other, and in the process, deepening the relationship between them. Soon she was trotting and it felt good for Dainn to stretch out his legs; and running alongside the horse, he too grew in confidence as his balance and posture improved. He put up little jumps for them and Ajeya learned to lean forward into the mane and grip with her knees. As the jumps got higher, so did her confidence and soon she was able to use her catapult whilst jumping over a low fence.

22

After two years Keao asked Red to marry him and it was going to be strange for young Ajeya to not talk about her day to him every evening.

'I will still come and visit you, we will only be round the corner. It's not like I will be leaving the camp.'

'I know, but already we don't practise together anymore, so it's just one more thing that will change.'

'But you have Dainn as your guide now; he is teaching you how to ride a horse and I saw you the other day knocking down a can with your catapult whilst riding.'

She wrinkled up her nose and he came down and sat beside her.

'I am not going anywhere Ajeya, I am still your big brother and you are still my little sister.'

She wrapped her arms around him and nestled into him.

'And you know what?' He looked at her with a kind face.

'What?'

'We both want you and Dainn to be our attendants and our ring bearers. Would you like that?'

She nodded her head and found it hard to hide the big grin that spread across her face.

'I am going to make you a beautiful dress for the day,' said Jena wearing her proudest expression. 'And Dainn will be wearing his finest clothes.'

Ajeya's sparkling eyes matched her beautiful smile and at last she began to look forward to her very first wedding.

Within a few weeks the stage was set; a stunning archway of jasmine, honeysuckle and creeping ivy, shimmered in the light of the sun and opened the way to the sacred Blessing Tree. In the sky above, shining like the sculpture of a bronzed god, a tawny owl looked down on the arrangement and carried on its flightpath towards the forest. Keao had donned a full length white robe held in place by two sashes. His ceremonial attire was complete with a grand garland of impressive animal tusks and he looked majestic waiting at the head of the aisle for his beautiful bride. Behind him sat Hagen and next to him was Jena, both wearing similar white robes with smaller garlands. Peira sat at the entrance of the gateway and ushered the clan members in with hauntingly beautiful melodies on the jaw harp.

The sun was at it highest point and Colom had taken his place in front of the Blessing Tree. On the other side of the aisle sat Red's mother and father, Flame and Gules respectively; and as the bridal party arrived and stood at the entrance, Colom's eyes lit up and the congregation knew what a vision she was.

She moved silently down the passageway with Ajeya and Dainn in attendance. Each of her bearers carried a clear obsidian stone; a piece of natural glass that bore a lighted wick; the glittering natural beauty rendered them sacred and were only used in important ceremonies such as this.

The bride wore a pure white silk dress that had been woven by her mother; her glorious red hair was loosely scooped up, secured with crimson rose buds, ribbons and elaborately carved grips. There were gasps of approval as she glided lightly past her audience, keeping her eyes focused as she approached the Tree. Hagen looked at Keao with unsurmountable pride and then focused straight ahead. When Red stopped, the attendants moved forward; Ajeya gave one stone to Red, while Dainn gave the other stone to Keao.

When all was in place, the ethereal music ceased and Colom opened the proceedings. 'Welcome everyone to this special occasion. It seems not that long ago we were welcoming Keao and his family into our clan and here we are now witnessing the marriage of this son and his chosen bride.'

Red and Keao breathed in the magic of the moment.

'Be sure in the knowledge that all our ancestors are here with us today in spirit and all those who have left this world and who want to share this day with us, they are all here amongst us.'

The congregation bowed in memory of loved ones and welcomed the spirits in.

Colom continued. 'Today is special because we are hailing a new dynasty, we look to the spirit guides and totems to take care of these two young people as they begin a new life as husband and wife and we ask the spirits to help you support them and protect them in whatever guise that might be.'

A few minutes silence transcended while the concretion held those thoughts and summoned loved ones who had departed and could not be here to share this auspicious spectacle.

'We begin with the two speeches of declaration; so Keao would you please start with yours.'

Keao choked back a hard swallow and touching her light with his own, declared his love. 'The gods looked down on me the day that my mother and father brought me here, because you were here waiting for me. On that first day we met, I was captivated by your beauty, and mesmerised by your compassion. As soon as Buttercup gave that final nod, I knew that she had chosen us for each other.'

Red could be seen wiping away a tear as she recalled that very first day.

'I will always love you and take care of you Red; you are my life, now and forever. My heart belongs to you my love, and now my body belongs to you. On this day, I take you, Red, as my wife. I will love you for an eternity and I will honour you with my life. I will walk with you and guide you, and as we tread our paths and overcome life's challenges, I will always protect you. I am your guiding light'. He bowed his head and prayed for a moment.

After an appropriate pause to allow the bride to compose herself, Colom continued: 'And Red, if you could respond.'

She had rehearsed this a thousand times. In her head it was clear and concise and without interruption. But in front of so many people it wasn't so easy; she had to steady her nerves. Colom sensed the affliction, so he closed his eyes and breathed slowly and deeply, encouraging Red to do the same. The air of contentment was like a spell; she inhaled the aura and that made her relax in an instant. As she calmed down she was able to continue with confidence.

'My dearest Keao, I knew you were special on the first day I met you. I felt your empathy with the animals and your love of nature and I knew that you were different from other men. Today I feel complete. You make me feel safe in a hostile kingdom, you make me feel loved in the family we call Clan. Today I am honoured. Tonight I will lay beside you, and in the morning I will wake up with you. I am proud to be your wife. I will bear you many children my love, and every day I will tell you how much I love you and tell you how happy you make me. I will love you for the rest of my life on earth and anything beyond this mortal kingdom. Keao, I will honour you with my life and my word and serve you as I walk every path alongside you. I am your guiding light.' She too then summoned her totems and gave thanks to them for this special day.

'Thank you Red and Keao,' said Colom

solemnly. 'Those beautiful words will resonate with your people and have been declared in front of the gods. Now, it is time for your totems to become as one.'

A knife nestled on an arm of the oak which he held it up to the spirits. 'With this blade and with your blessings, I seek to join these two people through their blood and let their totems mix and become as one. This will strengthen their bond, unite their bloodline and any children born unto them will inherit the strength of both guides.'

The edge was cleaned again on his robes and he took Keao's hand first. Turning it palm side up he made a quick incision along the pad of his left thumb, the blood ran freely so Keao held his hand up to minimise the flow. Then Colom took Red's hand and made the same incision on her left thumb. 'Now, press your thumbs together and let the blood flow freely round your souls.'

Keao and Red stood there, joined together, under the watchful gaze of the high priest and the congregation witnessing the marriage.

Colom put the blade back on the branch and spoke softly. 'Let nothing part these two souls. Let no man or woman come between them. Let the enemy weaken in their presence. When danger is near the other will know. When sadness is abound, the other will feel it. Their totems have become as one, their souls are now a single entity. This is the word of the gods.' He held up his arms to the sky and waited. After a few minutes of silence, Colom spoke again; 'Please, who has the rings.'

'I do,' said Dainn, looking visibly moved. He carefully took the obsidian stones and placed them on the blade. He then retrieved the rings and gave them to Colom who continued with the service.

'These rings are a symbol of your love. There is no beginning or end, love is everlasting and bound in these solid circles for ever. Keao, will you please place this ring on Red's finger.'

The captive audience held their breath as Keao held it to his heart and fulfilled his part of the pageant.

'And Red, could you place this ring on Keao's finger.'

She kissed the symbol and placed it on his finger.

Colom placed Red's hands inside Keaos'. 'And now please declare the covenant of marriage.' He held their hands together as they proclaimed the vow as one.

'By the Hill Fort Tribe we pledge our our love,
We swear by the soil and water and all that surrounds us.
We swear by The Owl and The Fox that protect us.
We swear by the gods and the spirits who look down on us.
We swear by all those who are present. This is our word.'

Colom bowed. 'I now offer you to tie your ribbons on the Blessing Tree. A small gesture for a life of plenty.

For this mighty oak is born from the tiny acorn, which, as a seed, is full of nature, knowledge and truth. Our Blessing Tree is an indication of the power of nature at an unseen level, for its very roots and life giving tendrils are as vast as the tree that we see above. We might start as the acorn, but we grow and age like the mighty oak as we advance through our own lives. Keao and Red, as you grow with knowledge and spread your wings, be sure to take care of that which is unseen, for that is the true meaning of life.'

The two newly weds approached the tree and Red took a crimson ribbon from her hair and tied it on a branch. Then Keao removed the smaller white sash from his waist and wrapped his ribbon next to hers. They then prayed to the spirits before Colom swore the concluding rites.

'In the presence of the gods and spirits and animal totems, and with these people here present, I now pronounce you husband and wife. Go and enjoy the day with your friends, enjoy the occasion with your loved ones and enjoy your lives as a married couple.'

After Colom's final words, the newly weds turned to walk up the aisle to their new life together. Before them went Ajeya and Dainn who brushed the aisle clean with fresh branches from newly felled trees and sprinkled new rose buds and recently opened petals to pave the way for a clear life that is blessed with good health and many children. The path led to the celebration enclosure where the musicians were playing and a wedding banquet waited.

Keao took Red's hand. 'Red, before we can share our wedding banquet with our guests, I have been practising something that I would like us to perform together alongside our friends.'

He nodded to a musician who started to beat rhythmically on the drum. The flutist tuned in after a few minutes and Keao adopted his opening stance. Red knew instantly what to do and affectionately followed his lead with a smile; she just wondered how Keao knew the dance. She held Keao's hand lightly in her own and her body tingled with excitement. She poised her body on her toes and nodding in time to the drumbeat they both began to move. First of all it was very slow as they dipped and turned, face in, face out, step in and step out. Turn around once, dip again and turn. Face in and face out, step in and step out. The constant drum beat keeping them in time. The congregation began to clap in time to the rhythm, others clicked their fingers or tapped a foot. Once the dancing started, Dainn noticed that the basic steps could be elaborated with a little imagination and an appropriate turn of footwork. He grabbed Ajeya and invited her to copy him, and as the music shifted to a different tempo, he shuffled and skipped his way around the dance floor while his steps were mirrored by his partner. Soon the flutes, drums and rattles were picked up by more musicians and Keao invited more people into the sequence. Hagen led Jena, Colom took Peira, and Gules escorted Flame.

The novices kept to the simpler choreography

around the perimeter as Keao moved to the middle and stepped up the pace. The spring in their feet, the grace of their posture, the strength in their control was mesmerising as the dynamics of the routine suddenly burst into a vibrant frenzy of intricate moves and complicated steps. The emotion of the dance was absorbing when Keao scooped Red up and held her there, a curved back supported a long thrown back neck and as he raised her up higher she reached out with her fingertips. The drumming stopped. The wooden pipes stopped. The people were silent. The supporting cast froze. Not a sound could be heard as he gently put her back down on her toes and let her spin around him, their index fingers touching all the time as if he were controlling the action. Everyone's eyes were on Red as she spiralled round and around. Then, with just a hair's breath separating them, the pipes whispered again and the drum beat like the ebb and flow of a wave. Red slowed, took Keao's face in her hands and held his gaze as the music stopped. Their beating hearts and short panting breath filled the silence. The crowd went wild. It was a spectacular sight to behold.

The music and dancing never stopped that evening; as long as the music was being played and the wine was flowing, there was no shortage of people wishing to continue. Dainn and Ajeya stayed the course and their movements got more intricate and captivating as the tempo shifted.

'That lad of yours has certainly got dancing feet. Look at him go.'

Gules' recognition was beautiful music to Peira's ears. 'I know. I always knew he had it in him.'

Flame smiled graciously. 'And look at the affection between him and Ajeya, it is truly wonderful.'

Gules and Flame bowed out while Peira and Colom continued to watch their son spin and twist and shuffle with his beautiful partner. It was a magical moment for them to observe.

Hagen took Jena's hand and led her even further away out of ear shot. He found a patch of lush green grass, the blades silvered in the sunlight and the blooms of the buttercups and daisies moved about joyfully as if they had been mesmerised by the dance.

Today the world was a joyous place, filled with the dawn of a beautiful spring day with its fresh new buds and rich azure skies. Neat little clouds puffed by quietly, only a light sprinkling from them would be required in the next few days. New stems rose from the ripened earth as honey bees threaded their way through the scatter of blooms strewn like jewels across the fields of the meadow below.

'Here, this looks a nice place,' he held her hand while she lowered herself to the ground. When they were settled and he was sure that no one could hear them he spoke again. 'Are you happy here Jena, do you feel safe now?'

'I am truly happy and feel very safe, and being part of this community with you by my side has made that happen.' She touched his knee. 'This is such a wonderful place for Ajeya to grow up, I know that we are very lucky.' She looked at him and sensed there was something else he wanted to say, something that had probably been on his mind for some time, and she didn't have to wait long to be proved right.

'Jena, you are the most beautiful, mesmerising woman I have ever met. You have made me laugh, cry, question myself, but above all you bring out the best in me. I have grown to love you where love has no boundaries. My love has no constraints. This love is limitless.'

She stroked his face and smiled.

He dipped his head and took her hand, kissing it gently then held it to his cheek. 'I watched with pride as Keao took Red for his wife, and I saw the love in their eyes and listened to the words as they pledged that love.'

'It was very beautiful,' she replied with a thoughtful thin smile.

'And it made me think of us and the only thing that is missing.'

She looked at him with wide eyes. 'I am too old to have another child,' her tone was one of shock.

He shook his head and laughed. 'No my dear lady, not another child.'

'What then?' her voice rose in disbelief.

'To be married Jena. I want you to be my wife.'

Tears came immediately to her eyes, her face flushed and she felt her heart quicken.

He responded quickly to her emotions. 'What's the matter, have I said something wrong?'

She sighed and sniffed back her runny nose. 'No Hagen, you have said nothing wrong. I love you with all my heart. Nothing would make me happier than to be your wife, it would be an honour and I would be so proud.'

'So, what's wrong?'

'I am still married Hagen, albeit to a man that I have not seen for over four years, but nevertheless I am still married, and the gods will frown on me and punish me. And after what I have already been through, I cannot risk further punishment.'

'The gods won't punish you my love, they know what you have endured, they are not there to punish. They are there to guide.'

She held his hands and looked into his eyes. 'When I know that the Emperor is dead, then I will marry you. Until then, I will serve you as any wife would. I promise you that.' She held him close and shut her eyes and prayed for someone strong to slay her ruthless husband.

23

Gradually daylight brought the landscape into sharper focus, driving the shadows out of small inconspicuous spaces. A grey pallor dulled the burgeoning meadows as though a dripping nimbus had washed out all the colour. Even the sky was a non descriptor shade of nothing, neither blue nor grey nor white. It was actually quite a dull day. A day for doing nothing she thought. Because that was what the day was like, a nothing. But she was already up and contemplating what to do when a familiar voice called from outside.

'Ajeya are you ready to go out for a ride?'

Suddenly her morning became full of colour and she rushed out excitedly. Dainn was standing there with her beautiful white horse and his dappled grey.

'See, Moonlight and Cloud are anxious to get out,' his smile lit up the day.

She ran up to the filly and wrapped her arms around her. Dainn had already tacked them up and helped her into the saddle as she patted the muscular neck.

'Thank you Dainn. Come on I'll race you to the forest before mother finds something menial for me to do.'

She crouched down and looked straight between the filly's ears and thundered across the plain. She loved riding fast, it fulfilled every longing that she had. To be at one with a horse was the greatest feeling ever, and to ride alongside Dainn, her other great love, formed the other part of that perfection. She always kept her reflexes sharp when galloping and was constantly aware of her surroundings. One mistake could be fatal; and her mount picked up on these transmitted thoughts. The signals between the young woman and the filly were subtle; it was as if her horse knew what she was thinking before she had even thought it. The animal became an extension of her own body.

Behind her, Dainn kept up on his own colt, shouting wildly and excitedly. 'You go girl, I'm right behind you.'

The ground from here to the forest was grassland. Fallow fields and low rolling hills, high meadows and stretches of plain between them. It was safe, but she still had to have her wits about her; so as she rode she sent out her signals and her horse responded.

With only a couple of years of learning under her belt she galloped across the land as if she had been riding for ever; with the wind in her face and her hair flowing behind her like the waves of a tempestuous sea. She felt the enormous power of the filly beneath as her strides stretched out to full capacity as she flew along. She could hear Moonlight panting with each motion and she could see her muscular neck reaching forward and lathering up with the excursion. T h e y   l u r c h e d across the summer plains, leaping hedgerows and ditches at this surging pace.

In the distance lay the forest; looming, monstrous and imposing and that's what she was heading for. She reined back to a canter when she reached the dense perimeter and laughed out loud from the exhilaration of the gallop. At her young age it was quite an extraordinary feat to accomplish, so her feelings were mixed; if her mother knew she was riding that fast she would have not been happy and probably tried to stop her. But where's the fun if you don't take a few risks she had thought.

Dainn caught up with her and whooped alongside her as he too relished the excitement. They slowed down to a walk as they entered the eaves and intuitively took note of their surroundings, and when her horse came to a halt Ajeya slid off her back. Moonlight billowed and snorted as she came to rest and Ajeya lifted the drooping muzzle with both hands and laid her cheek on the animals nose. Then she tucked the filly's head under her arm in a gesture of affection,

'Thank you,' she whispered. 'Thank you Moonlight.'

The horse tossed her head up and down as if to acknowledge the embrace and the appreciation.

The ride was a thrill she could hardly contain. The very idea of going along with a horse in full gallop filled her with a sense of wonder and unrivalled freedom. She had never dreamed such a thing was possible or that the feeling of power would be so intense, and the euphoria lifted her spirits to a place way beyond the gloominess of the overhead clouds.

'Shall we rest here a while?' she called out to Dainn.

'I think that's a very good idea, I need to catch my breath and so does Cloud. You both stretched us you know.'

The glen was a small oasis, an island surrounded by trees that stood to attention like a regiment protecting the silent pool. At any time of the year it was quiet and glistening with ripples that danced on its surface; a place where dragonflies and water boatmen skipped round the edges. Today it was more serene than ever. Dainn had packed a small breakfast and while the horses rested, the two youngsters sat down to feast on freshly baked crumpets and a bag of oat biscuits.

'This has to be the most magical place on earth,' she said, pulling up her legs to her chin.

'I know,' he replied, throwing stones into the water. 'I have always liked it here, but it's even nicer with you as company.'

She smiled at him with affection. 'Have you ever seen the fairies?' she asked him in all innocence.

'No I haven't, I didn't think they really existed,' he answered as best he could trying not to offend her.

'But they do,' she smiled at him tenderly. 'Keao

told me that fairies live in the woods.'

He sunk his chin into his neck in response. 'Really?'

'Yes, he said that deer are really fairies because they can disappear.'

'He furrowed his brow and stopped throwing stones. 'I don't think he means that literally Ajeya.'

'Oh, so what does he mean then?' her tone was one of surprise.

'He means that they are very clever and can camouflage themselves,' he tried to explain.

She thought about it for a moment. 'He has told me about that as well, that animals camouflage themselves. But he definitely said that deer were fairies.'

He looked at her with her chin on her knees, looking out onto the tranquil lake.

'Well I guess he must be right then,' and he carried on throwing stones into the lake.

'Perhaps you had better stop doing that,' her voice was one of concern.

'Why?'

'In case you hit a fairy.'

He looked at her and smiled. The girl who had just ridden like the most experienced horse woman in all the subject kingdoms, was still an innocent little girl at heart, and he loved her even more for it.

24

Three years later and Keao announced to the family that he and Red were expecting their first baby.

'That is such wonderful news Keao, a baby in the family at last, Jena was suitably elated.

'Congratulations son, it will make a man out of you to be sure.'

'What? so you don't think I am already? Keao teased.

Hagen smiled. 'You know what I mean?'

'That makes you an aunty,' said Red to Ajeya.

'Wow, can I teach it to ride a horse?'

The adults laughed.

'All in good time,' said Keao in joyful spirits. 'Maybe teach him to fire with a catapult and to make himself invisible first, then you can teach him to ride a horse.'

She found herself daydreaming about her new role, and from that moment on all everyone was talking about was the new baby. Jena made clothes. Keao made toys. Hagen made a crib. Peira went out foraging for all the berries and roots that would help Red during the pregnancy. Her own mother Flame, made garments for Red's ever increasing waistline and her father went hunting to make sure she was stocked up with protein and nutrition for the duration. And Red continually rearranged their hut and was constantly cleaning.

'This is so exciting, said Jena to Flame as they sat doing their needlework together.'

'I know Jena, there is nothing like a new baby to bring joy into the kingdom.'

'What would you prefer? A boy or a girl?' asked Jena.

'As long as it's healthy, I really don't mind.'

'Yes that's the most important thing,' and Jena carried on stitching and binding until a stack of clothes and blankets were complete.

The trimesters of pregnancy ticked by easily, and on that perfect sunny morning, an out of breath Keao suddenly burst in. 'Mother, it's coming. It's coming right now. Quickly, we have no time to spare!'

'Keao, we've got plenty of time, really we have,' but I will go and get Piera straight away.'

'Son, you come with me and let the women do their job,' said Hagen. 'A nice glass of fresh milk is what she'll need when all is done.'

'I don't want to miss anything father,' said Keao still anxious.

'You won't, we will be back in time. These things take ages you know.'

Jena went and got Peira and Hagen took his lad off to calm him down.

He remembered the events of the morning while he was laying in bed with his wife. 'I love you so much Red and if ever I thought I loved you more than life itself, nothing can compare to what I feel right now,' he kissed her head.

'I love you too Keao, and who would have thought that when we first met when we were milking those cows, that one day we would be married and looking forward to the arrival of our first baby.'

'I know, I just couldn't be happier.'

He put his hand on her swollen belly and smiled up at her. She felt a kick and moved his hand to where she felt the movement. 'It's nearly time you know, if my dates are right, it really is any day now.'

'This is truly a miracle,' and he felt the infant kick again.

The amount of activity inside her womb surprised her, there was never usually this much flurry - but then a pain shot through her abdomen and she groaned.

He moved his hand away instantly, fearful that he was pressing too hard. 'Have I hurt you?' his voice was anxious.

She grabbed hold of him. 'No you haven't hurt me, I think this baby wants to come out.' She breathed deeply and folded like scythed corn as a stab of pain sliced through her.

'I'll go and get help. Stay there my love. I won't be long!'

She shot him a withering look. 'I promise you I

won't be going anywhere,' and she creased up again as another wave came over her.

'Just don't do anything until I come back. You promise me.'

He heard her scream as he ran out of the door.

The women went in to find a contorted girl in the third stage of labour, bearing down, sweating profusely and being helped by her mother.

'Here, give her this,' and Peira gave her a concoction of raspberry leaf and marigold tea. 'It will help with the pain.'

Jena had a bowl of warm water and was wiping the sweat from her brow.

'I can't do this mother, I just can't do it.'

'Yes you can, just breathe and control your intake of air.'

Red screamed with the pain and then started panting.

'It's all right,' said Peira. 'You are doing so well.'

'I can't do it, I am so tired.'

The women looked at each other with concerned guises.

It was a long night for everyone that last day of summer. Flame, Peira and Jena never left her side. Hagen and Keao waited outside for hours. Dainn sat with Ajeya on the veranda and watched intently as the women went in and out of the room many times that night.

'Any news?' Keao would say urgently.

The women could only shake their heads despondently.

'I should be in there with her shouldn't I father?'

'I think it's incase there are any complications,' said Hagen trying to reassure him. 'When they know everything is all right you will be called in.'

'What sort of complications?'

'I don't know the intricacies, but your little one will be fine. You must not worry,' Hagen pulled his son into a reassuring embrace.

Keao looked at the sky for answers, there were none.

All of a sudden they heard Red screaming his name, Keao shot up from his seated position and raced to the door. 'I have to go in there, I have to, she needs me.'

Jena came out and ushered him in. He fell at Red's side and wiped her feverish brow.

'My love, my beautiful, I am here now,' his face was draped in concern.

Too exhausted to speak, she squeezed his hand and started to push. Sweat was pouring down her face and onto her chest. Her legs were pulled up and she had them spread wide. Her long gown was covering the baby's entrance, but it didn't hide the blood.

Keao was more than anxious when he saw the crimson sheets. He looked silently at Jena for answers.

Jena's tone was hushed. 'She is giving birth Keao, sometimes there is a bit more blood and sometimes it takes a bit more time.'

After a few minutes she screamed again and he felt her squeezing his hand and with gritted teeth she bore down to push with all her might.

He wiped her face and kissed her hand. 'I love you Red, I love you so much.'

She looked at him but still couldn't speak, instead another intense wave came across her and he could feel all her strength going into the push.

'I can see the crown,' called Peira excitedly. 'A mop of auburn hair, your baby is coming.'

'Red he's coming, come on, push him out, let us meet our son.'

She bore down and with one last effort pushed down to push her baby out. As he filled his lungs to bellow, their son made his presence known. Red fell back exhausted and Peira handed her the infant to suckle. Flame sat next to her and gushed over her new grandchild.

'Do you want to cut the cord Keao?'

'Yes - I will - thank you.'

Peira handed him a clean knife and held the grey and purple cord gently. Keao ceremoniously and proudly severed the life giving artery in two. 'It's a boy,' he cried out in delight.

He went outside the room to declare the news to the waiting family. 'I have a son, I have a boy. You are a grandfather.'

Inside, Jena and Peira were cleaning up Red and putting a clean gown and fresh bed linen on for her. When she was ready, the people waiting outside were allowed in. She was sitting up, looking radiant and happy with the baby content at her breast.

'What are you going to call him?' said Jena excitedly.

'This is Rufus everyone, meet little Rufus.'

'And his totem guide, have you thought about that?' Ajeya was keen to know.

'His totem will be the falcon.'

'A beautiful name and a very fitting totem,' agreed Hagen, nodding in appreciation. 'Both will serve my grandson well.'

25

It was now five years since Rufus was born, and Ajeya was fourteen years old. And Dainn, who at two years older, was teaching her to fight with a spear and develop her skills as an archer. But now she noticed how he looked at her in a different way. She had never seen anyone look at her the way he did. His eyes sparkled with respect and admiration when she spoke, his voice was always full of praise when she did something. He always put her first in everything they did. Sometimes she found herself blushing at his humbling words and found it hard to accept such praise; but for a young girl in the throws of adolescence, it built confidence at a time when she needed it, and because of him, she would always believe in herself.

'You are such a natural, all those years practising with the catapult as a youngster has certainly paid off.'

'That's down to Keao, he's the one who encouraged me from an early age.'

'Well he did the right thing, your focus is exemplary and your aim is always on target, that's why we should train together with as many weapons as possible.'

'I'm all for that, what shall we start with?'

'How about a spear?'

And while Ajeya could not match Dainn's mighty throw which gave him a greater range, he could not match her accuracy.

The spear was made from a light wood and he made her practise holding the spear in the palm of her hand so that she could find the balance point at any given time. Then, she was taught to raise the spear to her ear, so she could see the weapon through her peripheral vision; and keeping it a horizontal position she had to feel it connect with her arm until it was an extension of her own body. Envisaging the wood as a living entity with all the power from the tree from whence it had grown running through its shaft, would enable her to aim, throw and hit her target accurately. His strong overhand cast definitely gave him the advantage with his lift, so he spent hours and hours helping to improving her technique. Putting one foot forward and leaning back into the throw would give the greatest momentum in flight. Raising her other arm assisted the counter balance, and as she released the shaft, he told her to follow through every time; for a powerful cast was nothing without a proper execution.

She was also encouraging him whilst delivering her strategies for building his own accuracy skills. The padded leathers round the target tree didn't last very long from constant puncturing, and daily, another one had to be put up. Naturally, the more they practised, the better they became. He was the perfect companion and always encouraged her when she missed, and shared her triumph when her aim was on target. He always gave her advice how to improve and listened with respect and genuine interest to her suggestions.

An accidental touch made her warm inside and when he stood behind her to guide her, folding his strong hand around her own, or positioning her waist and hips for greater accuracy, it always made her gasp. And as they teased and joked and laughed together, the subtlest, most innocent gesture now took on a different meaning.

The next challenge for them was to improve accuracy with a bow and arrow and they decided to go to a cave for that rather than ruin any more trees. There they could light a fire and make tea, or cook a squirrel or a wood pigeon for supper. The cave was always a special place for them to train and as the days rolled into months, it soon became years.

'What happened to your face?' he asked one day.

She nearly choked on her tea. 'Where did that come from?'

'I am sorry, I didn't mean to embarrass you,' his voice was sincere.

'You haven't embarrassed me, you just took me by surprise.'

He couldn't resist, and he reached to feel the contours of her cheek. His touch held her motionless. She couldn't pull away. She felt his fingers as they traced the imperfection and watched as his eyes followed every blemish. He wasn't even aware of her breathing quicken as she tingled with the touch. He just thought of her as a beautiful woman with an incredible strength at her core and yet this disfigurement made her vulnerable and fragile, like a butterfly with a creased wing; and he knew that he would love her forever.

'You are an amazing woman Ajeya, and so very special; not only do you have a beautiful face but you are so strong and determined; you have a good heart, you are an exemplary horse woman and without doubt a most formidable warrior.'

She blushed. 'Thank you,' she felt her face and touched it delicately. 'I was born like this - and have faced my fair share of prejudice to be sure; but instead of disempowering me, it has defined me and made me stronger.'

He smiled at her humility.

She felt warm and safe next to him; with his statuesque height and broad shoulders and body covered in a soft golden down, he really was like a god, and any deformity at birth had healed long ago; nevertheless, she still found herself asking the question. 'So what happened to your legs?'

He stretched them out before him and tensed up the powerful muscles. 'I was born with twisted legs, though you wouldn't know it now. My mother and father insisted on splints and lots of muscle building exercises, so now I am strong and the same as any other man.'

'You are more than any other man,' she said with acumen. 'You have an extraordinary strength and a spiritual way about you. The way you see things, the way you feel things. It makes me wonder if people like us are given another sense, a special ability from a greater force to make up for our affliction.'

'Maybe we do,' he said thoughtfully. 'But maybe we just appreciate everything we have overcome and therefore see things in a different way.'

'Yes, maybe you are right.'

'I think we're both right. But we are both survivors.'

She felt humbled at being called a survivor, and thought it an exceptional accolade. Her mother was definitely a survivor and the real force behind her determination. So many women were at last finding a voice and a strength in a kingdom that was dominated by men and that made her smile.

Though the man sitting beside her was honourable, kind and full of humility, and she thanked the gods in addition to her totem for their guidance. But she soon realised that she didn't know everything about him and that despite talking about everything for the last ten years; she still didn't know what his guide was. And she asked that very question.

'What is your totem guide?'

'Well, I think you are going to have to guess that one,' he responded.

'Out of all the animals I know, how am I going to guess that?' her own response was not amused.

'What animal do you think best serves me?' he challenged her.

'Something powerful, so it could be a horse, or a good hunter; so it could be a heron, or something small like a beetle,' she questioned her pathetic attempts with a furrowed brow.

'Well it's none of those,' he raised his brows.

See, I am not very good at it,' she admitted her weakness. 'I thought that the hare was small and weak until Keao pointed out how powerful it is.'

'Yes, the hare has the moon as its home, the hare is very powerful,' he praised knowingly.

'So what is your totem then?' she persisted.

'It looks like you are going to have to marry me to find out aren't you. Because then it is all revealed.'
And he pulled her into his loving embrace and held her close; shrouded by the flickering fire reaching high into the vaults of the cavernous dome above where it displayed its unfathomable power and the incredible force it was born with.

26

For the first time in her life, Ajeya posed a real quandary for her mother. The Clan of the Mountain Lion were hosting The Gathering that year and she wanted to go.

'But I am old enough mother; Dainn is going, Keao and Red are going, even Rufus is going and he's only ten.'

Jena didn't take her eyes off the sheet she was folding. 'I'm sorry Ajeya but we left in such a hurry. There were terrible things going on and because of the difficult circumstances we couldn't say goodbye. I am worried that if Laith and Artemisia saw you then questions would be asked.'

'What sort of questions mother? It was so long ago now,' her tone was uncomprehending. 'Had you considered that they might not even recognise me.'

Jena tilted her head and raised an eyebrow. Ajeya grabbed an apple, threw herself into a chair, and bit off a large chunk. She knew that she would be recognised by anyone who had seen her as a young child. Her disfigurement had branded her and made her instantly recognisable.

'If it was anywhere else you could go, but not to

the Clan of the Mountain Lion, things might be said that I wouldn't want you to hear,' continued her mother.

So on that day Ajeya stayed behind and watched as Colom led his party off to The Gathering alongside her brother and sister in law, with Rufus and Dainn in attendance.

The wagons rolled through the hills exposing the great grasslands, displaying yet another facet of the renewing cycle as the Hill Fort Tribe travelled. Strands of amber, bronze and crimson stretched out for miles before them and the last pulses of colour were desperately holding on. Here, the feathered grass dominated the meadows, turning the land into waves of softly billowing silver; but already the plumes were dying off and the rich plains were turning from silver to gold.

Beyond the grasslands and the steppes, over the hills and round the mountain, a hundred marquees could be seen beside the river, and the clans gathered in their droves to take part in the Gathering. The splendour of it all took Dainn's breath away and he really had no idea it would be on a scale that was so spectacular and unlike anything he had seen before. The brilliant colours, the excitement of the crowds, the tents and banners flapping in the wind; the items that people had brought with them, but mostly the sheer amount of people. Many came on foot, some came by boat; several had pack horses loaded up with gifts for the host clan and produce to trade. Fine weaves and materials, freshly ground herbs and spices, exquisite jewellery made from amber and jet, tailored garments made from animal skins; trinkets, utensils and culinary delights. But the most exciting part for everyone, was the competitions; the competitions most of all.

'Are you going to have a go at the boxing?' shrilled Rufus excitedly.

'I might do,' he answered. 'I shall watch from the sidelines and size up the competition.'

Rufus smiled proudly at him and took hold of his hand as Dainn put his finger to his lips to indicate silence when Laith stood up to introduce the games.

'My dearest friends, guests, comrades, partners; it is with open arms that I welcome you to this years Gathering hosted by The Clan of the Mountain Lion.'

A round of applause rang out and a stream of nodding heads gesticulated to honour the hosts hospitality and the splendid array of entertainment.

'Let us pray for all our gods to watch over us and that our totems will be guiding us as we join together for this very special day.'

A few moments of silent homage was paid to the afore mentioned beings. Then Laith concluded. 'This day is for the young people, a day of fun and games before their lives change forever. Many will take leadership, all will make life changing decisions, and everyone will face competition. This gathering serves as platform to a challenging existence. So now, Clans, go and enjoy the celebrations.'

A rapturous applause echoed round the grounds, shouting and merriment broke the sound of Laith's trailing voice and the celebrations began.

No one really noticed Laith and the other leaders disappearing into the chieftain's hut for their regular talks. And not one person present on that day could have known that what they had to discuss would affect each and every one of them forever.

'We come with bad news Laith.'

'What has happened?'

'It's the General; he is under orders from the Emperor again.'

'Does this man ever give up? come fellow leaders; tell me what you know and what we should do.'

A young clan boy with a mop of dark black hair heralded his archery competition in a loud proud booming voice. 'Come on now, don't be shy. I have made lots of white wood bows and arrows for you all to use, and here is a magnificent mahogany bow for the winner. Expertly crafted by my own hands, planed for a smooth finish and polished with layers of beeswax for this deep red shine.' He held aloft his precious offering. 'All I ask is that you do not use the girls as a target.' And he looked towards the forest where, under the shade of the dappled autumn colours, the young women displayed their offerings on exquisitely vibrant stalls. He knew they were positioned far enough away though; he had shot a few arrows earlier in the day to make absolutely sure and nodded to a fellow clan member who was lining up a range of spears and rocks for his throwing competition.

Dainn went over to the boxing ring to check out the competition. Rufus stood by him as the rules were read out.

'Each boy is invited to take on the champion and try and knock him to the ground. Each opponent will have three minutes in the ring and then there will be a two minute break for the next competitor to prepare. If the champion isn't knocked down in that time then he will retain his crown. If he is knocked down, then the waiting boys will be able to take on the new victor until everyone has had a round. Does everyone understand?' Nods and grimaces acknowledged his words so he continued. 'Those of you who want to spar, then make it known to me.'

There was a crowd of boys around the make shift arena, all eager to watch and learn but mainly to have a go. Last year's champion was heralded into the ring amongst uplifting cheers and a riotous applause. Tore was a strong boy and paraded around the roped off circle to the adulation of the crowd. Namir dived under the rope to shake hands with his larger opponent.

'Good luck Tore.'

'Good luck to you too Namir.'

Namir and Tore were warming up in their corners while Bagwa rang out the rules. 'I will be watching for a fair game; there will be no punches to the groin; no high jumping or kicking, bare fists only. In the event of a tie I will make the final decision. If anyone breaks the rules they will be disqualified. My decision is final. There will be no contesting my authority, is that understood?' He looked around to make sure everyone acknowledged him and when he was satisfied, he exited the ring and gave the signal to start.

That year wasn't Namir's year, it wasn't Dainn's year either. He went in after being hounded and pestered by Rufus, and very nearly became that year's champion. But Tore had come in with a clean sweep right at the end and knocked him down in the last few minutes. That year Tore resumed his crown. 'Come back next year,' he said gallantly and respectfully. 'Try and take me then.'

'I will have to train a lot more before I return,' he said exiting the ring and nursing a swollen jaw.

'You will come back next year won't you?' Rufus was deadly serious.

'Oh I don't know. Maybe I will,' he was clearly tired and a return match was the last thing on his mind.

Rufus stopped in his tracks. 'You have to, it will look weak if you don't. You must not give in to him, you are stronger than him. Please promise me you will come back next year.'

Dainn looked down at the youngster. 'If it will keep you quiet - I will promise.'

Rufus sighed a happy smile and felt himself being lifted onto broad shoulders and taken to enjoy the much talked about tug of war.

The two teams were already in position. The

Marshland Tribe against the host clan, The Clan of the Mountain Lion. Each team had prepared themselves stoically and the grit and determination on these young faces brought a sense of pride to their respective clans. Eyes were focused, thoughts were powerful, muscles flexed and deep breaths were drawn in.

They took hold of the rope. The boys at the front had their feet firmly in the ploughed up soil. Legs were in the squatting position. Arms were out straight. They vied each other and mentally gave out strong messages of glory and defeat.

'Follow Namir's stance,' called out someone from the back.

'Take positions,' came the call to start.

'Ready boys, take the strain, dig deep with those legs and push hard into the ground.'

The rope snatched tight. The Marshland Tribe were strong. Their boys began pulling and shouting. Froth and spit burst from bellowing mouths. Sweat was already pouring down straining faces. Snot and phlegm mixed in quantities as veins popped out of developing muscles charged with energy.

'Stay focused,' a voice called out. 'Let them tire first, keep a grip, dig deep with your legs, they are pulling with their arms and will tire quickly.'

'Hold on boys, dig deep. Keep pushing into the ground.'

The Mountain Lion stood firm in the soil while the Marshlanders used up their energy with a pulling action. They seemed to be in a stale mate for ages with the red centre of the rope hovering over the line. Aching arms were burning just keeping it taught, such strenuous activity on this scale was hard. There was clearly a distinct variation in muscle size and strength between the groups.

The   Clan of the Mountain Lion began to gradually feel the tension of the rope edging their way as the Marshlanders grew weary. Their bare bloodied hands were losing the grip and another loud voice heralded a response to the thrown gauntlet.

'Boys pull now...'

They pulled hard.

'Boys dig deep take small steps back...'

They took small steps back in unison.

'Stay focused! Do not look up from the rope...'

They stayed focused

'And heave...'

More steps back. The tension was coming their way, the Mountain Lion had control.

'Stay focused boys - stay focused - dig those legs in firm - lean back - and - heave.'

Still the Mountain Lion pulled and heaved with all the strength they had having gained the advantage over the fatigued team. Low sitting thighs skimmed the soil with the exertion. Defined triangular calf muscles took the weight.

'Now big steps - move with the rope - keep momentum - and pull - and pull.'

They responded to the roars with their own deep guttural growls. Rivers of sweat poured down straining bodies, focused eyes squinted and teeth clenched hard, young hands were shredded and raw. With a final surge of exertion the Clan of the Mountain Lion strode back with giant strides and pulled the failing Marshlanders off their feet. They tumbled on top of each other, a sweating, heaving mass of testosterone with arms of useless jelly.

Exhilaration voided the exhaustion and they celebrated together, jumping and cheering and punching the air. The whole clan was dancing with joy while the other team applauded them.

'Well done boys,' they shouted together. 'Well done brothers.'

Winners and losers abounded that day, joy and exhilaration filled the dusky night air, and as each tribe made their way home, there wasn't one man, woman or boy who didn't think that they would be back next year to challenge for the glory.

When they returned home, Keao had gone in to speak with Jena. He knew that she would want news of her friends. Ajeya had been out in the fields all day practising with her bow and arrows and now was back to listen in on the conversation.

'It was a tremendous day, such a shame that Ajeya couldn't come. I watched a clan girl win the archery competition; she beat off all the opposition. You will come next year won't you Ajeya? It's at the Marshland Tribe next year.'

Ajeya nodded to her brother. 'You try and stop

me.'

Her mother smiled, she had waited patiently for Keao to spill out his enjoyment first. Only then did she ask him what was at the forefront of her mind. 'Did you see Laith or Artemisia?'

Keao was aware of her anxiety in waiting and only wished he had better news. 'I saw Laith, and I met his son Namir, but there was no Artemisia. I'm sorry.'

'Did you ask about her?' she said hopefully.

'Mother how could I have done that? I didn't see her at all. I was looking for her, I really was. I went round all the stalls and all the tents. I thought as a host leader she would be somewhere. But I really couldn't see her. And I couldn't ask where she was. It would have been too probing and possibly insensitive if something had happened to her.'

Jena looked sad, but understood his dilemma. 'Did Laith look well,' again she yearned for a positive reaction.

Keao bit his bottom lip to compose himself, he so wanted to tell her wanted she wanted to hear. 'Unfortunately not, again I am sorry, but I barely recognised him. He had aged so much. I remember thinking of him as a young man when I first met him and how much younger he looked than father. But now,' he paused at the recollection. 'He is half the man he was. I could see a sadness in his eyes. He was carrying a heavy burden.'

'Did you speak to him?'

'I didn't, because despite looking old, he did

look content amongst all his friends and I would have reminded him of a past which he was clearly trying to deal with.'

Sadness tinged the swollen hut. The man, who, in such a short time, had filled their hearts with so much hope and happiness, gaiety and laughter, was now fighting his own demons, and no one knew why.

Jena wiped away a tear. 'Something dreadful happened I know it, and it's my fault that we left them, and now I will never know what happened to them.'

'It wasn't your fault mother, you were protecting your children and you weren't to know. It was such a long time ago now; anything could have happened in that time.'

Hagen put an arm around her. 'Keao is right Jena, it was such a long time ago now, and digging up the past would have served no purpose. And besides, we all get old, just because he has aged doesn't mean that something bad happened to him. Cherish the thoughts that you have of them and be calm in the knowledge that they were all safe. Her son was at the Gathering, which suggests they were all together. Anything that happened after that was not down to you.'

She dried her eyes and wiped her nose. 'Thank you Hagen, I'm being a foolish old woman now. I'm sorry Keao, I'm glad you had a nice time.'

But Ajeya noticed the sadness in her mother's eyes and knew how much she yearned to know the truth. She had held on to the memory of that awful day for so many years now, and still didn't know what had happened to her dear friends. But as Keao had just told her, Artemisia's son was there. Laith was there. Perhaps she had died in childbirth or some other time since. No one would ever know for sure now. But Keao had an insight for these things. He had a sixth sense that he was blessed with. He could read people. He knew what they were feeling just by looking into their eyes. And if Keao sensed that Laith was carrying a burden, then he probably was. And that made her sad as well.

The journey home had been a silent one for Dainn. His father had barely said a word.

'Are you all right father?'

Colom looked at him in bewilderment as if he hadn't heard him properly. 'Hmm?'

'I said are you all right father you seem troubled?'

'We will talk when we are home son.' And he limply snatched the rein and stared at the debris being splattered across the path by the horses hooves.

The journey continued with Colom immersed in his own thoughts and Dainn wondering what on earth could be wrong. It wasn't until they were eating supper that evening, that Colom finally spoke. But his voice was heavy. 'This year's Gathering was another success for all, and as usual we welcome the chance to live side by side with our fellow clans and prosper in peace and harmony as we celebrate our good fortune together.'

Their nodding heads were in full agreement.

'Hear hear father,' said Dainn heartily. 'The Gathering installs peace in a time honoured tradition.'

'I know son and it also gives us leaders a chance to know what is going on the subject kingdoms and be alerted to anything that is unusual or what we have to prepare ourselves for.'

Dainn's face changed. 'Is there something you are trying to tell us father?' he looked at his mother.

Peira took up her son's uncertainty. 'Yes my love, if there is something troubling you then you must tell us.'

Colom leaned back in his chair and pushed his plate away. 'I do have some disturbing news and I want to keep it to ourselves for the moment. I do not want to worry the clan. So please, give me your word that you will not speak to anyone about what I am about to tell you.'

'I give you my word father, but what is it?' Dainn stopped eating and put his spoon in the bowl.

Peira nodded. 'You have my word also.'

'There is a General who goes by the name of Domitrius Corbulo, he works for the Emperor Gnaeus of Ataxata,' Colom's voice was hushed.

Dainn and Peira looked at each other, their faces ashen, their hearts racing in anticipation.

'He calls himself the angel of the gods, that he is a tool for cleansing the kingdoms of unwanted savages and parasites.'

'So how does that affect us?' said an anxious Dainn.

'We have been told that the Emperor has developed a new passion that he holds for a few weeks in the summer. He likes to please his people, his officials and his guests with his own version of the games.'

'What games are those?' asked Peira.

'He forces boys to fight in his new arena. He considers everyone outside his kingdom a savage and a parasite, especially the clans, and must only be used for his gratification.'

'What sort of fighting are we talking about here?' asked Peira.

Colom shook his head and breathed deeply to compose himself. He really didn't want to say the awful truth, but he couldn't lie to his family. 'We have been told they are known as the killing games,' he sighed heavily. 'We have reason to believe there have been deaths already, but we cannot be sure of the numbers.'

Peira and Dainn were shocked into silence. Colom tried to ease their obvious concerns.

'We do have an advantage,' he started. 'We are so far north that he might not even come this far. He would need food and equipment to last several days. He would have to go through the mountains and hazardous conditions to get here. It just wouldn't be worth his while, so I am fairly certain that we are safe. And I do not want to worry the clan unnecessarily, because it might not even happen. But I wanted to tell you just so that you can be vigilant and prepared.'

'Can I tell Ajeya?'

'Not yet son, please. It will worry her and she will tell her parents. So for now, just keep it to yourself.'

27

Another year had passed and all was well in the camp; no sightings of the General had been reported and so it was with an air of contentment that Dainn and Ajeya strolled through the small grove of deciduous trees towards their own flowering glade; a small luxurious meadow, a verdant piece of the landscape that sat beautifully amid the tranquil setting of the silent pool. They had been here many times, but none so much as the season they were in now, for the days were long and the midday hours unusually warm; so the clan were up extra early to get their jobs finished by noon, and escape the burning temperatures of the unforgiving sun.

'Be very still and look over there, near the water.' Dainn kept his voice low.

A heron was hunting, poised like a statue, ready to take its meal. It didn't flinch when they came into view. It kept still, unmoving and not once did it take its eyes off the prey. The keen observers waited as patiently as the heron; all they could hear was the sound of their own breathing and the mewing of the buzzard overhead. Suddenly the heron plunged its long spear of a beak into the water, brought out an impressive size trout and tipping back its head, swallowed the whole fish in one go so that you could see its very body being manoeuvred down its long thin neck.

'Now that's what you call impressive hunting,' said Ajeya in awe of the skill.

'An expert hunter, that's what he is; now where's that rope swing that we put up last year.'

He climbed the grassy bank to have a go on their thrill seeking apparatus. Below him a clear lake beckoned, its very base lined with a rich golden sediment and water snakes slithered through the reeds while fish blew out debris from the bed. He took hold of the rope, stood as far back as he was able and catapulted himself from the highest point and landed in the water in a seated position. The water snakes slithered away and the fish darted to the other side of the pool.

She laughed at him when he surfaced with a head full of green algae. 'You look like the monster from the deep lagoon,' her laughter was uncontrollable.

'Perhaps I am,' he teased, and raising his arms high above his head, came at her like a walking undead. She screamed at the sight of him, scrambled up the bank and then grabbing hold of the rope, swung herself into the water. Hers was an altogether perfect entry and barely made a ripple as her body glided through the surface in a streamlined fashion. She swam back to the shore and climbed out nimbly, then sat down and tilted her head back for the warmth of the sun to dry her off. Dainn came and sat down beside her and pawed at the blanket weed that was still stuck to his flaxen hair. He couldn't help look at her loose silk shirt clinging to the contours of her magnificent shape.

'You truly are a beautiful woman.'

She turned and looked at him and thought him to be the most beautiful man she had ever seen. With his broad shoulders, muscular chest, strong arms, working hands and skin tanned after spending hours in the outdoors, and the fine hairs that covered his body had turned golden in the sun. But then she looked at his grimacing face pulling at the green weed stuck to his head. 'Wish I could say the same about you.'

He looked at her lovingly and leaned in to kiss her. 'I know you don't mean it and that you love me really.'

The water had cooled them sufficiently on this hot summers day and after a week of high temperatures, it was usual for them to spend most of their afternoons by the lake; listening to the sound of crickets in the long dry grass and worker honey bees going about their day; and watching butterflies weave through the air and settle on vibrant colours fed by the heat of the sun.

They looked out over to the pastures where the horses were swishing away nuisance flies with their tails and shook their heads every time they raised their necks to take a look at the leaping deer that passed through their domain.

'This has to be the most peaceful place on earth,' she said drawing in a long deep breath of fresh air.

'I think so too,' and he leaned over to kiss the top of her head.

'I wish we could stay here forever and build a little hut in the forest, just you and me; hunting, trapping and living off the land. To just stay like this and not have to learn to fight to protect ourselves against the bigger monsters.'

'It's the way of the kingdoms we are living in.'

She didn't hear him, she was caught up in the moment. 'Isn't nature wonderful. I wish we could camouflage ourselves like the the insects and the animals, because everything they do is an illusion to protect themselves.' She looked at the scene around her. 'That butterfly over there with her beautiful painted wings, she has to blend in with the different colours of flowers so she is not eaten; and the cricket has to change colour to camouflage himself in the grass so he is not seized. And the deer in the meadow flash the white of their tails to evoke a sense of size. Everything in nature is an illusion to outwit and outmanoeuvre.'

'But we don't need those things, we have a much wider range of defences to protect us. Those smaller mammals and reptiles have to rely on another set of skills.'

She looked at the heron; solitary, still and undoubtedly aware of everything around it. 'I love the summer, everything is full of life and burgeoning with colour. The song of the bird, the hum of the insect, the call of the wild. Then by November everything changes: The stags fight for supremacy, the stallions kill for their harem, the animals get slaughtered for their meat. Birds have all but disappeared and hibernating creatures will have stuffed their last morsel of food.'

'Are you all right?' his tone was one of concern.

'I am just thinking about life, I hope we are safe here. I hope the blood month doesn't bring any monsters to our shores and into our lives.'

His face couldn't help but hide his surprise. Did she know something? Had he spent too long teaching her how to fight with a sword and train for hours with bow and arrows? No, it could not be, they had always done that for as long as he could remember. But she was the Hare, she was all knowing and could see things before anyone else. 'We will be fine,' he assured her. 'We are so far north that monsters don't even know we are here.' Her words took him back to a carefree time, more than a decade ago, and it made his heart melt. 'Do you remember the time when you told me that fairies lived in the woods?'

She nodded.

'Think about the nice things my love and the horrors will take care of themselves.'

She snapped out of her trance and smiled at him. 'Of course, you are right. Keao was always telling me to pretend. Even then he was probably protecting me. But I should be enjoying the summer while it's here, not envisaging the wrath of something that might never happen.' She kissed his face. 'Come on, I'll race you to the glen, we can conceal ourselves in there. You've got a boxing tournament to win in a few months and I've got an archery competition to train for.'

28

The sun was shining bright above them and the day was pleasantly warm for early autumn. The long hot summer had disrupted the seasons and even nature was confused. A horse nickered behind them and a buzzard mewed from above. On this fine September morning Colom had started out by setting a pace that he was accustomed to using when travelling with a large section of the camp, one that would not push the slower members of the clan too hard. The horses were used to this journey every year, though the Marshland Tribe was one of the closest clans and it made the journey so much easier.

Wagons rolled along, spewing up debris as they churned up the well worn path; they were carrying the gifts, trade goods and food for the day. The others carried their skills on them. Dainn and Ajeya trotted along together at the helm followed by Keao and Rufus who were eager to watch the rematch. They stopped by a small river to rest and they had their breakfast in a large field partially surrounded by trees. Dainn practised his punches with Keao while Ajeya took Rufus into the forest to help with her shooting.

'He will win today won't he?' asked the young

lad.

She nocked an arrow to her bow and sent it pulsating through the air. He went running after it and snatched it out of the trunk she had aimed at.

'I'm sure he will Rufus, he has been training so much these past twelve months.' She sent him scurrying after another one that had been deployed into a notch in an old oak.

'He is ready for anything now isn't he?' Rufus came back with both arrows.

'I think he is. I think we both are.' Another quiver hit the acorn out the hands of a bewildered squirrel.

Rufus laughed. 'You two can take on anything.'

'Well thank you Rufus, it would be amazing if we were both wearing a crown by the end of the day.' And she finished off with a quick round of six that were sent into the stub of a tree branch.

The sun was high when the clan approached a large settlement situated on a broad natural terrace which ran alongside a wide swift river. Banners could be seen flying as more travellers emerged from the green of the wood and from a steady flow of floating vessels on the river. Ajeya watched from atop her horse on the crest of the wooded ridge that overlooked the settlement, with its mill, houses and stables. The trees were full of golds, crimsons and browns now, and the few withered flowers that still clung on to the branches did little to obstruct her view. She could see the archery tournament being set up quite clearly and then her gaze took her to the arena where Dainn would be heading.

This was the rematch that everyone had been waiting for. The champion Tore and the man that had nearly taken his crown the year before. There was a large crowd around the make shift arena, all eager to watch and learn but mainly to see if Dainn took take the crown from the three times champion. Last year's winner was heralded into the ring amongst uplifting cheers and a riotous applause. Tore paraded around the roped off circle to the adulation of the crowd. Dainn dived under the rope to shake hands with his opponent.

'So you are back then?'

'Yes I am.'

'I hope you've been training and got yourself fit.'

'I certainly have Tore, I can't take another beating like last year.'

Toro smiled. 'Good luck my friend.'

'Good luck to you too Tore. May the best man win.'

They retreated to their respective corners and waited for the sound of the drum.

The fight started and they vied each other, feeling the energies around them and willed the power of the spirits into their veins. Above them, the plumped up clouds marched across a clear blue sky, and seemed to stop every now and then to view the unravelling spectacle.

An invisible chord held them together as they bobbed and ducked around the perimeter of the ring. It wasn't long before the first move was made and with a double left as he walked outside his jab, Dainn had the upper ground; but then Tore came back with a right hook over his jab. It caught him unawares and he had to refocus. A few moments relapse and Dainn leaned his head to avoid the punch back and threw a left uppercut to his opponents exposed body. Tore tried to get another jab in response but Dainn dipped out of the way.

They parried and danced around each other, the invisible chord tight, fists raised, light feet barely making any impression on the ground, holding the gaze, not flinching, undeterred, neither giving anything away. But then Tore came in with a right hook against his own right cross and they stood there, locked together, beads of sweat congealing and then they separated again.

The crowd swelled and enjoyed the parry, yelling out encouragement to their favourite to win. Dainn raised his concentration levels; he tried to think, he tried to feel. The moves got quicker. Jabbing, hooking, striking as they hopped and skipped round the arena. Each yielding nothing, holding perfect concentration and the tension grew. Grim faces around the perimeter urged them on. Which one would concede first and lose the fight?

Tore tried a succession of sweeps but Dainn blocked with strong arms and protected his head. He responded with a two fist strike but that was also defended well by Tore. They parried round the ring and Tore launched with a full arm thrust. Dainn recoiled again and returned with a clean sweep. He caught Tore on the jaw who staggered back and shook the surprise from his swelling face. Dainn launched in again with the other fist and Tore only just blocked it in time.

They refocused and eyed each other, dancing and jabbing with continual movements. To them nothing else was around except the time ticking by. They didn't even notice the excitable voices getting louder and louder, giving advice, making remarks and spurring them on. Tore was still giddy from the knock but he came back into the game with a swipe that knocked Dainn off balance. The invisible chord was still taught, but Dainn staggered and lost his footing. He took a step back to get his composure and refocus his game. He raised his eyes to Tore, concentrated all his energies on the man's stomach, and struck. His own body remained perfectly still, but the blow landed with such force that Tore was sent sprawling backwards; he stumbled around for a while trying to find his balance, he was stunned and shaking his head in disbelief.

Dainn was inspecting his own fist. He hadn't really thought about what he was doing, or how he was going to do it, he had just felt a huge surge of energy and had deployed it. He wasn't aware of the chants urging Tore to get back in the game and wasn't aware of anything apart from the elation he was feeling. He was incredulous of his own strength and took his mind off the task. So much so that he wasn't prepared at all when Tore came back at him with a left hand to the body and a right hook to the jaw. Dainn had the wind knocked out of him and with waves of disorientated flowing through his body, he was rendered motionless.

Time stood still.

But to the shock of the crowd, he raised his stance again as a rush of exultation fired through his body. His power was growing and with a surge of strength pumping through his veins he launched in with a straight lead left. It was fast, it was strong and it was unpredictable. He didn't hesitate, he knew exactly what to do and where to punch. He gave Tore no time to think and with that punishing strategy, Tore was sent flying. Last year's champion was knocked out as his head hit the floor and he had to be revived. He sat up dazed and shook his head. Dainn helped him up and embraced him.

'Hope I didn't hurt you Tore.'

'Nothing that won't heal. My ego is permanently damaged though.' He rubbed his jaw and grimaced. 'But thank you for a good fight Dainn, you are a worthy champion.'

They shook hands gracefully and Tore ducked out of the ring. Dainn then went on to knock out every other opponent that came into his domain and take the championship. Rufus punched the air in admiration and they both went off to watch Ajeya win her archery competition.

The leaders had gone in for their yearly talks and it transpired that the General hadn't been heard of for some time.

'Just as I thought,' Colom said easing a heavy heart. 'We are too far north for the General. It just isn't worth his trouble.

'I had thought the same at last year's Gathering,' came another voice from the back. 'There are many miles between us and Ataxata, and many zones full of wild animals and hazardous terrain. Only a madman would even attempt the journey.'

29

The horizon was grey on this morning and overhead an obscured sun peeked out timidly through low scuttling clouds and tried desperately to brighten an otherwise forlorn day. The wind blew cold and Ajeya could hear the gushing rush of water and the creak of the mill's great wooden waterwheel. There was a smell of rain in the dawn air, but no drops were falling yet. Smoke was rising from the chimneys indicating another chilly November day. Children's shrill voices could be heard coming from the homes.

A wagon carrying a crowd of boys was on its way to the fields; she heard Storm, Malik, Durg and Tay, shouting and laughing as it went off. She waved to them but they were too engrossed feasting their eyes on the pretty girls feeding the chickens and geese.

Ajeya smiled as she watched them go and as she followed their path with her eyes, she could see the rich and fertile land filled with orchards of trees yielding the fruits of autumn; and further on she could just about make out the tilled fields, many still tawny with the stubble of a late harvest; and adjacent to that, the keen farm workers already starting their day, driving teams of plough horses or digging up roots and vegetables.

Jena and Hagen had left even earlier on their wagon that morning. Catching fish at this time of year was always profitable and a good supply of nutritious vertebrates could be guaranteed. How she loved fresh salmon for dinner and felt the pit of her stomach growl as she anticipated a rich meal that evening. For now, a chunk of bread and a bowl of last night's left over stew would have to suffice, for in a few hours she would be out hunting with Dainn for the rest of the day.

But as the wagon of boys disappeared out of view, there came the roar of horses hooves followed by a loud thud. An army of soldiers had thundered into the village, overturned a wagon and set fire to it. There were cries and jeers as they upturned more. And then came further devastation as flaming arrows shivered through the morning mists, trailing pale ribbons of fire, and splintered into the wooden huts. A few smashed through shuttered windows, and soon there were thin tendrils of smoke rising between the broken shutters. Ajeya ran forward and without a second thought shouldered her bow and snatched her quiver of arrows leaning against the door.

She could hear fighting from the stables now; shouts mingled with the screams of stricken horses and the clang of steel as the metal on metal rang out across the settlement.

She saw Dainn in there wielding his sword in a desperate fight with an armour clad guard. She loaded up her weapon and sent an arrow through the burning building and ended the fight for that soldier. Dainn

227

looked up, nodded to her and got the horses out safely as the old dry wood blazed with a fierce hungry light. Another man came through on a charger and was swinging an axe in both hands. With his first blow he smashed one of the struts of the water wheel, with his second and third blows he demolished even more. The water gushed without the struts and the power was depleted. But then Dainn came from nowhere and threw himself at the man, the soldier fell to the ground gasping, winded and barely conscious; Dainn knocked him out with one swipe and Ajeya sent another arrow to finish him off.

She turned on her heels to see a man take an arrow through the chest as he tried to torch the Blessing Tree; she heard him scream as he fell and looked over to see Colom reloading. The smoke was heavy now and a series of arrows sped back and forth as Peira fed more shafts into the wrath of her husband's bow. Suddenly there was a great rush of bodies, noise and panic. Those that could, ran into the siege to help, while others were barged out of the way by men on horseback as they ran for cover.

On the hillside above, Keao was driving his herd of cows, riding in a horse drawn wagon that carried the days supply of milk. The agitated lowing of his herd had alerted him and now he was coming down to help; bringing the cows, his wagon and the churns of milk. As he got downside he emptied the churns and let the rich creamy liquid gush out of the containers and into the path of the soldiers. Their chargers began to slide everywhere and couldn't be controlled. The cows began to stampede and forced the army back. More liquid made its way to the burning buildings and soon the rich smoky smell of burned milk filled the air.

Thunder rumbled in over the hills, spots of rain could be felt. A flash of light could be seen in the distance. Dainn and Ajeya looked at each other desperately and nodded to Keao as he went to round up his herd of stricken cows and help with the terrified horses. Colom was standing there with Peira and the other villagers who could only look on in shock at what had just happened.

Suddenly a clap of thunder tore across the sky with such a force the vibration splintered the earth; the clouds opened and a wall of rain swept in battering down the last few remaining flames. Lightning struck in such ferocity that it lit up the true horror, and through the mists of rampage and the stench of fear, a tall, stately man appeared on a charger and brought hell with him.

Behind him came the captains and behind them came four drawn wagons which carried the cages full of slaves, the rations for the men and the provisions for the horses. Storm, Malik, Durg and Tay, who thought they were on their way to the fields that morning, were already in one of the wagons and clung onto the prison bars. Their mothers screamed when they saw them and cried pitifully into their aprons unable to do anything.

Colom stepped forward. 'What do you want from us?' his voice was bristling as he stood amongst the carnage.

'Well that is no way to greet a General now is it?' the fiend cocked his head and sneered. 'But as I am in a fairly good mood, and we don't appear to have lost too many men,' he looked coldly at the strewn corpses of his fallen soldiers. 'I am going to be very lenient today.' His white gloves steadied the reins of his black mare and a gold helmet covered a strong face. A blood-red cloak fanned out behind him and trailed like a burning flame.

Colom stood there, his face contorted with anger. For he was a mere pawn against this army and he couldn't risk another assault on his village.

'I know what you are thinking,' the General tilted his head to one side in a mocking fashion.

Colom shook his head, trying desperately to hold back the venom he wanted to deploy.

'You are thinking that you can't attack me because otherwise you will put your entire settlement in danger.' The General smirked and looked back at his captains who responded to his goading. 'And of course you would be right,' he sneered again. 'This is nothing to the hell I have unleashed on other clans,' he let the words sink in.

'So what do you want from us?' Colom's voice grew louder and impatient.

'I want you to know my name so that you will remember who I am and know what I am capable of.'

Colom sighed loudly in response, he was getting tired of this man's games.

'I am the General Domitrius Corbulo and I work for the Emperor of Ataxata and I am instructed to take boys from your clans for our games in Ataxata. No questions asked. No answers given. If they please the crowd, they will return. If not...' he looked back and curled a grimace at the terrified youngsters.

'You can't do that!' Colom's voice was raging.

The General kicked his horse into a walk and drawing out his sword held it to Colom's throat. Peira screamed, Dainn moved forward, Ajeya got her bow ready.

The General spun his head round and barked out an order. 'Take him!'

Within seconds Dainn had been frogmarched to the waiting wagon and thrown in with the other boys.

'I can do what I like and you had better not forget that! You are peasants, you are nothing. You are here to serve the Emperor and nothing more. Do you understand me?' His voice gathered momentum, his face contorted with loathing.

Everyone had their head low, only a handful stood their ground.

He then went over to Ajeya and flicked the hair from her face with his sword. 'You really are disgusting aren't you.' His words were slow and controlled. He studied her face carefully. 'I should put you out of your misery right here and now. What kind of man could ever want you? Maybe a monster, maybe a savage; but certainly no man!' He taunted her with his blade and ran the tip down the side of her disfigured face. She

231

stood and glared at him.

Rufus jumped forward and put himself between her and the General. 'Don't you touch her!'

Dainn shouted and bellowed from the cage and rattled the bars until his hands bled.

But the General wasn't interested in what he was saying, he was already a prisoner.

'How touching. So you are going to give your life for that deviant? What a brave little boy.' His smile was sickly. Then he leaned forward and held his face within a fingers breadth of Rufus. 'Well more fool you.' He sat up. Brushed down his cloak, and bellowed out another order. 'Take him as well.'

'You can't take him, he's just a child,' Ajeya was raging.

The General spat at her. 'Are you telling me what I can and cannot do again? Just keep that poisoned mouth shut!' He jerked his horse sideways on a vicious rein and spurred it into a canter to the head of the procession.

Red came running over and raced towards the wagon's. 'Rufus!' her screaming voice was cut off with a torturous bayonet and she sunk to the floor.

Ajeya reached for an arrow and loaded it in her bow. She raised it up and took aim. Just one shot at the beast, that's all she needed. But then she felt someone's arm on her own.

'The soldiers will set fire to those wagons if you kill the General and then those boys will have no chance at all.'

'But I can't just stand back and do nothing Colom. Dainn can at least fight back given half a chance, even the four farm boys are strong. But Rufus can't. Look at him. He's a child.' She raised her bow again and took aim.

'Ajeya, please!'

The words rang deep. She slowly dropped her bow and swallowed the pain. 'What I am I going to tell Keao? What am I going to tell him?' She stood defiantly while her throat ached with unshed tears. And as the wagons trundled over the hill she could see Dainn mouthing the words 'I love you' and a bloodied hand was on his heart.

30

The community were left stunned, a village awash in gloom. Red led the chorus of grieving mothers where even their husband's words of comfort and awkward optimism fell on deaf ears. Others picked their way between crumbled stone and blackened timber. The carrion scavengers were already squabbling and shrieking as they fought over the charred and mangled corpses amongst the wreckage. People were coughing and disorientated; colliding with each other in their stricken state, shouting out the names of loved ones, stumbling as they searched, while others staggered about clutching on to a few meagre belongings.

Keao came back from the fields and his gaze fell on the slaughter and his wife sobbing uncontrollably.

'What on earth has happened here?' his voice was stricken.

'They've taken him Keao, they've taken our boy.'

Keao could hardly make out what she was saying. 'Who's taken him Red, what are you talking about?'

The General has taken him, taken him and Dainn,' she was inaudible with sobbing. 'When you went to herd up the cows, the General came with wagons,' she was shaking uncontrollably as Keao strained to understand. 'He took Dainn, then he took our boy,' she broke down again and Peira comforted her.

'I don't understand,' his bewildered voice needed answers. 'How could this General take anyone?'

'After you had gone he marched in with his army,' Colom started to offer some kind of explanation, but his voice was slow and inaudible as well. 'We were outnumbered, totally outnumbered.'

'Did anyone try and stop him taking our child?' He demanded to know and looked round sternly at all the forlorn faces. 'Did anyone try and stop him? Did you? Or you?' He pointed at each one in turn. Then he stopped at his sister who was still clutching her weapon. 'Why didn't you stop them Ajeya? Why didn't you stop them? What good is this bow if you are not going to use it?'

Tears ran down her face in quantities. She had never seen her brother so distraught and there was nothing she could do. She couldn't even speak coherently as he shook her by the shoulders. 'I'm so sorry Keao, I'm so sorry,' she let him take his anger out on her and tried to unload his pain.

'I stopped her,' said Colom, taking away the blame. But his voice was pained and tight.

Keao turned. 'Why did you stop her Colom, why?'

'Because the General is no ordinary man, he is a madman intent on wiping out clans. With him dead, the soldiers would have set fire to the cages.'

He had revealed too much. Peira looked at the floor.

Keao's face contorted with disbelief, his eyebrows met as he faced Colom. 'You knew about him and didn't warn us! You let me go off and take care of some wretched cows while my wife and son were in danger!'

The whole village was deathly quiet. Only Peira spoke out in defence of her husband.

'Would anything have been different if every one of you had known about the General? I think not. He had an agenda with a bigger force and we have all paid a price.'

Colom stopped her with his arm. 'It's my fault,' his voice was faint and tiny. 'I didn't want to alarm anyone, I thought we were too far north to be attacked. I thought we were safe.' He hated himself before he said it. 'But six of us have lost a precious son today.'

'Six?'

'They took Storm and his farmhands,' said Peira.

'But those sons are men. Mine is a little boy.' He slumped to his knees and sobbed.

Red came over to comfort him and helped him up.

Ajeya stepped forward. 'We couldn't have done anything about it Keao, we were totally outnumbered. Your heroic actions held them back for a while, but that General would have still carried on and executed his plan. There were only a few of us here that had weapons and could fight. Remember that we are a farming community, these people are not warriors.

'The General said that other clans had suffered far more losses at his hands. We should take some comfort from that Keao. Please, I understand your pain but Colom did the right thing. He really did brother.'

Keao looked right through her, it was almost as if he didn't see her, and as the community made a silent aisle for him, he led his distraught wife back to their home.

'Rufus will be safe,' she called out after them. 'Dainn will take care of him; I promise you. Dainn will bring him back.' Her voice trailed after them and then disappeared into the stench of smoke and fear.

For the first time Ajeya sunk her head in her hands and wept; and a weak voice begged the spirits to take care of all the boys and bring them home safe.

Jena and Hagen arrived in time to see Keao leave the enclosure. Having witnessed this type of attack once before, they knew the trademark signs. They left the trap where it was and ran over to Colom.

'Is this the Emperor's work?' asked Hagen, his voice shaken.

'No, it's his henchman, the General.' But Colom couldn't speak any more. He turned and went back to what remained of his hut, followed by a weeping Peira.

Ajeya was left to explain everything.

But no one asked questions about how Hagen knew it was the Emperor's work.

Colom immediately thought Dainn must have

told them; after all, Ajeya's fighting skills were superb that day.

Ajeya thought that Peira had told Jena. They told each other everything.

The whole community thought that Hagen and Jena had been given prior knowledge somehow.

No one raised the question.

The only person who sunk to an even lower state than everyone else was Jena, because she knew it was her husband's work; and after all this time, he was still alive and still haunting her.

31

The village was numb now and people moved about like slow grey moths. The broken bridge was drowning in the stream and most of the huts had been destroyed in the fire. Families had to double up, or treble up in some cases. For those poor souls their homes were a graveyard of ashes and memories buried deep within layers of dirt, soot and mud. Nothing of the beautiful apple orchard remained, that was trampled flat and bare. The rows of bee hives were burnt out, those residents would have sought other accommodation elsewhere. Poles, splinters and nails protruded like hideous charred skeletons. It was like walking into hell itself. The slow grey moths picked their way about the tattered village, muttering and contemplating that life would never be the same.

But then the people gradually began to find hope.

'All is not lost,' said one brave soul. 'Most of the stone walls are intact, albeit fragments and charred, but the foundations are probably still strong and can be used again.'

Another voice added to the melody. 'The wooden stable block is burned to a cinder, but that can be repaired.'

'There is so much stone and timber in the surrounding forests, what is stopping us?' echoed another.

'We can build the hives again,' came a woman's voice.

'And clear the orchard,' said another.

And one by one, the slow grey moths discarded their heavy shrouds and began to salvage their community. Stronger new fences went up to replace those that had burned down. Then the collapsed roof of the Meeting House had been cleared away and a new one raised in its place. The huge arms of the water wheel were lovingly restored and once again the harmonious splash and rumble could be heard across the village.

The only thing that had been left untouched was the Blessing Tree, and that had been saved by Colom as he protected it with shaft after shaft of poison tipped arrows. Now it loomed over the village with a blaze of life, light and beauty. An island of peace in a sea of chaos. Its vibrant ribbons shimmering with colour where everything else stood grey. The ground around it was fertile and lush and its small hard scaly bits of bark represented the thousands of people who had stood by its side seeking strength and asking for protection. It twisted up to the sky from a myriad of life giving roots and hair like tendrils. It breathed the air as the branches swayed and called people over to hang even more ribbons on its fingers, to count their blessings and pray for the safe return of the boys. One by one the villagers heard the calling and at any time of the day and night at least one person could be seen immersed in their own private vigil and securing another ribbon on the Blessing Tree.

Winter was upon them now and they continued to put their village together whilst preparing for the coldest most unforgiving season. Because while the haunting devastation of the General's wrath was still evident in quantities; life had to go on.

As time went by the sluggish grey moths discovered that each of them had a tough colourful exterior; and a stronger, more imposing fort rose higher out of the ground than ever before.

The community had already gathered an abundance of wild food and preserved the meat and plants for the torturous winter months ahead. And yet there was still the menial tasks to do in the camp while the temperatures plummeted; string bows, fletch arrows, sharpen spears; gather firewood, milk the cows, feed the animals, and still find time to restore their fortress.

Whilst everyone took on the guise of some hideous monster draped in their heavy winter coats with oversized hats and wore scarves that stuck to their faces and shivered as the snow fell around them, Ajeya found herself thinking about Dainn and Rufus and wondered how they were faring in this freezing weather. Did they have enough clothing, had they got enough food. She remembered that they had been taken with the lightest of clothing and it had been still warm then. No, she must not overthink. She had to remain steadfast in thought. Of course they were all right. They were strong with powerful totems looking after them. They were somewhere safe with a roof over their heads. They were warm. They were fed. They were safe. Of course, they were all safe.

32

By spring, all hopes had risen. Faith had been restored. Trumpets of the earth heralded the return of this spectacular season and the long fingers of the sun's rays fanned across the fields to open up an artist's palette of rich hues, blushed tones and a blaze of colour. The sweet breath of a westerly wind flew in from the wings of the sun and the pulse of the earth returned to camp. Birds, bees, butterflies and dragonflies were increasing in numbers, while trees released their buds and flowers opened their blooms. Within the village a brand new fountain splashed, the restored waterwheel rumbled and the gurgling stream under the bridge had been drained. Spring was always a turning point and with new life pulsing through the earth, a community was considering its next move.

Ajeya had called a meeting and asked everyone to attend. The Meeting House had been carefully restored and proudly exposed an even bigger seating area with a wider platform for the speakers. The sun shone brightly through the shutters and as the rays streamed in they lit up a richly furnished chamber. Luxurious woven carpets now covered the floor instead of rush mats, and in one corner stood a small blessing tree, standing in an ornamental pot where its branches were trimmed and cut so it would not overshadow the stylish decor of the room. The walls were decorated with paintings and scenes of nature and the banners of the Hill Fort Tribe stood proudly on display against the back wall. Ajeya stood strong wearing a deep purple doublet, the figure of a golden hare had been embroidered on the breast; the handiwork of her mother and she wore the garment with pride. She welcomed everyone in and then took her place on the raised dais.

'Firstly, I want to welcome everyone to our brand new Meeting House, and what a Meeting House it is.' She gasped in awe at the workmanship and skill that had gone into this prestigious building. 'I want to thank each and every one of you. For despite overcoming such dreadful circumstances you have pulled together and restored our fort to a scale that only a few months ago, could only be imagined.' She scanned around the room and invited the people to applaud with her.

'This clearly demonstrates what we are capable of. And at a time when spirits were low and all hope had gone, we all rose above it and have excelled ourselves. We should be proud. We have had to rise above the scale of destruction and have found it within ourselves to rise up even higher than ever before.'

The congregation were processing this information carefully.

'I truly believe that our boys will return unharmed. I truly believe that. I believe, that with all our focus and energies they will be returned home.'

The crowd nodded and a rumble of murmurs echoed round the room.

'But now I want to step up our game further. I want to draw on other skills that we have and I know that each of you have those skills.'

The murmurs rumbled louder, anxious faces wore the guise of uncertainty. What could she possibly mean?

'I am fearful of the future. We live in changing times and from what I have witnessed recently, we need to be prepared incase of another attack.' She looked at the concerned blank faces; most didn't fully understand what she meant, so she drew breath and shouted it from the rooftops. 'I want to avenge what the Emperor and the General have done to our people. These rulers are a disgrace to humankind. They instil fear and force their way in by brandishing the blade. They lead by destruction.'

A cheer went up.

'I want to show them that they can't just thunder in and take what is not theirs, that they can't wreck havoc on an established community and bring it to its knees.'

People were on their feet now.

'I want every man, woman and child to take a weapon and train until they can pick it up and launch it without even thinking about it. I never want to see our community ravaged again. I never want to see that type of fear instilled again. Never again will anyone, from anywhere, descend on our land and tell us what to do!'

The roof nearly came off with cheers. She could hardly hear herself speak. 'We start today. We start right now. We are The Hill Fort Tribe. And we will conquer! We will prevail! Our boys will return to a tight, secure fort, where everyone, and I mean everyone, is skilled - in the art - of warfare!'

The applause sang into the rafters and the tribe were fired up with grit and determination amongst such powerful words.

Colom approached her from the side. 'I admire your spirit Ajeya; you are still so young but so incredibly strong.'

'Thank you Colom, that means a lot to me.'

'You were meant to come here,' said Peira with admiration. 'You and Dainn were brought together by the spirits, and when he returns, he will see many changes.'

Ajeya smiled at the thought of him returning. She had missed him so much. His smiling face, his warmth, his effervescence, his passion for life. His totem was keeping him safe. She would never give up hope.

Jena and Hagen were the next to join her side and were too emotional for words, all they could do was to hug her and smile with copious amounts of pride.

And then Keao came up and she stretched out her arms to greet him. 'My dearest brother,' she embraced him warmly.

'I'm so proud of you Ajeya, you really have pulled this tribe together.'

'It's not my doing Keao, they have done it all on their own. I am just extending that determination,' her words were humble.

He continued. 'I turned on you at a moment when you were dealing with your own demons and your own loss. I reacted badly and I am so ashamed,' his voice was tight.

'You've apologised already brother, and I understand that you were shocked and traumatised. You spoke out of anger and not from your heart.'

'But I shouldn't have said the things that I said to you or to Colom.' He shot a look at the leader who bowed his head low and placed his hand on his heart.

'Colom knows you didn't mean it.'

'Yes, I have apologised to him as well.'

Ajeya put her hands on his shoulders. 'Keao, I want you to know that it's because of you that I stood here today and ignited that fire into our people. It's because of you and your disappointment and wrath with the tribe for not trying to stop the General. You were right to be angry and we were wrong to just stand there. That should never have happened and our weakness was our own demise.'

He took her hands and kissed them. 'But we are farmers, as you said back then, no one but you and Dainn and maybe a few others could actually fight with a weapon.'

She rose up high to his small voice. 'I never

want to see that happen again though Keao. You have instigated the change and I want you to help me. I want you to teach the children how to camouflage themselves, how to remain still and poised, how to focus and stay calm and still be accurate with a catapult, or an arrow, or a spear. All those things that you taught me, I want you to share.'

'You really mean that?' his voice was incredulous and brimming with pride at the same time.

'Of course I really mean it. There is no one better for the job. I am who I am because of a handful of people; and you are one of them. It is your teaching of nature and your perception of our senses that has carved me and defined me, so we need to share that with everyone here.'

He kissed her hands again. 'I love you so much Ajeya; thank you for giving me a reason to live again.'

'You have a son out there who will return, you have a wife here who needs you. Every day you have a reason to live.'

'When shall we start?' he was eager to get going.

'We start right now Keao, we start today.'

33

Colom and Peira, Hagen and Jena watched in awe as the new troops manoeuvred on the plains around them. Listening to instructions, forming close knit groups and practising all day every day; hour after hour with little time for rest, so passionate was their determination.

Basic weapon training had been followed by war games; carefully orchestrated strategies and what to do in an attack. They had mock manoeuvres where the defending troops were made up by one half of the clan and the attackers consisted of the rest. Even the musicians were brought in with the drums as Colom said that the instruments could be used to intimidate their enemies; so anything that made a noise, a beat or a rhythm was used to give instructions and orders in the heat of battle.

Skilled metal workers forged even more swords and lances, while the women weaved protective garments and made shields out of layered animal hides. Day after day the clan trained hard, practising tight formations and forming shield walls, attacking each other with blunt wooden swords. This exercise had been executed with such force that if the wooden swords had been real, the General's army would be depleted in an instant by the spitted lances and curved sabres.

Ajeya had led a regiment of archers and spent most of the daylight hours practising on a prepared shooting field. The butts used mounds of earth for targets and the archers sent wave after wave of arrows to stand like flags of honour in the dug up ground. Farmers, gardeners, shepherds, unused to such materials, trained so hard that their fingers bled; so the women made leather finger guards for their protection. Nothing was left to chance and anything that could strike a blow, was excavated to be used.

They collected chunks of weighty rocks to bombard invaders in stronger more efficient catapults and stacked them in metal carts. Ballistas were camouflaged with nets and foliage but easy to get at. Weapons used for hunting the stag and the boar now became longer and more powerful with razor sharp edges and toughened welded shafts. Spending long hours in the forest aiming and targeting objects with spears and daggers; they had learned to lift, aim and throw an assortment of spears rocks and arrows. And Keao instilled the emotional focus of their craft.

'Everything in nature is an illusion to outwit and outmanoeuvre. So look to the skies to see the nimbus, smell the direction in the air and feel the pace in the breeze. For only then will you become aware of your surroundings. Only then will you hear the different sounds and feel the change. Only then will you survive.'

Within a few months the Hill Fort Tribe had become accomplished warriors, they could feel, breathe and see a disturbance in the air. They could grasp a weapon and make it become an extension of their own bodies. Their eyes and instincts instructed them, protected them and alerted them for anything untoward and threatening. They worked as a team guided by sounds and noises and taught to have panoramic vision like the animals.

But on this day,Ajeya could sense something in the air and she could feel a change; and by dusk the mood was heavy with anticipation. Because somewhere, out of the crevasse of the mountains, in the vast wilderness, coming through the mist, came the familiar rumble of horses hooves.

34

The men had been travelling north for several days now, they all felt hot and sticky, disgustingly dirty and almost sick with hunger. It was the hottest month of the year and insects in the north were just as troublesome as those in the south. And while the blood sucking monsters fed on their malnourished bodies, none of them could remember the last time they had eaten a proper meal.

The Hill Fort lads had started upstream along the watercourse that flowed near a ravine, then they began ascending the mountain along a tributary creek forcing their way through heavy underbrush. They stopped by a steep rock wall, over which the creek spilled in a cascading spray. The wall presented a barrier that ran parallel to the gorge and they had to circle some distance before they found a gap large enough to admit the horses. They followed the course of the gorge and then began to follow it upstream again. Then they began their ascent up the challenging stocky glacier. Back in the forest, the crest of the mountain could be seen; now they were on it and home was the other side. It wasn't far to go, but the only way was up and over the rocky edged perimeter; an arduous course which required the skill of the horsemen to guide their animals round to the other side in safety. As they edged forwards and round, an expanse of land unfolded and the party remained speechless as they absorbed the spectacular vision.

Pine and spruce dominated the higher elevation which was home to a range of squirrels, birds and bats; the boys embraced the smell of freedom as the wind picked up and trees thinned out to a familiar sight. An expanse of land whose far end terminated in the grey brown rock of the mountain, sparsely covered with clinging growth, soared into the mouth of a cave. Specks of light that come with dusk fell on the rock formations. They danced on the wind and into the entrance of the chamber. This was easily recognisable, this was Dainn and Ajeya's domain and Dainn felt that he wanted to weep for the lost time and the miles that had kept them apart.

The river they were following gushed into a stream and beyond the stream was their camp. A falcon had followed them like a personal guard heralding their return with a haunting cry and saluting her praise for uncovering a sleepy vole. A blanket of dazzling dew continued round and highlighted their path to where the village and the colour of peace and tranquillity merged. Their goal was right in front of them. At last they were home. They looked at each other. They were safe. And for the last time on that journey, the once six captive lads galloped home for a clan's welcoming.

'I can smell the dinner cooking,' cried out Dainn.

'Me too,' echoed Durg.

'I hope they've got enough for all of us,' shouted Storm.

'I can't wait to see mother and father,' cried Rufus.

'I'll race you Malik,' challenged Tay.

The clan were out preparing dinner when the first sightings were made.

'Open the gates! It's Dainn and the boys, they have returned to us.' Came the call from the watch tower.

The gates were hauled open and after the initial shock, a hundred throats roared them home.

'Thank the gods, thank the gods.' Ajeya crumpled on to her knees to give thanks to her hare totem. She wailed into the sky and wept tears of joy.

And gradually as each mother saw her child through the gates, they fell on their knees and sent prayers to the Blessing Tree. The fathers and children followed the howls and when they saw the reason for the excited screams, ran towards the galloping racers. There were cheers and jubilations amongst all of them and an excited Keao just about managed to outrun Red as they raced towards their son.

'Praise be to the gods,' hailed Colom. 'And praise be to our totems that have protected our boys.'

The horses were trotting by the time they reached the arms of the open gates that had been swung wide for them, and the entire Hill Fort Tribe were lined up in jubilation to welcome them home.

Colom and Peira were first in line to greet their son. Dainn jumped off his horse and ran to his mother's arms. 'Mother, I have missed you so much.'

She hung on to him and wept until her tears ran dry. Dainn wiped her face and then embraced Colom. 'Oh father, how glad am I to see you!'

'And me too my dearest boy. And me too.'

'What happened to you all?' asked his agitated mother. 'I saw many boys taken that day. Is everyone safe?'

'They are all fine. We were saved with moments to spare by a remarkable woman.'

Peira smiled knowingly.

'And of course I will tell you all about it in due course, but for now I need a bath, something to eat; and most importantly, I need to see my Ajeya.'

'Of course you do my love. I will heat up the water for you right now and get everyone preparing to celebrate your return, but my dear boy, give me one last hug.' She wrapped her arms around him and held him like she would never let him go. But she knew she shared his love with another, and wiping away stinging eyes, hurried off to attend to her duties.

He watched his mother scurrying off and his heart sang after her.

'Where is Ajeya father?' Dainn said looking around. 'Is she well, is she all right?'

'My dear boy, Ajeya is without doubt one of the

strongest, bravest women I have ever known,' and Colom looked in her direction.

Dainn followed Colom's gaze towards the courageous young woman. She was embroiled in her own emotions as she welcomed home Rufus alongside Keao and Red, taking it in turns to hug him and shower him with an avalanche of kisses. Tears of joy ran in quantities and such emotions were heartwarming to view. Then she felt his eyes on her and she turned.

She froze as she looked at him, and he somehow looked even more handsome and more strong than she had remembered. His beautiful golden hair had been cut short in a primitive fashion; who had done that she wondered? Her displeasure was obvious. His clothes were that of a stable boy; where had they come from she thought? He did look tired and drawn with a covering of dry dust from a barren path, but he was still her beautiful Dainn and how she loved him. They held the gaze and the umbilical cord of love started running with life again. It twitched and pulsed and she could feel herself moving towards him with trembling legs. She walked slowly at first, fearful that her unsteady limbs would buckle beneath her but also terrified that she was dreaming and scared that he would be snatched away from her arms again. They were so immersed in their own vacuum that not a sound outside of their trance was audible, not a quiver could be felt; just the umbilical chord that held them together that was reeling her in. She felt herself walking quickly. Then she began to run. Faster than she had run before. Faster than a horse. Faster than the wind. She felt as though she was flying. Her feet didn't touch the ground. But it was Dainn twirling her through the air and holding on to her for dear life.

'How I've missed you,' and he kissed her face a thousand times.

'I didn't stop praying for you. I knew you would return, I knew I would see you again.' She could barely speak through his bouquet of kisses and her rivers of tears.

'You are the hare Ajeya, the all knowing and powerful hare that can see things before anyone else.'

She smiled and cried and gave thanks to her totem. 'I've missed you so much.'

'So tell me what have you been doing my little hare. I have had to imagine it for the last nine months, so now you can tell me.'

'Apart from missing you and sending powerful thoughts to protect you, you mean?' she hugged him.

He laughed.

'Come with me, I will show you what I have been doing. Let me take you around the camp. Let me show what our people have done. It is truly incredible.'

She led him around the impressive fortress with the high gates, stone towers and timbered keeps, where a deep ditch and solid walls were part of the reinforced defence system. Ballistas and huge catapults stood like sentries. A stone courtyard was surrounded by outhouses, storehouses, stables, a blacksmith and sheds full of weapons. The pastures were green and lush with oats and barley; with the smell of pollen on the wind amid the sweetest detection of wine; and fields yielding fruits that stretched away for miles. A squadron of bees could be heard as they darted through the air, drawn to the subtlest scent of herbs and plants. And the solid lodges were now reinforced and built with stone upon granite foundations.

'Have I been away this long?' his voice was pitched in disbelief as his eyes looked on in awe.

'Yes you have and it's been far too long.'

She took his hand and led him to the cavernous Meeting House with a watchtower at one end rising twenty feet above the Blessing Tree and loomed over the magnificent waterwheel.

The hall was sombre and quiet. She took him to the smaller blessing tree that clung on to its own small ribbons of hope and fortune.

'I came here most evening for my own private vigil,' her voice was tight. 'I never gave up hope, I never stopped believing.'

'Neither did I my love, despite everything, I never gave up hope. You were my shining light at the end of a very long tunnel and I looked up to the hare in the moon every single night.' He kissed her face. 'When I was imprisoned I dreamed of the day that I would be holding you in my arms. I would close my eyes and imagine us standing on a marbled balcony of a gold encrusted palace, the walls and floors adorned with jewels and mirrors, and the brightest, biggest moon was looking down on us.' Ajeya had half closed her eyes.

'We both wore the crowns of royalty; you were an Empress and I was an Emperor and we governed the subject kingdoms where everyone admired us for our compassion, our fortitude, our strength and our leadership.' His voice lifted with a passion at every octave and his head rose with it.

She looked at him out of the corner of her eye, a smile tugging at her mouth. She tried to press it back as it broke across her face. He caught her trying to stifle the outburst and then he was laughing with her. Then, without either of them seeming to move, she was in his arms again, giggling and sobbing and clutching each other.

'Don't get me wrong Dainn,' she croaked through her tears. 'I don't doubt that we would make a fine pair of monarchs; but really,' she giggled again. 'I think we will have to make do with leading the Hill Fort Tribe.'

He laughed with her until her next question bought him back to the realms of reality.

'What happened to you in Ataxata?' she asked, wiping her eyes with the back of her hand. 'What really happened out there?'

'I will tell you all about it one day my love. But for now all you need to know is that all the stolen boys are safe and well. We were saved from the pits of a hell by a courageous woman like yourself; her name is Skyrah from the Clan of the Mountain Lion. We believe that the Emperor and his forces are now weakened by her intervention. But we will strike back, we have to

259

strike back because it isn't over.' His voice was grim and his face was blank. 'We have to get an army together now and attack the Ataxatan forces. We cannot risk anything like that happening again. We are weak against them. We have to step up now. We have to prepare ourselves. We have to fight back.' His breathing was shallow and he clenched his fists at the thought.

She held onto his arm. 'I have been training our people,' she began. 'In case those soldiers came back again. I have been teaching everyone how to fight. Keao has been helping me. All the men, most of the women, and lots of children, they have all been taught.' She was on a roll and her voice tripped effortlessly. 'I can take you to our armoury. You have seen our weapon store. We are ready.'

He looked at her in wonder, his face was full of admiration. 'So that's what father was talking about when he said that you were the most incredible woman that he had known.'

'Alongside Peira and Jena and most of the women here,' she smiled humbly.

'Yes, there are lots of strong women; I just happen to think my love is the strongest.'

She smiled at the accolade. 'So when do we fight?'

'It will be soon, I know that. Messengers are being sent out right now and word will get to us within the next few weeks. We believe the Ataxatan force is weakened right now, so we have got a passage of time. But for now I want to put all of that behind me and celebrate coming home. I want to enjoy my first evening back here with you again and forget about what happened in Ataxata. We have all the time in the world for that story another time.'

She reached up and kissed his face. 'Of course, only when you are ready. Today is the first day of the rest of our lives; let's get ready for the celebration.'

The food was incredible that night; in place of gruel with stale bread and rotten meat; they dined on fresh caught fish and bread still warm from the oven with cured mutton, fresh carrots, potatoes and wild mushrooms. And for afters; apples baked with ginger, blackberries soaked in honey, wild pears simmered in ale, and all the wine they could drink.

The huge outdoor fireplace burned hotter and hotter as more ash and wood was added and formed a centrepiece as the clan began to move away from the tables full of food and into the centre to celebrate with song.

A drum began to beat rhythmically and people began to tap on anything that was near; the ground, a mug, a knee; then the wind pipes came in; a haunting melody that was lifted by the breeze and transcended around the camp like a plume. Women began to hum a high octave while the men thrummed a deep guttural sound. A woman's voice began to sing out with passion and the beating got faster and faster. Then the same woman put an instrument to her mouth and began playing on a jaw harp. The most incredible haunting sounds seemed to connect all of nature and its surrounding cosmos in a staccato of octaves.

The harp trailed off as the drum took over and in a burst of exuberance, Dainn landed in the centre of the group with his feet thumping and his hands clapping; he pulled Ajeya into the centre and together they danced in perfect time with each other. She moved forwards and backwards with him, meeting together then out again, taking a turn round the edge of the circle, skipping, jumping, but laughing most of all. Round and round they went and then started the whole thing over again. Dainn lifted her into air amid a cacophony of shrill excitement and then put her down gently when Keao entered, and in an amazing display of high kicks and long leaps, began to weave his way round Ajeya. The crowd were shrieking with laughter as the two men linked arms and in a series of acrobatic moves and dare devil antics, entertained the throng with their much admired theatrical displays. There were shouts of joyous approval, feet stomping, hand clapping and those who still had a beer in their hand, slurred it all over the dance floor in unrivalled appreciation. Women began to join them, the children were dancing as well, and as the music changed tempo again, everyone by now was moving in time to the beat.

Hagen and Jena sashayed and swayed to the rhythm in beautiful intoxicating moves. She tingled within his warm embrace and held onto his strong arms tightly. But Hagen had something on his mind; something of high importance to discuss and it couldn't wait any longer. So, in a series of intricate Samba steps, he led her out of the circle to a patch of lush green grass. He held her hand while she lowered herself to the ground and then sitting beside her, took in a long deep sniff while he orchestrated his words. She knew what he was going to ask. They had been in this very same position eighteen years ago and she picked at the daisies while she waited for him to punctuate his words.

Finally he was ready and he took her hand. 'Jena, I asked you once if you would marry me, and you said when the Emperor is dead that you would do me the honour of being my wife.'

'She nodded her head. 'Yes I remember Hagen, I remember it well.'

'Well here we are, eighteen years later, and I am an old man now. I feel that sometimes I can barely move, but every beat of my heart beats for you Jena, and you are still that rare jewel and the most beautiful, mesmerising woman I have ever known.'

She stroked his face.' My handsome, beautiful Hagen. How I love you.'

He kissed her hands. 'So my love. My Jena. I ask you once again, in light of what has happened; the boys return amid whisperings of the Emperor's demise, and I am sure they must be founded. So please, my Jena, will you do me the very great honour of becoming my wife?'

Tears came immediately to her eyes, her face flushed and she felt her heart quicken.

He responded quickly to her emotions. 'What's the matter, have I said something wrong again?'

Her voice was shaky and she wiped away a tear. 'No Hagen, you have said nothing wrong. I love you with all my heart. I should have married you years ago, but I always thought the gods would punish me even more. But they never did punish me did they. Everything was a gift to make me stronger and set an example for my beautiful, strong, courageous daughter to follow. Even the boar attacking me was a sign and the scar on my leg is a reminder of my own humility and my own destiny. I can see that now.'

He kissed her hands. 'I have always believed in the gods' judgement, no matter how difficult it seems at the time. But you had to find that out for yourself.' He kissed her face. 'The boar found you Jena and gave his life for you. He is your totem guide.'

'Yes, it's taken me a long time to find that out,' her voice was humble.

'Sometimes it takes people longer than others.' His hand was placed reassuringly on her knee. 'But we found each other. Ajeya and Dainn found each other. Red and Keao found each other.'

'All because of the boar,' her smile broke through.

'Yes all because of the boar,' his grin was even wider. 'So, are you going to keep me waiting even longer for my answer?'

'Of course it is a yes,' she beamed. 'And even if the rumours about the Emperor's demise are untrue, I do not fear any reproach now, and nothing would make me happier than to be your wife.'

That same evening Dainn and Ajeya had disappeared into their cave and Dainn lit a fire, and as Hagen and Jena slept under the stars on that bright starry night, Dainn and Ajeya cocooned themselves in front of the bright dancing flames.

'Do you remember the time you were trying to guess my totem?'

'I do,' she responded, feeling the warmth of his arms around her.

'And in all this time have you thought about it any more?'

She reached up to touch his face. 'I have been a little busy actually,' her voice was playful and full of love.

'So you are telling me that you still don't know then,' he answered the question for her.

She kissed his hands. 'I think I will wait for that special day to find out.' And she pressed his hand to her cheek.

'That's exactly what I was hoping you would say.'

The flames matched his elation and rose high into the crevasse of the canopy.

'So, are you asking me then?' she finished the question for him.

'I am Ajeya, I am asking you to be my wife.'

She turned round to face him. The glow of the flames lit up his face and his golden hair looked like a halo against the dark backdrop of the cave. His piercing blue eyes shone out at her and the strength in his heart matched the passion in hers. She kissed him passionately and held his face in her hands.

'Of course I will marry you. I love you.'

35

The double wedding was held in the Meeting House exactly two weeks later. The congregation was still in high spirits with all of the boys safely returned. Keao and Rufus took the honorary position of ring bearers while Red had been selected as attendant for Jena and Ajeya. Inside, the intricate weavings of Peira's ensemble music drifted from inside the cavernous complex and spilled out onto the manicured lawns amid a sensual aroma of rose and pine.

The centrepiece and epitome was undoubtedly the magnificent waterwheel which was festooned with climbing ivy and entwined with a rambling rose. The structure's cog turned and rumbled as its very heart pumped water through its veins and a cascade of shimmering lights festooned with golden particles brought an abundance of beautiful flying creatures attracted to the structure.

Hagen and Dainn entered the hall by way of the huge double doors at the front where even more jasmine and fragrant honeysuckle could be seen wrapped around the ornate gold and turquoise carved oak pillars; and the sunlight bounced off bronze copper vases ablaze with the rich vibrant colours of a summer's day. Intricate tile work ran across the ceiling in patterns of gold edged flowers and looked down onto a thousand mahogany chairs below. The occupants of the tribe were seated and Colom stood by the Blessing Tree waiting for them at the end of the aisle. Hagen and Dainn walked slowly through the Meeting House where they acknowledged those people furthest away with a wave and shook the hands of those that were nearest to them. They were preceded by Keao and Rufus who held aloft the rings on small plump cushions and when they reached the altar, took their places on the grand thrones set aside for special occasions. With the sound of a drum beating softly and a hushed flute chanting melancholy in the background, they waited for their brides.

The two men spent a few moments taking in the atmosphere and ambience and sat quietly immersed in private conversation with each other. Then, as if by magic, all chatter was interrupted by a gasp from the congregation and they knew that there was nothing more elegant in the room. Jena and Ajeya stood at the back and shared a smile as they began the long walk to take their places at the end of the aisle. Colom stood there waiting for them, his eyes as bright as The Blessing Tree which was ablaze with colour and almost sang out in harmony with the sounds from the ensemble.

They both wore a dress of ivory samite and lined with a silver satin, the silver and gold threads blinked in the sunlight as it poured through the stain glass windows and lit up the outline. Jena's was a tight bodice with a full skirt; pulled in securely with laces at the back, her dark hair was scooped up in loose curls and she wore a single purple orchid in the side. Her hands clasped a bouquet of violets entwined with the lilac gossamer of a thistle, and she wore the subtlest fragrance with a hint of lavender.

Ajeya's stunning golden locks shimmered against the thread in her dress that clung on to every curve and emphasised her magnificent shape. The amber necklace that she always displayed complemented her elegance and sent spectrums of brilliance across the pavilion. She wore a garland of daisies in her hair and held a spray of primroses secured with a wreath of lemon braid. Her fragrance was one with a hint of citrus which blended in lightly with the posy she carried. Behind them followed Red in a blushed silk satin robe with her auburn hair tumbling down her back in soft ringlets; and she scattered fresh petals of purple and yellow roses where their soft doeskin slippers skimmed the voluminous floor.

The music stopped as they reached Colom. Both men looked upon their women with pride. Hagen thought his heart had missed several beats, while Dainn had momentarily stopped breathing.

Both couples took their places on the ornate thrones. Red took the bouquets and sat behind them. The hushed audience eagerly anticipated Colom's words.

'Honoured guests and fellow countrymen, I am

so very privileged and honoured to welcome everyone here to witness a very extraordinary but beautiful union of these people into the special bond of marriage; and to perform this union inside this magnificent Meeting House fills me with immense happiness, pride and exultation.'

Nods and hushed whispers echoed round the hall.

'A wedding such as this, where a mother and daughter share this auspicious and grand occasion is a joy, and we thank the gods that Jena and Hagen, Ajeya and Dainn were destined to meet each other and we pray that they will live a long and happy life together.'

The couples acknowledged Colom as he continued; 'Marriage means so many things to different people; so I ask Hagen to speak first and tell his bride why he has chosen her to become his wife.'

Hagen took Jena's hand and spoke with love and affection. 'Once in a while, right in the middle of an ordinary life, the gods give us the person who will make their lives whole again; a person who will fill a void that had been so empty for so long.' He took a deep breath in memory of Keao's mother.' I have loved this woman for eighteen years, and for eighteen years I have waited for her to say that she will marry me. However, during all that time I knew that she was part of my soul; the woman who completes me and I will continue to honour her, protect her and love her with all my heart.'

For the first time in eighteen years he had

thought of Raine, his beautiful wife who had died in childbirth. She would be looking down on him now, with a smile on her face and a glint in her eye, she would embrace this union and she would love Jena as much as he did. He felt the warmth in his heart and knew she would be happy for him. He kissed Jena's hands and lowered his gaze while she composed herself to offer her accolade.

'And Jena,' Colom look at her with smiling eyes. 'Please will you respond with your words of love for Hagen.'

She had to wipe away a tear and sniff back the sting in her eye. She was such a fortunate woman, and the love in her soul was immeasurable. Taking a deep breath, she spoke from the heart. 'Hagen, you know how much I love you. You know that you are my destiny and that I was meant to find you; and though we have waited eighteen years for this day, nothing would have been different had we married all that time ago. I love you for enriching my life and making me a stronger person. I love you for bringing Keao into our lives, a young boy who helped Ajeya all those years ago and who has now given us a beautiful grandson. I love you for being you, for your kind heart, for your passion and because I know that no one could love me as much as you do.' She too kissed his hands and lowered her gaze to the floor.

Ajeya was so proud of her parents in every way. They had loved her and supported her, especially when she had wanted to practise training with Keao as a little girl. And Keao, what a fine brother she had; she couldn't have wished for a more loving sibling. But the reference to eighteen years made her think. Was Hagen not her father? She could not remember a time before him, and everything she could remember included him. But he had said eighteen years and she was twenty years old now. Keao was thirty. It didn't make sense. Perhaps he had made a mistake. Of course, he had blurted out an error in his excitement. That was the answer. Of course it was. But wait, her mother had said thank you for bringing Keao into our lives. The young boy who helped me as a young child. I don't understand. He's my brother. What does that mean, what could it all mean?

Colom's voice brought her out of her quandary and she faced her great love.

'And Dainn, could you please continue why you wish to take Ajeya as your bride.'

'My beautiful Ajeya, whom I have known since I can remember; who, as a small child had me mesmerised with her strength, her knowledge and her beauty. From the first time I met you I knew there was something special about you. A warm, loving, beautiful girl who has shown me on so many occasions the true meaning of love. And then we were cruelly parted - but it only served to make me love you more - and my time in captivity made me realise that being deeply loved gives you strength, but lovingly deeply gives you courage - Ajeya, I will love you forever.'

The congregation felt the warmth of his

sincerity feed around the hall. Peira wiped the tears from her cheeks, having wondered on so many occasions if he would find true love; and now she couldn't be happier.

'And Ajeya if you could respond to Dainn.'

She looked up to him and smiled. 'My strong courageous Dainn, who I have learned so much from. We are so in tune with each other that I can sense how you are feeling even when there are hundreds of miles between us. We have shared so many memories that they are stored in my heart for ever. I want to have children with you and share our knowledge and our love and secure a dynasty that is made up of trust, loyalty and respect. I trust you, I respect you, and will always be loyal to you. And with every beat of my heart, I will always love you.'

Jena listened to her sentiments, she heard every word. She warmed hearing the reference to children and remembered that the Emperor had told her all those years ago that no man would ever love Ajeya or want to have children with her; for they would be too repulsed by her disfigurement. And yet here she was, about to marry a man amongst men, a leader amongst leaders and a spirit who loved her daughter as much as she did. No one saw the disfigurement any more. All they saw was a fine young woman, who was courageous in spirit and steadfast in commitment. They saw a woman who's beauty radiated love.

Colom's voice filled the auditorium again. 'Thank you, all of you, those words are timeless and

273

heartfelt. They support the tribute of why marriage is so special to those who love and want to share their devotion. So now we will bond these people with our customary ritual - Keao, could you bring me the sword.'

The young father stepped forward and lifted the guilt edged sword from its resting place and gave it to Colom. The body was wiped with the ceremonial ribbons and the couples knelt before the weapon. At the same time they pressed their thumb on an opposite blade and waited for the blood to run. Then they pressed their thumbs together and felt their bodies become one.

Colom lifted the sword and proclaimed: 'Today we have witnessed the joining of these people. They have declared their love in front of honoured guests and loved ones. The spirits have looked down on them and have blessed them all.'

He gave the sword back to Keao to wipe clean.

'Let nothing part these souls. Let no one come between them. Let the enemy weaken in their presence. When danger is near the other will know. When sadness is abound, the other will feel it. Their totems have become as one, their souls are now a single entity. This is the word of the gods.' He held up his arms to the embossed ceiling and waited. After a few minutes of silence Colom held out his hands to conduct the next part of the ceremony.

'Who has the rings that will bind these people in marriage?'

'I do, I have the rings,' said Rufus. And he

placed them on the blade that Keao held so proudly.

Colom took each ring in turn and blessed them. He then handed the sword for each couple to take their respective ring. 'These rings are a symbol of your love. There is no beginning or end, love is everlasting and bound in these solid circles for ever.'

The captive audience held their breath as each couple took their ring, kissed it and placed it on their betrothed's finger. Jena's ring displayed the image of the boar, carved out to remind her how this animal changed her life, while Hagen had the eagle engraved to symbolise his freedom. Ajeya looked at the fine workmanship of the hare chasing on her band, epitomising infinity and everlasting love, and Dainn's bore the image of the stag; for strength, intelligence and valour.

Colom placed Jena's hands inside Hagen's.
'And now please declare the covenant of marriage.'
He held their hands together as they proclaimed the vow as one.
'By the Hill Fort Tribe we pledge our our love,
We swear by the soil and water and all that surrounds us,
We swear by The Eagle and The Boar that protect us,
We swear by the gods and the spirits who look down on us.
We swear by all those who are present. This is our word.'

They stepped back and allowed Ajeya and Dainn to step forward. Colom placed Ajeya's hands inside Dainn's. 'And now will you two please declare the covenant of marriage.' He held their hands together as they proclaimed the vow as one.

'By the Hill Fort Tribe we pledge our our love,
We swear by the soil and water and all that surrounds us,
We swear by The Stag and The Hare that protect us,
We swear by the gods and the spirits who look down on us.
We swear by all those who are present.
This is our word.'

Colom smiled at the union. 'I now offer you to tie your ribbons on the Blessing Tree. A small gesture for a life of plenty. For this oak is born from the tiny acorn, which, as a seed, is full of nature, knowledge and truth. Our Blessing Tree is an indication of the power of nature at an unseen level, for its very roots and life giving tendrils are as vast as the tree that we see above. We might start as the acorn, but we grow and age like the mighty oak as we advance through our own lives. And all of you, as you grow with knowledge and spread your wings, be sure to take care of that which is unseen, for that is the true meaning of life.'

The newly weds approached the tree and Jena took a purple ribbon from her bouquet and tied it on a branch. Then Hagen removed a small green cord from his pocket and wrapped his offering next to hers. Ajeya stepped forward and secured a lemon braid from her posy and Dainn took a golden strand from his wristband and secured it next to hers. They then prayed to the spirits before Colom swore the concluding rites.

'In the presence of the gods and spirits and animal totems, and with these people here present, I now pronounce you both husband and wife. Go and enjoy the day with your friends, enjoy the occasion with your loved ones and enjoy your lives as married couples.'

After Colom's final words, the newly weds turned to walk up the aisle to their new life together. The path led to the celebration green where the musicians were playing and a wedding banquet was waiting.

Under the protection of the outdoor Blessing Tree, the first few notes of the reed pipes began to shiver across the lawn and the guests formed an arch. Not taking their eyes off each other and keeping their pierced thumbs together, they crouched through the arch amid the calls of well wishes and cheers. The women of the congregation picked up ribbons of pure silk and made circles around the two couples; entwining them and binding them as the material brushed against their bodies. Dainn had Ajeya's hand and pulled her closer into him; Hagen led Jena and together they paraded round the enclosure as the ribbons curled wildly and passionately casting a rainbow of colour at every turn.

Children threw petals at them; the men threw

coins at them, the drums beat like a hundred hearts and the flutes whispered through the silks. And above the festival of love, the gong sounded its deep sonorous call, bursting into a wave of shrill tones which echoed across the throng.

In the courtyard the spit was turning, the cauldrons were simmering. The smell of freshly baked bread, pies and cakes were wafting. Sweet aromatic fragrances of infused wine, of orange and ginger deserts, of cinnamon and lemon cakes, tantalised the tastebuds. And amid the raucous laughter of speeches, anecdotes, renditions and song, the bridal party celebrated until the early hours, and when it was time to sleep, those who couldn't make it back to their lodges, were happy to just lay where they fell, under a canopy of stars and a bright full moon.

36

Over the next few weeks Dainn and Ajeya were so engrossed in military tactics that they barely had a moment in the day to enjoy their time together as newly weds. Ajeya attended meetings and training sessions while Dainn discussed logistics and troop movements. Hardly an hour passed when either one of them wasn't embroiled in the finest details from overseeing the operation of the newly constructed Ballistas to the best method of transporting the rocks onto the battlefield.

The tribe were preparing for the biggest battle in the history of clan life. The men had begun to feel restless now and eager to get on with their tasks and rid this General once and for all. Mothers and wives began foraging and preparing vast amounts of wholesome nutritious food to build them up. The massive cauldrons were continually simmering on the hearths with something gastronomically delightful. The stables were restocked with fresh straw and hay daily. The horses were constantly pampered and groomed, put out to grass in the day and brought back to their warm stables at evensong.

The blacksmith and newly appointed armourer had made a selection of mail shirts, mail leggings, protective headgear, gauntlets and a collection of weapons that included a two handed sword, a battle axe, a mace, a dagger, a lance, as well as reinforced spears and double edged swords. The best archers would use the mahogany bows with ivory tipped arrows. Foot soldiers were drilled with the use of shields. The cavalry were instructed to charge.

Stroking the proud arched neck of her horse Moonlight, Ajeya called out to the recently assembled cavalry. 'I know that these beasts can be easily frightened and they become skittish at the slightest movement, but a trained cavalry horse is quite a different thing.'

She stood high in the saddle and instructed her foot soldiers to stand their ground with their shields in place. 'Do not falter, do not waver, stand your ground.'

She wheeled her horse around and cantered back some distance. Then wielding her sword gave the battle cry and galloped towards the shield wall. Moonlight felt her passion and determination and with the sight of the outstretched sword in her peripheral vision kept charging towards the wall until Ajeya turned her off to the side. She reined her horse to a halt and addressed the cavalry chargers.

'Yes these animals are gentle giants who eat only oats and grass, but with your strength and courage they will give themselves to you and will be your guides as we attack our enemy.'

As the hours became days, the cavalry had mock battles on their chargers and learned to become as one; guiding their horses with their knees and shooting a hail of arrows into the raised shields. Other targets had been placed adjacent to the shields and the riders would turn in their saddles to fire even more arrows into those targets. Every man who took part in the displays was fuelled with the power of revenge and each target became the face of the General or the heart of the Emperor. And while Ajeya looked on from the sides, atop of Moonlight, they both embraced their fellow warriors. The Hill Fort Tribe had gone from simple farmers to an elite army in a matter of weeks and with Ajeya and Dainn at the helm; every man, woman and child felt unbeatable.

The day was warming towards noon when the sighting was called from the watchtower. The two approaching men were the messengers on route with the long awaited news. They were in full gallop by the time they reached the fort on the far side of the forest.

37

The General's party had a two day ride. Behind him marched a thousand soldiers, half on horseback and half again on foot. His spies had informed him that there was no army in the region and so he was revelling in his glory already; for victory had been his at every turn. He rode at complete ease, his hands loose on the rein and his white gloves crisp and clean without one crease or blemish.

This was the man who instilled fear at his very name and had brought the clans and royalty to their knees; killing some, enslaving many, but with no regard for human life whatsoever; and now with the Empire of Ataxata, its provinces and all surrounding land within his grasp, his greed and hunger had no boundaries at all.

He had decided to go through the pass of the Giant's Claw which took them past rivers, ravines and mountains on their course back to the borders. This was Clan domain and it had to be taken at all cost, this would become part of his growing Empire now. All subjects would be massacred; not one infant would be left alive to come looking for him in years to come. He didn't want to spend the rest of his life looking over his shoulder. No, they all had to go. The cavalry clattered its way along the palace roads and out of the city at dusk. Lights were on in the small pink houses and curtains twitched nervously as the entourage rode out of town. The hard stone road that gave away the cavalry morphed into soft green verges and a light summer breeze pushed small dark clouds to shower and bring the scent of primroses from grassy mounds.

Compounds of condensation billowed from wide nostrils. Rustling armour and chain mail signalled a dense layer of bodies and beasts. Each soldier and captain strode forward, navigating the others uniformly. They were focused, anxious, silently praying and preparing for the discipline of battle. With the army behind him immersed in their own thoughts, the General reined his horse to a halt.

'We must rest now,' he said at last finding a dense area of forest with the mountain range on the horizon. 'We must collect our thoughts and remember why we are here. Remember no man or boy must be left alive and the girl must be taken alive to be my prisoner. Do you all understand that?' He looked at them severely as a thousand faces nodded to him. 'If anyone harms that girl I will personally disembowel him.' His smile was cruel as he savoured the image. 'We will leave at first light. Any man not in line when I am ready to leave will be hung by the neck.'

'When do we attack the clan my lord?' asked a rogue dweller, eager for his first taste of blood.

'We attack at dusk. That is always the best hour

283

in my experience. They are seldom prepared and never expect a twilight raid. So rest now; for tomorrow will be a long day for all of us, but remember, it will yield the greatest prize.'

They all dismounted and loosely tied their horses to the branches, the soldiers and captains helped with the weapons; they took off most of their cumbersome clothing and made themselves as comfortable as they could. The down and outs, rogues and thieves made jests in hushed voices, they didn't care what lay ahead or who they killed, they just wanted to sever some limbs and be paid handsomely for the joy of it. But the soldiers and captains who had sworn allegiance to the Emperor in waiting knew that those men would not be paid at all and most would not return home anyway.

The tall soldier pines and gnarled old oaks closed around them. The trees were huge and dark, menacing and threatening. Their limbs wove through one another and creaked with every breath of wind and their higher branches scratched at the hare in the moon. The woods were full of whispers and even the nocturnal animals and insects hid away from them.

As General Domitrius Corbulo and his army turned in for the night, a group of six clan men went unnoticed as they slid down the trees and made their way to a concealed river. They took delivery of their horses and split into three directions.

'May the gods be with you,' Kal whispered. 'I will go to the Clan of the Giant's Claw with Jonha.

Sable and Godan go to Hill Fort Tribe. Nema and Bray go back and tell Laith at the Clan of the Mountain Lion. The General is on the move and will attack at dusk tomorrow.'

'To Freedom!'

They all raised their arms in a salute and disappeared into the night to deliver their news.

38

The gates were dragged open and the men cantered in sending a hail of dust on their arrival, the first one dismounted quickly before his charger had come to a full stop, the other pulled his horse's head into an arch before jumping off. Dainn had already been alerted and was there ready to greet them. Storm had also spotted them and was the next to arrive. A groom rushed over to take the reins and led their drenched snorting horses to the stables.

'We come with news,' said Sable catching his breath.

'Come, we shall go to the Meeting House at once,' said Dainn, guiding the way. 'Storm, gather everyone. We must all hear this together.'

Peira and Jena prepared the welcoming drinks and were busy making fresh bread and mutton pies for the entire congregation.

Sable and Godan were in grim talks inside the yawn of the doors with Colom and Dainn as Storm and the other imprisoned boys rushed back and listened in on the proceedings. Shaking heads were interspersed with concerned gasps, and nodding heads met with thin smiles.

Worried faces filed in amid murmurs of raised whispers. Speculation and trepidation filled the room and the air of discontent could be split with a knife.

When all of the tribe where seated, Dainn called for hush. The varied tones trailed off and at last he could introduce the men. 'Thank you everyone for coming here so quickly; and I know that this rushed meeting has caused concern for most of you. We live in troubled times and there have been so many changes; so I thank you for your cooperation.' His anguished smile tripped round the hall. 'So without wishing to keep you waiting any longer, I would like you to welcome our guests Sable and Godan from the Clan of the Mountain Lion. These men have brought us news of the General and I now hand you over to Sable who will endeavour to fill you in.'

Sable bowed to Dainn, and standing next to Godan, began to share what they had been told.

'Good afternoon good people of the Hill Fort Tribe, my clan send their warmest wishes and want to share their gratitude with the gods for bringing our boys home safely.'

Stamping feet and raised voices acknowledged his well meaning words.

'I know that we share a common enemy that must be eradicated.'

Murmurs of agreement echoed round the chambers.

'We recently had a visit from someone who worked at the Palace. This informant is to be trusted and comes to us amid concerns for the safety of our clans.' His voice remained stern and grim. 'We all know of the Emperor's and the General's reputation. We are afraid of them. They are both cold, ruthless and vicious in character. They have instilled fear amongst people who thought it was the wolves and bears that deserved our fear. But not so. The Emperor and The General are the most wicked of predators any of us have had to deal with.'

'They are barbarian's,' came a voice from the back.

Jena shivered at the mention of her husband's name. Hagen put a loving arm around her shoulders.

Sable continued. 'For too long the Emperor and the General have been invincible. They have rendered us all helpless with their warfare of fear and dread. They have preyed on the weak and vulnerable. They have attacked the unarmed and the unprepared. They have imprisoned some of our greatest men. ....But today, that regime ends.'

A roar from the crowd went up as Godan stepped forward and waited for the crowd to settle before he could share what they had overheard.

'For the boys that were held captive and treated so appallingly, this news will be welcome, for only they truly know more than anyone the true depravity of the Emperor's rule.'

Once again Jena shuddered and this time her response was matched by Hagen. A hushed crowd awaited the news.

'The Emperor is dead!'

Jena turned to Hagen and sank her head in his embrace with relief. The boys stood and cheered, the roof of the hut nearly came off with the jubilation. They were dancing and swirling Rufus around with such vigour and excitement the leader had to step in.

'Calm down boys there is more to be heard. Please, let Godan finish.'

The clan sat down again amid waves of mumbled excitement tripping along the rows.

'But all is not well,' his voice was solemn with a feeling of apprehension. 'The General survived!'

Groans rumbled around the room.

'He has now been made Emperor in Waiting. With the Emperor's son, Cornelius, missing, General Domitrius Corbulo has been bequeathed the title. When he is sworn in he will have control of the palace, all the estates and all the subject kingdoms.'

'May the gods help us,' Storm's chilling tone came from the side of the room.

'We are the messengers that were sent out to follow him and we now know that the General has summoned an army of a thousand men. A ruthless army from what we have seen; it is made up of rogues and undesirables who are as depraved as their leader.' Godan's voice started to tremble as the next point was waiting to be delivered, so Sable took over.

'He will then take down all the clans and all the people in them. Men, women, children and babes in arms. He believes we are vermin that need to be

289

exterminated.'

The women looked up fearfully to their men.

'How long have we got?' Tay's voice was thick.

The two messengers looked at each other.

Godan found his strong voice again. 'They will attack at dusk tomorrow!'

Gasps went up.

'Are you ready to fight?' shouted out Sable.

A cacophony of roars boomed back at him with vigour.

'We are!' shouted Ajeya, her voice rising above the chorus. 'We are ready!'

The clan were stamping their feet and punching the air as Ajeya led them out of the Meeting House. The two messengers followed her outside and went to speak with the rest of the clan and answer any questions while feasting on the gourmet offerings from the elder women of the tribe.

Keao approached Ajeya. 'So tomorrow it is then. I have been looking forward to this day for so long. At last I can howl my battle cry and drive a sword into that General's heart.'

Ajeya looked at him in horror. 'Keao, please, no, you can't!'

'What do you mean I can't?'

'You have a son and you have only just been reunited. Think of Red. How worried is she going to be?'

'I am doing this for Red,' his voice was waning.

'The General is a monster with deviants in his

army, I do not want you to risk your life Keao. You have done enough. You have trained everyone here, you have instilled powers that they never knew they had. You have completed your part to get revenge. Please stay at home with your wife and your son where it is safe.'

He was shaking his head in disbelief. 'So I am supposed to stay back and watch you go off to fight alongside many of the other women, and await your triumphant return knowing that I did nothing to help.'

'But you have done so much Keao. You taught me everything. I have shared that knowledge with Dainn. You have shared it with the clan. You have done everything to help.'

He was shaking his head again. 'No. No, I am fighting with the rest of you. I have scores to settle. And you may think that I am too old and too weak to fight now and that I have lost my edge.... and you may be right.... but I have to do this for my son and for my wife to show how much I love them.'

She took his hands and kissed them tenderly, she had seen the passion in his eyes and heard the strength in his voice. Who was she to stop him? She sighed heavily in defeat. 'I'm sorry, forgive me. It will be an honour to fight alongside you on the battlefield.' She hugged him tightly and sniffed back the tears, but from that moment on she would beg her totem, and his, to watch over him as he sought justice against the General of Ataxata.

39

Brilliant sunshine hailed the November morning that day, dappling the land in a dazzling display of moving light and shadow. The wind had dropped to a mere whisper and in the stillness a rich earthy scent caressed the anxious soldiers. Men were sharpening their weapons again and had smeared themselves with the indigo of ground woad mixed with animal fat. Peira said the anti-bacterial properties would protect them and give them extra healing powers. The foot soldiers had been deployed early to secure their posts with their own instructions ringing in their ears; to operate in line for maximum impact and not be outflanked by the opponents, and every soldier had sworn an oath to never make another man his shield. With these words ingrained onto their souls, the battle was now their focus.

The cavalry were waiting anxiously, their mail rattling and their war horses pawing in anticipation. This was an historical moment for the tribe as Dainn and Ajeya had prepared them for victory; to set a precedence and end the brutal regime forever.

Dainn spoke like he had never spoken before; he had the heart of a warrior and had taken his position like a true leader; valiant, strong and determined. 'Let us go now as warriors and those who give their lives for the safety of the clan, may your resting place be divine and may you be richly rewarded in your next life.' He bowed his head solemnly and prayed to the gods and spirit guides for strength and fortitude. His gaze settled on his comrades. 'Until we meet again!' He saluted his people and he embraced Ajeya and Keao. 'Fill your souls with fire! Fill your lungs with determination! Fill your hearts with passion and together we will be victorious!'

As dusk stained the steppes a vivid hue of crimson, Ajeya and Dainn urged forward the first canter of the newly formed cavalry. The rumble on the ground cleared the aisle of anything in their path; ground squirrels scampered for cover as grasses leaned out of the way, while birds and insects flew in the other direction, even hundred year old oaks drunkenly supported each other as they parted the way for the masses. Ajeya thundered across the plains with an odd mixing of elation and fear. She shot a look over to Keao. He was so strong and valiant, but did he still have his instincts about him, could he still conceal himself and focus to have the invisibility of his totem? Mastering weapons technique on the training ground was one thing, but how would he perform in battle? He had worried about her for so much of her young life, and now it was her turn to be concerned.

She felt the flats tremble beneath her and the

horses hooves rumbled ever closer to their destination. Onwards they went, an entire force of clans and their allies, all intend on ridding the stain of the Ataxatan Empire for good.

They picked up the pace. Keao waved the banner and then the opening to the battle field could be seen. They filed in ceremoniously and slowed when they saw the other clans.

'Thank the gods,' Dainn exclaimed pulling up his horse. 'The Clan of the Mountain are over there, and look how many men they have gathered.'

The Hill Fort Tribe whooped and yelled in absolute elation.

'There's Namir waving the banner leading his troops, look how tall he sits.' said Dainn.

'And I can see Lyall beside him, oh how he has waited for this day,' cheered Storm.

'And look who sits alongside them both,' yelled out Ajeya seeing another girl.

'That's Skyrah, she's the one who saved us,' said Dainn.

'Another remarkable woman then,' Ajeya nodded her head in appreciation and admired her strength from afar.

Dainn gripped her hand with his own and kissed it tenderly.

'Look at Tore and Lace,' said Ajeya recognising them straight away. 'They are coming from the other side and just look at the masses they have with them.'

They all stared at the vision before them; their

spears a hedge and their shields a wall, and then the tumultuous shouting and yelling began with the banging of shields and the armies moved forward.

The General wouldn't have seen the joyful faces in front of him and he wouldn't have seen the sheer mass of young men and women filing in from the flanks. His army was still charging through the very centre of the pass. The clan's torches kept on coming baring flags and banners of power. The Ataxatan army looked beaten already. From that moment they knew that the clan's soldiers could out do the General's and that they could slay twice as many as their own number. That's what gave them unfathomable strength and determination as they stood their ground defiantly.

Dainn breathed in the enormous power from the generating wind and bellowed out his order to move in. Three hundred blades left their scabbards in flight and the entire force of the clans leaped to the attack, storming over the battle field towards the General who was rushing towards them like an angered flood. The ground shook with the stampeding sound of horse's hooves thumping rhythmically into the grass lined plain and the earth trembled as a thousand foot soldiers ran in to support them. They didn't have time to panic; adrenalin and a much greater force took over and carried them along with a concoction of excitement and fear.

Ajeya's voice rose in power above the din of the galloping horses, shouting out her war cry. 'Fill yourselves with vengeance, for only then will vengeance be ours.'

A great roar went up from the soldiers and they surged forward to meet the ranks of the enemy. She leaned in to Moonlight's quickening pace, tightening her grip on to her reins as she urged the filly on. Foot soldiers with spears and daggers ran in first to cause as much chaos and slaughter as they could.

Dainn reached for his weapon whilst in a gallop and swiftly fixed a bow to the string of his crossbow and sent it flying through the air into the jugular of his first victim. Another arrow was taken that followed the first into the heart of another assailant. Godan came in with the advance and sent in a squadron of archers to deploy their weapons. Ajeya sped off in another direction with Keao and Storm, firing their arrows and catapults as they moved in.

Moonlight set her hoofs in the ground while Ajeya dismounted and nocked an arrow. She let her mind go dark and focused like she had been taught all those years ago. Nothing else mattered now. 'Be like an animal,' she told herself. 'They slow their heartbeats to a near standstill, so their body heat drops and their scent disappears. They become invisible.' The smell of death buzzed around her; dirt and the ravages of war landed on her face and in her hair, arrows flew so close that she could feel the whisper of its flight. Grass ants crawled up her legs and bit her, but she didn't flinch. To them, she was nothing. To them she was invisible. To the soldiers she was an animal in the grass.

A soldier was standing close, sniffing the air

with his nose, looking for a victim, searching out something to kill. He had spotted Dainn. Ajeya stood her ground; invisible, silent, unmoving. This human couldn't be detected. She sent the swiftness of the hare into her arms. She drew back the arrow, let it loose and it thundered through the air straight into the chest of the unsuspecting assailant. Dainn looked up and nodded to her. He was safe. She looked around for more to slay, she drew again and released the arrow, another one dropped in his path.

Out on the plain the enemy came on, and as soon as they came within range, Ajeya launched another attack on the advancing horde. Every few minutes the hiss of arrows were sent pulsating through the air causing the advancing line of soldiers to topple and sink as they fell under the continual fire. But still they came.

Ajeya leapt on her horse and drawing her sword, called out the war cry of the Hill Fort Tribe again. Further along the line the General's soldiers were being pushed hard by a massive phalanx of spears, thrusting through the shield wall, slashing throats, piercing eyes and severing limbs.

Dainn was locked in a battle with a soldier, they leaned on one another for support as they parried each blow. Both were tiring. The captain of the guard saw his opportunity and took aim with a spear. Keao spotted the impending assault and shouted. 'Dainn, look out!' But Dainn was battle weary now, he had fought so hard for over an hour. Sable saw the minefield unfold in front of him and ran towards the second in command but something hard hit him on the head and he slumped to the ground pitifully waving in a frugal attempt to stop the events. The captain's spear realigned its destination and the weapon left his grasp. It cruised through the air like a missile and hit its target. Dainn collapsed. Ajeya pulled back her bow and hit the captain full on in the chest. He dropped down on the spot clutching the shaft that was rooted to his heart and searched with narrow eyes for where the arrow had come. A tall strong woman stood there, ready to fire again if the first had not been fatal. Storm ran in and plunged his dagger into the captain and rushed to Dainn' side, he was injured but he would survive. Enraged, Godan stormed towards the General's men coming in to finish his comrade off. He swung his sabre into a vicious arc taking a man's head clean from his shoulders. He then went on to decapitate half a dozen others with the force of his blade. As the captain died, Ajeya saluted to Godan and Dainn.

She saw Sable grip his arm in pain as the General's soldier tried to hack it off, she sent an arrow swiftly into the eye of his attacker. That soldier would fight no more. As she remained invisible and concealed she charged through the centre of the fighting, slicing through the enemy with her sword, sending arrows to soldiers to meet their doom. Cutting them down before they knew what had hit them. Longbows began to whisper all along the defences as flights of arrows were shot into the sky and curved in flight to unseat the enemy. The demons ran in all directions like headless chickens looking for a way through.

The struggle continued with neither side giving ground, but then the General's beleaguered army began to yield. Whether it was from pure fatigue of the journey and the fighting, or the effects of the poisoned liquor that still ran through their veins, they began to fall and the General yelled out foul mouthed obscenities as he watched the massacre of his men. Under the grip of panic, many vomited in the soil, it was like watching day old lambs being slaughtered by a pack of wolves. Those that were left were surrounded on all sides and suffered further casualties in their masses. The General called for the cavalry to regroup but they were now further beleaguered having fallen into an explosion of flailing limbs and weapons. One by one the Ataxatan army fell and if one of them was seen staggering, then a punishing blade would finish him off.

He had watched the struggle for more than an hour, his face unyielding any emotion until it was time to act and show everyone just how powerful and fearsome he was. He dismounted his charger and sucked a spear out of a lifeless corpse. The exhausted troops were aimlessly swatting at flies now as the General stood menacingly poised with pure venom pouring through his veins. Arrows deployed into the air hit nothing except a wall of emotion and a static avalanche of loss. The atmosphere was putrid amidst the wrath of war simmering down to a haze of dying groans and men searching inside themselves for redemption. And now, under the enormous pressure of the enemy's numbers, there was no one left from the opposition.

Ajeya was frantically looking around, searching for assailants, her bow ready, her sword at her side, a bloodied dagger in her boot. It was then that she witnessed a disturbance out of the corner of her eye. Dainn was attending to Keao; he was hurt.

Keao had stopped for a second, just a brief moment to collect his thoughts and try to refocus. It was important to concentrate and channel his energy. He had lost some of his vitality in his advancing years and he was not as nimble and fast. She had seen this change in him, she knew he wasn't a man to fight on the field and kill men; to see them suffer slowly and watch their tortured souls beg for mercy. He should have stayed back. She had told him not to fight. She had told him not to go in with the younger men, but he wouldn't listen to her.

Keao's eyes were avoiding the General's direction and he did not notice him dismount his horse and get ready for the assault. The General prepared for an ambush, it was now predator and prey, he was going to take this opportunity. Keao had let his guard down, he was not invisible, he was not camouflaged. He was not taking heed of his own teaching. He had become disorientated by the sounds of war. The screams and shouts of terror, the noise and chaos of battle, the sound of death, the sight of blood; they had stripped him of all his power; and just like any powerful animal, when faced with something it is not accustomed to, loses its intuition and becomes irrational.

Keao, who had responded to nature all his life and could hide and conceal and hit a target just by focusing all his senses at once, was in a completely alien environment, and his hearing, his sight, his smell; once so finely tuned, had abandoned him. He had become the hunted instead of the hunter. Dust had obscured the sun and turned the air a putrid brown. The smell of death horrified him. Looking around him all he could see were piles of bodies and severed body parts. The fallen lay sprawled across one another, their red stained weapons abandoned around them. The reek of blood and gashed corpses had encouraged the carrion birds to start their feasting and they got in his line of vision as well. Sweat and dirt ran down his face and collected in wells in the rim of his eyes. Rubbing and blinking made them worse. Only a few figures were stumbling around in the battle field now. Many of the opposition just sank were they stood, gripped by fear and apprehension as they watched the General prepare for an ambush. The ground had become a patchwork of crumpled corpses, and the ones that were left standing, swung their swords aimlessly as if drunk on battle. Abandoned screaming horses were fleeing the flats. Others waited on the perimeter. All Keao could see was the blood of battle and all he could hear was the distortion of death.

The hunter slowly gripped his spear, his eyes locked on the vulnerable unsuspecting victim. With cunning perseverance and without arousing suspicion, the General found the balance of his weapon. Calmly and carefully he raised the murderous shaft until it was aligned with his eyes. The victim was the perfect target; the eyes were focused elsewhere. The predator kept the prey in sight and with a perfect stance, leaned back, took aim and followed through with immense power. He exerted a force so strong that it separated the heavy blanket of brume and knocked away several arrows on its path. The breath of the flying weapon was heard by Keao's ear as it struck him. The weapon was much faster than his reflexes. His life flashed before him and everything that might have been. Everything that he had been through, everything that he had taught Ajeya. Be silent, be vigilant, be invisible. Never become a target, never take your mind off the task. Think, feel and survive. He knew that he had let the clan down, he had let himself down, but mostly, he had let Ajeya down. The long stem was all that could be seen as it impaled him on the unforgiving steel and he sank to the ground.

Ajeya sprang off her horse and ran over to him. 'Keao, Keao!'

By the time she reached him his breathing was getting more laboured. He was struggling. She was holding his hand, willing the life he so desperately needed. 'Don't leave me Keao, please don't leave me. You are strong; you are the owl remember; I watch out for you and you watch out for me.'

He looked at her and breathed in deeply, he

302

remembered what he told her all those years ago.

'The owl is the greatest predator of the forest. It has total awareness of its surroundings so it can hunt in the dark using sound alone to guide it to a kill. It will watch the movements of its prey for hours before choosing the right moment to strike. It has perfect patience and perception and its stillness makes it invisible.' He looked at her. 'Have you ever seen the bird behind the call?'
She shook her head.

'That's because it is special and can hide. But the hare can see it, the hare can see everything. It will be a very special guide for you Ajeya because it will know where everything is, good and bad, and it will protect you.'

He coughed meekly and blood spurted out of his mouth. He struggled to speak and she held his hand. 'I am no longer the owl Ajeya, it does not live in me any more. I am a fraction of my former self and I should have listened to you.' He coughed again.

'Don't speak,' she told him. 'And never forget that you are the owl Keao, it does live on in you.' She looked around with wild eyes.

'Quickly someone, get help!!' she screamed out the order.

Twenty men rushed over but he waved his hand to dismiss them and his voice was barely a whisper. He struggled to say the words and each sound took all his strength.

'It's too late dear sister. It's too late for me - but

303

not for you. The skills I taught you live on in you. You are the hare Ajeya - the hare can see everything. The hare is all powerful. Much more powerful than you know - it will protect you.'

'Don't you leave me brother, don't you dare leave me, don't you dare.'

'I'm sorry Ajeya,' he rasped. 'But I will look down on you - from wherever I am. I will continue to guide you - in spirit form - I won't ever leave you. But look after Red for me. Take care of Rufus.' He groaned with the pain and his breathing was shallow. 'Tell them I love them - please tell them.'

'You are not going anywhere. We are going home together and you can tell them yourself. We will practise together again, just like we used to, do you remember? Do you hear me Keao, do you hear me!'

But he had already gone. Somewhere he was flying above her, looking down on her, trying to give her strength, trying to pull her up and look at the man by her side. But she wailed and sobbed as if she would never recover from her loss. All that Dainn could do was to put his arm around her and try and take away some of the pain.

As the fighting ended and the injured were escorted back to the Clan of the Mountain Lion, a melancholy Storm approached him. 'When you are ready comrade, I will take you to get that mangled arm treated.'

He looked down at the butchered appendage hanging at his side, he hadn't even realised he was hurt.

'I have to help my wife, I can't leave her.'

'No Dainn, you go with Storm,' said Ajeya wiping the tears from her eyes and trying to find a strength within. 'We need to find out what happened to the General and only Namir or Lyall can tell you that. I will take my brother back with me on Moonlight, and you stay here with Storm.'

'Ajeya, I really don't like leaving you here on your own,' he protested.

'Dainn, I am not on my own. I have my brother, albeit in spirit, but he is still with me. And besides, look at your arm. Storm is right, you probably won't even make it back. And I can't lose you either.' She stroked his blood stained face. 'There are lots of men and women waiting for me now. I will go with them. I will need to speak to my father, to Red and Rufus and tell them how valiant this man was in battle and that he was a true hero to the end.'

Dainn hugged Ajeya tightly as if he would never let her go. 'You really are the most courageous woman I have ever met. And I love you so much.'

'I love you too Dainn, I love you very much.'

A dozen men helped put her brother across her horse, and as she watched her husband being escorted towards the Clan of the Mountain Lion; she led the way back to the Hill Fort Tribe.

If she thought hard enough, she could bring him back to life. If she could pretend and camouflage and vanish, surely the opposite worked as well. So she brought him back to life in her thoughts and soon she was sitting beside him in the cart on that very first day when he held her hand. Then she was running with him, chasing butterflies and bees. Throwing snowballs at each other. Running through the grass firing a catapult like he had taught her. Hiding in the wagon when he told her to keep her head down. Sharing the same bed and feeling so safe with him by her side. She remembered it all so well, and a whole lifetime came flooding back. At a time when spirits should have been so high and filled with the adrenaline of winning the battle, they marched back in unison in a sombre mood and her tears fell silently on to her brother's back. But he was more than a brother to her; he was her soul mate, her teacher, her mentor, her guide and he was the first man to call her beautiful; she would never forget him.

40

Two iron braziers filled with charcoals had burned in the Meeting House throughout the morning, taking the bite out of the November chill. Ajeya came in early with Jena to replace them for the ceremony. Heavy tapestries covered the windows, blocking out the grey afternoon. The vaulted chamber was dimly lit, which made Keao's face look warm and glowing as he lay in his long narrow box on a supporting table with Red whimpering over him and Rufus comforting her. Ajeya looked at Colom standing on the dais, stooped and gaunt, slowly arranging the ceremony vessels by the Blessing Tree and wearing the guise of a withered old man in the autumn of his life.

In front of the long box stood the thrones made out of rich mahogany and red wood and at that moment were the strongest presence in the room. Hagen was already sitting on one, his face looking straight ahead, his hands in his lap holding the solitary feather from an owl. Jena had never seen him look so frail as he did right now. The huge doors opened, and silently the forlorn faces of the tribe filtered in. Stone expressions, fixed glares, cotton handkerchiefs held against snuffling noses, swollen puffy eyes wet with tears;

worn by all. Those who had fought the war were now struggling with their consciences and asking themselves: could they have done more?

For Ajeya, she had wept a thousand tears that morning alone and shook her head despairingly at the long wooden box in front of her. 'If only he had listened to her. If only he had stayed back with his wife and son. If only...'

Colom lit the lanterns by the Blessing Tree and guided Red and Rufus to their thrones in front of the long box. Jena and Ajeya then took their seats beside the family. When they were seated Colom raised up his arms and closed his eyes to bring in the spirits. The congregation bowed their heads as the omniscient powers entered. Red's heart began to race as she knew they had come for her husband. Hagen stopped breathing as he felt a chill on his neck; for him, Keao had already gone.

'Friends, family, loved ones, sisters, brothers, sons and daughters,' Colom began. 'It is with much sadness and deep regret that we meet today to say goodbye to one of our own.' He paused as he too felt the chill. 'One of our family has been taken to the next life, where he is needed to move on from this mortal life.'

The tapestries twitched and a whisper of breath was felt by all.

'Keao was a strong man, a proud man, a courageous man who gave his entirety so that we all may live in safety. And forgoing all fear, he has shown us what bravery and courage really means.' He stopped to compose himself. 'Sometimes we cannot find answers, sometimes there are none. For Red and Rufus the explanation may never come. But be secure in the knowledge that Keao led a good life and made a difference to so many; and we all know that his memory will live on in the people whom he touched and that his bloodline will continue in Rufus.' His words weaved round the echoing chamber as he invited Keao's widow to the front and held out the blade of a sharpened knife. 'Your blood flowed as one when you were joined in marriage. Now the spirits ask for your blood in death.'

Red rose to her feet, dazed and unsteady, though thoroughly prepared. She looked straight ahead and held out her warm hand over Keao's cold body.

Colom made one swift movement and the blood dripped from her palm over his heart.

'This will protect him in the afterlife.'

The blood ran down the side of his body and spooled into an ever increasing circle on his white shroud. Colom then gave her a white ribbon to wipe her hand and tie it on the Blessing Tree.

Her eyes were focused on the soft, smooth white material that was now stained with her blood as she wound it around a branch. She was aware of someone weeping behind her and took in a deep breath of air as Rufus tied his pure, untouched ribbon next to hers. The rest of the family were then invited to leave gifts in the long box. The mourning family stood up. Ajeya tried to stay strong for her mother. Hagen prayed that Keao was in the arms of his mother.

A strand of hair from a cows tail was offered by his son who had entwined it with an auburn curl from his own locks. Hagen followed next and placed the owl's feather in Keao's left hand; Ajeya wrapped his right hand around a catapult. Jena was the last to make an offering and had made woven figures of his family and placed them around his body, on his head, his heart, and his arms; representing peace, love and strength. Each one of the family prayed for everlasting life and asked for the spirits to take care of him on his next journey. The lid was closed for the final time and Colom put his hands on the cover.

'A man such as Keao is a fearless man. He will be safe from all because the body is covered in wood and the soul is covered by the defence of honour. This soul, that is now on another journey, will fear nothing, for he is protected by the blood of the living and the gifts that will escort him to the next life. The spirits favour this man.'

Colom bowed to acknowledge the end of the ceremony.

The pallbearers stepped forward to take him out to the fields where a plot had been decided by Red. On a hill overlooking the valley, his final resting place would lie beneath a century year old oak that was home to a magnificent tawny owl. It was the place where they used to sit when they first met and the place that he loved the most.

41

The air was warm and heavy with the scent of flowers on this beautiful day in spring. The small party of Keao's family were gathered by the site of the funeral mound that stood under the old oak tree. It was covered with the tumbled colours of wild blossoms and a whispering breeze caressed the land. Dainn stood alongside Ajeya and laid his wreath of fresh blooms on the grave. It was the first time that he had visited the site having only returned home a few days before.

'I am so sorry that I was not here for you all,' his voice was faint and tiny.

'My love, we know that you were here in spirit, and you were the first one to get to him before he died,' said Ajeya, fighting the sting in her eyes. 'You comforted him and held him until I got there.' She held his hand while her words stood strong.

'It seems like only yesterday that I was talking to him,' he was still void of strength.

'I know,' said Hagen. 'I think that time stands still when someone you love has died, it always seems that no time has passed since their last words.' He took hold of Jena's hand. She knew what he was referring to. Hagen laid a spray of owl feathers next to the wreath.

'It gives me comfort being able to touch the wings of an owl,' his voice was melancholy. 'It makes me feel closer to him.'

Red touched his arm as she led Rufus back down the hill. Hagen and Jena followed, and last came Dainn and Ajeya. She always looked behind her, hoping to see a glimpse of the bird, even a wing or hear it call....... but she never did. No one ever saw the tawny owl; he concealed himself and silently soared, only once in a while leaving a feather to show his presence.

By October, Dainn had been summoned away again. His assistance had been requested by the King of Durundal who needed his help in finding Namir, King of the Clans. The leader had been missing for several weeks now and his aide had been discovered washed up in the river. When the messenger told Dainn and his family it was the Emperor Cornelius who was now considered a possible threat; Jena's face was ashen with a stark horror and this time Ajeya wanted to know why?

'The past always catches up you at some point,' Jena's eyes were sad and her smile was dry.

'What do you mean mother? The past always catches up with you.' Ajeya's voice was anxious and fuelled with uncertainty.

Jena looked at her daughter, a fine young woman who would be twenty-two next spring. She thought about her own life and how many years did she really have left? She looked over at Hagen, he was day dreaming in the rocking chair on the porch and had taken to smoking a pipe in the winter of his life. His old wrinkled face creased into a smile when he caught her looking at him.

Colom and Peira were attending to their herb garden; stooped and slow, their creaking bones and sagging skin evidence of a lost youth. Everything takes its toll eventually.

But now it was time. She had to tell Ajeya everything, because this proud intuitive woman was beginning to sense that all was not as it seemed. It would be wrong to dismiss her with false statements; her daughter was worth more than that, she needed to know the truth about where she had come from and where her ancestral roots lay.

'Come with me my darling, let us sit by Keao's tree a while and he will be with us as I share this story with you.'

Ajeya's face froze with concern but she followed her mother as requested. Hagen took in a long draw from his pipe just as Peira lifted her head to watch the two women disappear up to the brow of the hill. They both knew what she was about to do.

42

She leaned back in the chair and relaxed. 'So that is my story. My mother told me all of this eight months ago and left it up to me when I came to see you. It was a lot for me to digest at that time, but mother was most insistent that we pledge our allegiance and commitment to you.'

The men looked mesmerised and couldn't speak for a moment so she continued.

'Dainn arrived home a month after being asked to join the search party,' she said looking at Lyall. 'And we got word of your safe return after the thaw,' she turned to Namir. 'I wanted to wait until you had settled in and fully recovered from your terrible ordeal before I came here, so that is why I have left it until now.'

Namir nodded at her foresight.

'So Rufus is your nephew and Dainn is your husband - what a small kingdom we are part of,' said Lyall, obviously moved by the saga.

'And so intricately entwined with each other's lives,' said Namir.

Ajeya nodded her head with pride.

'Does Dainn know you are here?' asked Namir sensitively. 'Does he know who you are?'

'Yes he does. As soon as he returned I told him everything. My mother wanted me to tell him. She didn't want me to keep secrets from him, and I couldn't have done that anyway.'

'So will you ever tell him who his real father is?' asked Lyall beneath the concern of a raised eyebrow.

'I think I will have to,' she replied, fully understanding the sentiments of his question. 'I think everyone is entitled to know where they come from and who their real father is. It doesn't stop me loving Hagen any less. He is my father and Keao is my brother. But I still had a right to know the truth. I still had a right to know about my blood father the Emperor Gnaeus and about my blood brother, Cornelius.'

Lyall and Namir offered their agreement by way of a nod and a mutual understanding.

'It is indeed a stoic story,' hailed Namir. 'And you have my fullest admiration and praise. Your mother also has my deepest respect for being so honest with you and protecting you as she has.'

'Hear Hear!' echoed Lyall. 'And I offer my heartfelt thanks to you, your family and your clan in supporting us in our fight for freedom and the war for justice.'

Namir nodded in agreement and Ajeya raised her head in pride.

'With you and Dainn ruling over Ataxata, peace will prevail, and all the clans and non clan dwellers will be safe in that knowledge,' Namir's praise was high.

Ajeya fell silent and she felt a whisper curl

round her face. She looked out of the window to see a tawny owl fly past; it looked at her for a split moment before disappearing into the abyss again. Tears came to her eyes and she felt her heart miss a beat.

'Thank you for your humble words and depth of honour.' She took a deep breath. 'But with your kind permission, there are still a few things that I don't know; things that haunt me and keep me awake at night and I know that you can provide the answers.'

Lyall raised an eyebrow, Namir cocked his head.

She took their expressions as a sign to continue. 'Please tell me what became of Laith and Artemisia, so I can ease my mother's aching heart; she carries the torment like a heavy burden and I can see the unknown weighs her down.' Her eyes were sad. 'Also my brother Cornelius; what can you tell me about him - my mother always worried about him and she needs closure now - however painful that may be.' She drew a pained response. 'And what really happened in Ataxata? My dearest husband has given me patches of the story; possibly to spare me the details of my father's deadly rise to power and his heinous crimes in getting there, but I need to know the truth.'

Lyall looked at Namir with his customary raised eyebrow. Namir tilted his head is response and the two men fell silent as the events of what she had just spoken about raced through their memory banks and fired up a distant past.

'Of course we can fill in the gaps for you, if that is what you wish,' said Lyall. 'We understand your need to know the truth - if you are ready for the truth.'

Ajeya's heart beat faster with trepidation. She had opened a can of worms now and there was no going back.

'Perhaps Lyall should begin our story and I can end it for you,' said Namir, and looked at Lyall for his response.

'Yes, perhaps I should,' Lyall was already reliving his past. 'As it does begin with me.' He paused for a long breath while he collected his thoughts...

He looked out of the huge windows as if he was searching for something on the brow of the hill. The mountain range crowned the vista and immediately it was moving towards him, bringing his past closer and closer until the vast glittering wall was right in front of him. He was standing on the edge of a great precipice and below him was his life spread out like a moving quilt, a sea of motion awash in the colours of his memories. He breathed in the spectacle that was teasing old wounds; stabbing and tearing and wrenching them apart until they all began to resurface. Suddenly he felt a grip of pain and his memory banks flew open.

'My life was quite ordinary until I was fourteen years old, living in this very castle, with the King and Queen of Durundal.' He looked around in awe. 'And then everything changed. Everything. And it all started on that dreadful night in November. The blood month.'

To be continued in - 'A Wolf in the Dark.'

I was a very frightened fourteen year old boy back then; too frightened for my own good by all accounts. My father desperately wanted me to succeed him as a strong king with absolutely no fear of anything or anyone. A tall order back then. He used to tell me stories and I hated them. Because night after night, I had the same recurring nightmare, the same disturbed dream and even now as I speak, it's as real today as it was then.

It is pitch black and my heart is hammering. I can't control my vicious panting. The tunnel closes in and I crouch against the wall. My fingers can feel every crevasse on my shrinking tomb as I slide along the cold, damp, ancient, stones.

And then I feel it. Something cold reaches for me and I instinctively recoil. The thing groans and wails as it claws at my flesh. I manage to break free and start to run; but fettered legs are weak. I am weak. I cannot breath. I cannot move. The creature closes in. A long forked tongue licks along the sweat of the walls and I can feel its icy breath on my neck. I scream and sit bolt upright, trembling in my bed.

Printed in Great Britain
by Amazon